The Mummy's Curse

Afterlife Calls

K.C.Adams

ISBN: 9798483875352

First published in 2021.

Cover design by 100 Covers.

1
Edie

'Hold her still!'

'I am!'

'Can we hurry up please, this is hard!'

'I'm *trying*!'

Who's idea was it to exorcise Melanie again?

Oh. Mine.

Don't get me wrong. I hated Melanie. She was my arch nemesis's sidekick. That meant I hated her by default.

But nobody deserved to have control of their body taken away from them by a ghost. Bitch or no bitch.

So, ever since finding out that Melanie was possessed, Mum, my boyfriend, and I, had been trying to come up with a plan to exorcise her.

And now that we were enacting said plan, it was going terribly.

A ghost flew around the cubicle, trying to get us off Melanie. He kept moaning, pushing into us, but mostly floating through people. Except me. He kept bashing into me. I ground my teeth together, trying to ignore the pain each time he smashed into me. Mum and Josh didn't know I could touch ghosts, and the middle of an exorcism felt like the wrong time for that conversation.

'How much more potion do you have?' asked Mum. She was pinning one of Melanie's arms down, while Josh held on to the other, and I forced her to drink the exorcism potion.

'It's kind of hard to see when I'm ramming it down her throat!' I said. The ghost inside of Melanie, and its companion, weren't making it easy, but I was determined to help Melanie.

Now there was a sentence I never thought I'd say.

Melanie choked, convulsing. That was a good sign. It meant her body was starting to fight off the spirit.

We were fairly sure the ghost who wouldn't leave us alone was the partner of Melanie's ghost. Giving up on attacking us, he changed to hovering behind me, watching, screaming. It was as if he could feel her pain. Cute, but not great for my concentration.

'Start chanting!' said Mum. I followed her instructions and our voices fell into harmony. 'Two spirits inside one host, expel the one that should be a ghost, protect the soul that belongs in here, keep them safe as this host we clear.'

An exorcism was always risky, but it was rare for a spirit to leave a body without a fight. Mum had tried many ways to get ghosts to give up their hosts before she'd quit ghost hunting, and exorcisms were the only things that worked.

I was so glad she was ghost hunting again. And letting me help her.

This ghost had really attached itself to Melanie, even dragging her out of bed at one o'clock every morning to visit a grave. I didn't know whose grave it was, but she cried there every night, and the ghost who was currently trying to get to her was always there, too. His love for her was palpable.

We'd decided not to exorcise her then, since it was too noisy and risked waking up anyone nearby. There were too many houses in the area.

Instead, we'd cornered her in the college toilets. Classy, I know.

As Mum and I repeated the spell, Melanie's body twisted and turned in unnatural directions. We let go, resting her on the floor by the wall. No one used the disabled loo, so it was probably the cleanest floor in the whole damn college.

If the potion failed, this time, we had a backup. We'd learned the hard way what happened when you didn't have a backup spell and potion. That wasn't something we'd ever do again.

Melanie screamed. Or, rather, whatever was inside of her did. The second ghost echoed her wail.

Thankfully we'd found a silencing spell in our Book of Shadows, so nobody outside the room could hear anything.

Melanie's back arched; a plume of grey smoke gushed out of her mouth. I pushed Josh back, wanting to keep him away from the spirit. What did grey mean? I'd never seen grey before.

Instead of disappearing, like usual, the smoke morphed into a ghost. She was a scruffy woman wearing a baggy skirt which covered a pair of trousers, with her head wrapped in a tartan scarf. Her skin was covered in dirt. I had no doubt she was one of the ghosts from the local mine that had collapsed in the 1800s.

Her partner's face lit up when he saw her. They were about my age, which was a terrifying thought, but I could tell how much they loved each other. Would that be Josh and me one day?

He grinned, embracing her for the first time in what was almost two hundred years. A circular light formed behind them. It looked like it was really close, but also really far away. A silhouette appeared in the light, cradling a baby. I couldn't make out what the figure looked like, but peace and happiness radiated from her, and from the light itself.

Holding her partner's hand, the two of them ran towards the figure, took the baby from the figure's arms, and disappeared into the light.

I looked behind me towards the toilet, wiping a tear from my eye. I didn't want Mum to see me cry and think I wasn't cut out for ghost hunting if watching a couple cross over made me emotional.

'Well. That was…unexpected,' I said to fill the silence.

Melanie's body relaxed. Mum went into her bag and got out some Lucozade. After that ordeal, Melanie's body would need all it could get to repair itself. A sports drink felt like a good start. Personally I'd have preferred a gallon of Coke, but it wasn't me in charge.

'Indeed,' said Mum. The way she'd said it told me the discussion was closed. Her focus was on the living, not the dead.

Melanie opened her eyes and looked around. 'What the—?' She started to sit up, but rested her head against the wall instead. 'Why am I so dizzy?'

Mum crouched down beside her, cradling her head and handing her the open bottle of Lucozade.

'Thanks,' said Melanie, taking the Lucozade and drinking half the bottle in one go.

'What's the last thing you remember?' asked Josh. Aw, he was learning. That was the question Mum and I often asked after an exorcism. It was Josh's first exorcism, and we hadn't even wanted him to be a part of it, but the extra muscle was helpful. Especially when we'd been battling two ghosts instead of one. He was curious and open-minded even though he couldn't see ghosts, and that was the kind of attitude we needed in the people around us.

'The last thing I remember clearly is the earthquake. But there are fragments of other stuff, too.'

'What kind of fragments?' asked Mum.

Melanie unfastened her thick, dark brown hair from its ponytail. It was a subtle sign, but the ghost who'd been possessing her seemed to prefer her hair tied up, while Melanie had always styled it down. Small changes can be big signs that something is wrong. I hadn't known Melanie well enough at the time to notice. Isn't hindsight wonderful? 'Did I—did I go to a graveyard really late at night?'

'Yep,' I said. 'A lot.'

She wrinkled her nose, squeezing her eyes shut and reopening them a few times. 'What the hell happened to me? Why can't I remember anything properly?'

'You wouldn't believe us if we told you,' I said.

Josh scratched a spot under his blond hair. 'She might, actually. She believes in ghosts.'

'*Ghosts*?' echoed Melanie, her brown eyes wide as she stared at Josh. 'Are you saying I had a ghost inside of me?'

'A Victorian miner,' I confirmed.

'That explains it,' said Melanie. She didn't seem shocked or scared. It surprised me, given the fight that ghost had put up. Mum and I were so used to people reacting sceptically to finding out we could see ghosts. Even Josh had needed time to process that we could see ghosts, but ever since he'd accepted it, he'd been equal parts supportive and curious.

We all looked at Melanie, confused.

She chugged some more of the Lucozade, then continued: 'It was like I was filled with this never ending pain. It pulled at every part of me. I think whoever she was, she lost a child.'

Mum shook her head. 'Oh, the poor thing.'

'That would explain the grave thing,' I said. 'And what we saw as she crossed over.'

'What did you see when she crossed?' asked Josh.

I always forgot he couldn't see what I did. It was all so clear to me, the thought of someone not seeing it was almost inconceivable. 'Someone came from the light to get her and her partner. Whoever they were, they were carrying a baby.'

'That's heartbreaking. But sweet. But…why is this so complicated?' said Josh.

Mum laughed. 'You'll get used to it.'

Josh rubbed the top of his head, then returned to checking on Melanie. It was probably easier for him to deal with. 'Do you remember anything else?'

Melanie smacked her lips together. She was slowly starting to sit more upright the longer she was awake, which was a good sign. It meant the exorcism hadn't done any permanent damage. The more we did them, the more I worried about one going wrong. Especially since we seemed to need to do them more and more lately. This was my third exorcism in less than a month, and that fear of hurting someone while trying to help them was always there.

Which was worse: not being in control of your body, or getting injured – or killed – while being set free?

'Just feelings, really. So much pain. But love, too. Love for some guy I saw a couple of times.'

'You can see ghosts?' I said.

Melanie shook her head. 'No, I don't think so. But I could see him. Or at least, *she* could see him.'

'If the ghost is in control of her body, it makes sense it would change what she can or can't see,' said Mum. 'She'd take on the abilities of the spirit inside of her.'

'That's…weird,' said Josh.

Yes, yes it was.

Despite all the research I'd done to find a solution, everyone was susceptible to getting possessed. There was nothing we could do to prevent it. Not that anyone we knew could find, anyway. And with so many ghosts hanging around town, we'd all been looking for solutions.

Ever since there'd been an earthquake a few weeks ago, we'd been on alert. It had unleashed a worrying amount of ghosts into our hometown, and we had no way of knowing where they'd gone. Or how many were really out there. So far, we'd exorcised the one inside of Melanie and her partner, and one who'd possessed a little girl on the other side of town.

Melanie squeezed her eyes shut and massaged her forehead with her palm. 'Why me?'

Mum flashed her a sympathetic smile. She'd probably heard this question a gazillion times before. 'If only it were that simple. It could be proximity, age, appearance, emotions, or sheer bad luck.'

Melanie wrinkled her nose, hugging the Lucozade bottle to her as if it were a teddy bear. 'What do you mean by emotions?'

Mum started pacing the small room. Her back was probably going to seize up if she sat down for too long. 'Well, if they're feeling something similar to you, they'll be drawn to you. Like attracts like.'

'So she was latching on to my grief?'

'It's possible, yeah.'

Melanie lowered her head, swirling what little was left of the Lucozade around in the bottle. 'I had an abortion. It was the right thing to do – I'm not ready for a child of my own – but I still think about them every day. What if they could've cured cancer? What if they could've become prime minister? What if, what if, what if? You know?'

'I understand,' said Mum. 'Looks like the ghost did, too. Abortion was legal back then, although it had very different rules.'

'Abortion was legal in Victorian times?' said Josh. He rested one of his legs against the wall. Here's hoping his shoes were clean and it wouldn't leave a muddy footprint…

'Up until eighteen weeks. After that it was considered murder,' said Mum in her usual matter-of-fact way.

He widened his eyes. 'Wow. I had no idea Victorians were that progressive.'

'Depends on the topic,' I said. They didn't exactly have a great track record for women's rights. Mum being a ghost-hunting, DIY-doing, single parent would've made her even more ostracised in Victorian times than in the twenty-first century.

Josh flashed me his trademark smile. Butterflies filled my stomach. I still couldn't believe Josh was my boyfriend. After everything we'd been through and how long we'd known each other, we were finally together.

It still didn't feel real.

'What happens now?' said Melanie.

'You should go home and rest,' said Mum. 'You've been through an ordeal. We can take you to the nurse and say you collapsed, if you like.'

'Won't they find it weird you were on campus?' said Josh.

Mum checked her watch. 'I'll just say I was coming to meet you both for lunch, when we saw Melanie collapse.'

'Damn, you're good at this,' said Josh.

Mum grinned. 'I should be after forty bloody years.'

*

The nurse didn't question our story and practically shoved us out the door when Mum offered to drive Melanie home. Josh and I insisted on going with them, since it was the first time Mum had met Melanie and we wanted to make sure she really would be fine. She'd been through a hell of a lot, and she was bound to have questions. Heck, I had questions. I'd never exorcised someone who could remember being possessed before. The last two exorcisms Mum and I had done had been young girls possessed by much older spirits. Well, one had been a spirit. The other one was something I was trying to forget.

'I really do appreciate your help,' said Melanie. 'If there's anything I can do to return the favour, let me know.'

'How about you get your friend Tessa to back off Edie?' said Mum. Ugh. Seriously? Talk about embarrassing.

Of course Mum would bring Tessa into things. Tessa was my nemesis. And Melanie's best friend. She made my life hell. She'd cut my head open *and* damaged my coccyx in the space of about a week. And not even been remotely sorry for it. To call her a bitch was an understatement.

It didn't help that she had a thing for Josh. If anything, that had made her jealousy worse. But she had confronted me a little less since the head teacher had called her into his office. Frankly, she got off lightly if you asked me, but I told Mum to drop it. Tessa had ran out of his office crying on the day he'd spoken to her. Seeing her do that in a corridor full of people was pretty satisfying, not going to lie. She hadn't come into school for a couple of days after that.

To make matters even more cringeworthy for her, the head teacher had made her apologise to me in front of Melanie; her other crony, Laura; my mum; her parents; and Josh. It had taken a lot of strength for me to not look smug that day.

But my mood had been dampened by the fact that I knew she didn't mean it. She was doing it to save face; to win favour. If she didn't show remorse, she'd get kicked out of college. Bye-bye dreams of becoming a lawyer.

If the performance Tessa had put on when she supposedly apologised was anything to go by, she'd be a great actor if her dreams of being a lawyer fell through. It was a shame Mum and I didn't buy her apology, since, as I'd told Tessa before she'd pushed me over the second time, bitch can't be cured.

Melanie nodded. 'I'll try. To be honest, Laura and I don't like that she does it anyway. But when we try to argue back, she takes it out on us.'

'She sounds like a lovely person,' said Mum.

'Eight months and we're done with college, and I can move to Bristol for uni, never to see her again,' said Melanie.

Eight months couldn't come soon enough.

2
Niamh

After dropping Edie and Josh back at college, I stopped off at Maggie's to pick up some food, then went to Mrs Brightman's. She was a client of mine who'd turned into a friend. I sometimes left our dog with her during the day so that they both had company. Tilly seemed to enjoy chilling on the sofa watching TV with her, and she also seemed to understand that she couldn't jump up at the almost-blind and sometimes wobbly octogenarian.

'Brought you some of Maggie's leftover casserole,' I said, walking into Mrs Brightman's house.

I nodded in greeting to her husband, who haunted her. He smiled back. 'Thank you. She hasn't been eating much.'

The last couple of weeks, it had looked like she was wasting away, which was why I'd asked Maggie to make a casserole for her. Nobody would thank you for my cooking, but I knew she wouldn't be able to say no to Maggie's cooking. How could you when it was homemade casserole, put together by a professional chef?

If I'd told her Maggie had made it especially for her, I knew she'd get annoyed at me, so we frozen a couple of portions for Maggie's family to make it look like it'd been eaten, then I took the dish over to Mrs Brightman's. She had a cupboard full of plastic tubs.

'Bless you both,' said Mrs Brightman as I walked inside. Tilly jumped up at me in greeting. I bent down to fuss her, holding the casserole in my other hand. Mrs Brightman tried to take it off me, but I wouldn't let her. Her wrists weren't as strong as she made out, and I didn't want her to get hurt.

We went into the kitchen, where Mrs Brightman reached into a cupboard for her plastic tubs. There were so many I thought they might fall out, but it was a surprisingly organised cupboard.

'How is Maggie?'

Maggie was still freaked out by her daughter having been possessed by a demon. But I couldn't tell Mrs Brightman that. 'Good, thanks.' I put the casserole dish on the cookertop, and found a serving spoon out from a drawer.

Tilly watched us, hoping to grab herself anything that we dropped. Nice try, westie.

'Isn't Edie courting her son?'

It was words like 'courting' which reminded me of the totally different generations we'd grown up in. I suppressed a laugh.

'Yeah, for about a month now.'

She smiled. 'Young love. So adorable.' A whimsical look crossed her face, as if she were reliving a memory from long ago. I left her to it, starting to separate the casserole into the tubs she'd laid out.

'We met when we were about their age,' Mr Brightman informed me.

I smiled at him. I couldn't speak to him while she was there, but, since her eyesight wasn't so good, I could communicate with him using expressions and gestures instead. He didn't seem to mind I only spoke to him when she wasn't around. Then again, what would he do otherwise? He'd have nobody to speak to and a freaked out wife. And she'd probably cut Edie and I out because she'd think we were complete weirdos. No thanks.

Mr Brightman watched us dish up the food, a wistful look on his face.

'What does it smell like?' I asked Mrs Brightman. She'd once been a school cook, so she was great at identifying what Maggie put in her food.

Mrs Brightman lifted up one of the plastic tubs of food and sniffed it. 'Coriander. Thyme. Parsley. Onions. White ones, I think.' She paused.

Mr Brightman grinned, leaning in as his wife spoke.

'Beef, and red wine. I can't tell what kind, though. I don't know red wine well enough.'

'Wow. It's amazing how you can do that,' I said.

'Thank you,' said Mr Brightman.

I smiled at him. It was hard for him, not being able to taste or smell anything. Senses we took for granted when we were alive. I hoped that his wife's description would help him imagine what it tasted like, even if he couldn't actually taste it.

Mrs Brightman and I continued dishing up the food in a comfortable silence.

'Good afternoon?' she asked as we finished.

'Busy,' I replied. We put the casserole into the fridge, then went into the living room to sit in more comfortable chairs.

'Always so busy. You need to leave time for yourself too, you know.' She sat in her armchair. Tilly jumped up, curling up on to her friend's lap.

'I do. I get home and I watch TV.'

Mrs Brightman rolled her eyes. 'That's not what I mean.'

'What do you mean?' I said. Where was the conversation going?

And where had Mr Brightman gone? Usually he stuck around if Edie or I were there. That wasn't a good sign.

'There's a gentleman from my church you'd be a great match with.'

My eyes widened. No. Oh no. I was still recovering from my last relationship, and now my dead husband had discovered how to visit me whenever he liked. Dating so wasn't on my radar. It was so far down my radar I hadn't even considered it.

Was that why Mr Brightman had gone AWOL? Was he hiding from my wrath? Chicken.

'Um, thanks. I'll keep that in mind,' I said.

'I can set you up with him, if you'd like.' There was a glint of excitement in her eye, as if she got a kick out of playing Cilla Black.

'Thanks, but I'm not interested in dating right now. I've got too much going on with Edie and her exams, and starting my new job. You know how it is.'

'That makes it the perfect time to meet someone new! Everything is already up in the air!'

Which is exactly what I *didn't* like. I liked being able to control things, thank you very much. I had so little opportunity to control anything in my life, the last thing I wanted was someone else playing matchmaker.

'Not for me it isn't. I really just need some time to myself. Especially after such an ugly divorce.' Which was only a half-excuse. It was true. I still wasn't over how my ex-husband had made me feel when he'd filed for divorce. 'I'd better go. Tilly needs feeding.' I grabbed the dog from her lap and scurried out without even putting Tilly's lead on her. She didn't need feeding for another couple of hours, but I couldn't think of a better excuse to get out of there so fast.

*

I was on edge after Mrs Brightman's ambush. The last thing I wanted was to be set up with some random guy who'd balk the minute he found out I could see ghosts. It was bad enough that's what my ex-husband had done. We'd been together seven years. I didn't have it in me to let anyone else in.

I didn't have the energy for dating, either. I was too old for that nonsense.

She wouldn't actually set me up, would she? I loved the woman, but she needed to pull her head into the twenty-first century.

On my way home, I stopped off at the library to return a book. Fine. And as an excuse to see Ben. I didn't like him in that way. It was just nice to have a grown-up friend who understood when I had conversations with what looked like fresh air to most people. Honest.

When I got there, he was already talking to someone. The long, thick black hair and tanned skin looked familiar. The figure turned around. It was Jaya, the historian who'd helped us with the history of the local mines after last month's earthquake. Why did I feel a pang of jealousy, and not just because her hair was so much nicer than mine?

'Hey,' I said, pretending I was fine. 'Good to see you again, Jaya.'

'Thanks. You too. How've you been?'

'Same old, you know. You?'

'I was just telling Ben – I found the pay roll for First Pit. It's got all the names of everyone who worked at the mines on it, and it looks like the names of everyone working the day of the collapse, too.'

'Huh,' I said. 'That's cool.' I met Ben's gaze again and smiled. It was hard not to get excited about it. It was what we needed to track down every ghost that had been released when the building site in town had disturbed the ghosts from First Pit. We could then make sure they were either crossed over, or otherwise not causing trouble for the living.

'Oh! Almost forgot.' I dug into my messenger bag and handed Ben a book. It was a novel I'd borrowed last week. I hated leaving books lying around if I'd finished reading them.

Ben removed his glasses and wiped the lenses on the edge of his shirt. 'Was it any good?'

I shrugged. 'Pretty average. Not sure I'd recommend it.'

'That's a shame. I guess they can't all be page-turners,' said Jaya.

'Yeah,' I agreed.

There was an awkward pause as the three of us hovered around the desk. I felt like I'd crashed a private conversation. What had they been talking about?

'So see you tomorrow night in town?' Jaya said to Ben. My stomach fell. They were going on a date. Why did it bother me so much?

'Yeah,' said Ben, smiling.

*

I busied myself making dinner, opting for a cottage pie as I could take my stress out on chopping potatoes and carrots.

Edie did her homework upstairs while I cooked, preferring to stay out of the kitchen and away from my bad mood. I didn't really blame her. I was chopping those potatoes pretty aggressively.

I'd just put the cottage pie into the oven when someone knocked at the door. We weren't expecting anyone, but sometimes Maggie or Josh turned up unannounced. I washed my hands, then went to answer it. Ben was standing on the front porch, holding a canvas bag.

What did he want? I'd assumed he'd spend all night at home flirting with Jaya via text, ready for their date tomorrow night.

A part of me was annoyed at him, but then common sense kicked in and reminded me it was his life, we weren't in a relationship, and he could do whatever he liked. I may have been older than him, but I wasn't his mother. Or babysitter. Or partner. Or…anything that allowed me any kind of judgment. Especially since we'd only know each other a month or so.

'Evening,' he said, a broad grin on his face.

'Evening.' I stepped aside to let him in. The contents of the canvas bag clattered inside as we walked into the kitchen. An excited westie followed us, jumping up at Ben's legs and almost knocking him over.

'Tilly! Off!' I said. She stopped jumping up, sitting at his feet and lowering her head.

Ben put the bag on the breakfast bar as I flicked on the kettle.

'Take a look,' he said, bending down to fuss Tilly.

Our ghost cat, Spectre, remained nonchalant, floating above the kitchen table and looking bored. Sometimes he played with Tilly, but mostly he just hovered above objects, judging us.

I opened the parcel and inside were three things wrapped in bubble wrap.

'The pirate one's mine,' he added. Now I was really confused.

I opened the first one to reveal a garden gnome dressed in snorkelling gear. The second was a pirate, wielding a sword, and the third was a mooning gnome. Classy.

'Um, thanks?' I said, totally confused. I made us both a cup of tea as he continued to cuddle an excited Tilly.

'They're gargoyles.'

I snorted. 'I've seen gargoyles. Those are not gargoyles.'

'My options were limited,' he said as he pulled out a chair, Tilly now in his arms. He wasn't letting go of her, and she didn't want him to. It was cute. 'But I thought any extra protection right now would be good. These were all I could find.'

Edie walked in, staring at her phone. She looked up when she noticed someone sitting at the breakfast bar. 'Hey Ben.'

'Hey Edie.'

'Can I get a tea, please?' Edie asked me.

She'd no doubt heard the kettle boil and realised if she timed it right, she wouldn't have to make her own drink.

I got another mug from the cupboard and started making her a drink, too.

'What's with the gnomes?' Edie asked, picking up the mooning gnome and examining him.

'They're gargoyles,' I told her.

Edie lowered an eyebrow. 'Gargoyles? Don't they go on churches?'

'They can go anywhere, and, in theory, can be anything,' said Ben. 'They're designed to protect the people inside from evil. I couldn't source any actual gargoyles, so I got someone to make them using the next best thing.'

'Garden gnomes are the next best thing?' I said.

'They're inconspicuous and cute. How are they not?' He picked up the pirate and examined it, wiping off a bit of dust from its shoulder. He seemed attached already.

'One for you, one for us, and one for the Morgans?' said Edie.

Ben nodded. 'The pirate one's mine.'

'I want this one,' said Edie, hugging the mooning gnome. Sigh. Of course she wanted the rude one.

'Could you really see Harry allowing this one near his house?'

'I can't see him allowing anything this twee near his house,' I said.

'Good job it's Maggie's too, isn't it?' said Edie with a smirk. She was smart, that one.

I smiled at her. 'We might have to hide it in the hedge.'

'Will that still work?' Edie asked Ben.

He shrugged. 'If it's close enough to an entrance it should. But I don't know if they'll work regardless. A friend made the spell up. It's a combination of a warding spell and an amulet enchantment.'

Edie turned the gnome upside down. 'That explains the runes on his feet.'

'Yeah. Like I said, he improvised.'

'Is there any way of testing them?' asked Edie.

I put our teas on the breakfast bar. Ben picked up the Westie Mum mug and sipped his. Edie put the gnome down and gulped hers from an *Aristocats* mug.

'Not that I know of. Unless you know anyone who means you harm.'

'Does Tessa count?'

I laughed.

'Sadly it will only work against magical evil. As far as I know, anyway. But you never know,' said Ben. He put his tea back on the table, but kept his hand on the mug.

'Shame,' said Edie. 'I'll call him Moonie.'

'We're not naming the gnome,' I said.

'Gargoyle,' Ben corrected.

'We're not naming the gargoyle,' I said.

'I already did,' said Edie with a smirk. She picked up her tea and walked off.

*

'I'm sure Mrs B didn't mean anything by it,' said Maggie as Tilly and I walked into her house the next day.

'You mean she didn't want to interfere?' I said as I removed my coat and muddy boots. The end of autumn was upon us, and winter was on its way. The crunchy leaves had turned to mulch, and it never stopped raining. Just stepping outside and walking five minutes down the road was enough to make you feel like you'd gone for a shower in your clothes.

'Well, I'm sure she meant that,' said Maggie, picking up Tilly and hugging her. Tilly responded by licking the end of her nose. 'But she didn't mean to offend you. She's from a different generation. She just sees a lonely woman.'

I glared at my best friend.

'Not that I think you are. Or anyone who knows you.'

'Except her, apparently.'

'Yes.'

We went into the kitchen, where Maggie put Tilly on a chair, then flicked the kettle on. Honestly I couldn't remember the last time I'd visited her and we hadn't immediately started making a hot drink when I walked through the door. Heat was so rare, even in the summer, we practically had tea on a drip.

Tilly walked in circles on the chair a few times, then lay down.

'Bugger, I forgot to bring the gargoyle for you.'

Maggie froze, her hand halfway to the mug cupboard. She turned to face me, her eyebrow lowered. 'Pardon?'

'Ben got someone to make gargoyles out of gnomes. To protect us. He's got a pirate, we've got a mooning one, and you have a snorkelling one.'

Maggie snorted. 'Now there's something I never thought I'd hear.'

'Tell me about it,' I said. 'He's not even sure if they'll work. But he wanted to give us all some extra protection.'

'Tell him thanks anyway. Any protection we can get will offer me some peace of mind. I can pick it up tomorrow after the cinema if you want.'

'Yeah, that's a good idea,' I said. Before all the ghost activity and Abigail's possession, Maggie's family and mine had been doing weekly cinema trips, since our return to Hucknall at the start of the year. We were finally resuming them now that all the craziness had calmed down. 'What will you tell Harry about it?'

'To get a sense of humour, because the gnome stays.'

'It has to go out the front somewhere,' I added.

'Why?'

The kettle boiled, and Maggie continued making our cups of tea. She also got a metal tin of homemade biscuits from the cupboard and placed them in front of me. 'Gingerbread.'

'Thanks.' My favourite. I opened the tin and started munching on one. After swallowing, I continued: 'So that people have to walk past it to get into the house. In theory, it will stop anyone from causing harm to anyone inside.'

'Why in theory?'

'Like I said: they haven't been tested.'

'Let's hope they won't be,' said Maggie.

'I'll eat biscuits to that,' I said, raising a gingerbread. Not that I needed much encouragement to eat them.

Maggie picked one up and tapped it with mine.

'What time did Edie get here?' I asked, changing the subject. She'd spent so much time with Josh since they'd started going out I barely saw her anymore. I didn't mind, though. She was happy. And it gave her a distraction from all things ghost.

While I'd come to accept she would always have ghosts – and ghost hunting – in her life, that didn't mean I had to like it. Or that I couldn't be grateful for anything that delayed her embracing her inner ghost hunter.

'Beats me. I was still in bed.' Maggie yawned as she put the two cups of tea on the table. 'Worked late last night. Friday nights are such a bitch.'

'Least you're off today, right?' I said.

Maggie nodded and yawned again. I couldn't help but copy her. Stupid yawns. 'Off work, but never off-duty as a mother. Too much to do around the house. Although it's Harry's turn to take Abigail to dance and swimming lessons, so at least I'm not rushing and waiting around.'

'How does a five-year-old have more hobbies than us?' I asked.

Maggie shrugged. She picked up her tea and gestured to the living room. 'Comfy seat?'

My joints protested as I got up out of the wooden chair, but I knew they'd be grateful for a more cushioned seat on the sofa.

Footsteps echoed through the floorboards. Edie and Josh were moving about upstairs.

'Should we go check on them?' I asked, twiddling my thumbs as Maggie and I sat on my sofa.

Maggie laughed at me. 'Relax, would you? They're good kids.'

'But what if—'

'What if, what? They had sex?' she scoffed. 'Please. You know how long I was sleeping around before my mum even figured out I wasn't a virgin.'

'How is that helpful!'

'Because Edie's a better kid than I was. More responsible, too. So's Josh and you know it. You can trust them. You have to, or they'll hate you.'

I sighed, leaning back on the sofa. Tilly jumped on to my lap and fidgeted on it, trying to find the perfect position to lie on me. It was like getting the leg massage I'd never wanted, while she tried to get comfy. Eventually finding it, she spun one last time, then lay along my lap, facing the TV. She loved watching it.

'Why is parenting so hard and how are you so good at it?'

Maggie patted my leg. 'Just trying not to repeat the mistakes my parents made.'

'Why didn't I think of that?' I asked.

'It's not like you didn't have a plan,' said Maggie.

'Marrying your high school sweetheart and setting up a ghost hunting business is hardly a plan. More like my genetics meant I felt like I didn't have a choice.'

Maggie narrowed her eyes at me. 'Is that why you're so protective of Edie?'

'Ever since she saw your dad's ghost, and Javi warned me…I panic when I think about her. It's like she's tied to train tracks, and I can see the train hurtling towards her, but my legs won't move so I can't run over to help.'

Maggie sighed. 'I mean, you could just be paranoid.'

'I got two warnings from the Other Side. They don't throw out warnings for laughs. Even Javi wouldn't joke about that.'

Maggie pursed her lips. 'Yeah, I guess you're right. Well, whatever it is, we'll figure it out. Together. After all, what are friends for?'

What would I do without Maggie? She kept me sane among all the craziness in my life. It was nice having a friend who couldn't see ghosts; it added a sense of normalcy to my life, especially with her being happily married with two kids. You couldn't get much more normal than that.

'How are things with Ben, anyway?' Maggie asked, giving my knee a playful shove. It shifted Tilly, causing her to turn and glare at Maggie. She rubbed the little dog behind the ears. Tilly quickly settled back to where she was lying on my legs, paying more attention to the TV than we were. I swear she got the most use out of it.

'What do you mean? There are no "things" with Ben.'

'Come on, Niamh. I'm not blind. The sparks fly between the two of you like someone's stuck their wet hand in a plug socket.'

'Sounds dangerous.'

She glared at me, but what else was I supposed to say? There wasn't anything to talk about. We were friends and he'd been helping me with ghost-related things. It was handy having a grown-up friend who could see ghosts and had a degree in parapsychology. Outside of my deceased husband, I'd never known someone my own age who could see them before. Almost my own age. He was five years younger. But anyway.

'There's really nothing going on?' she said, sounding disappointed.

'No, there's really nothing,' I reassured her. 'Besides, he's got a date.'

She pouted, as if I'd just told her the most disappointing news in the world.

'A date? With who?'

'The historian who helped us with some ghost stuff last month without knowing she was helping us with ghost stuff.'

'Oh. That's a shame,' said Maggie.

Why was everyone so obsessed with me being in a relationship? What was wrong with me being single and raising Edie alone?

'He's one of the good ones, you know,' said Maggie.

I resisted the urge to roll my eyes. 'That's not the point, Mags.'

'Why isn't it?'

'Because my focus should be on protecting Edie right now, not on my love life.'

'What if he can help you protect Edie?'

He knew more than me. I resented admitting that, but it was true. And if he could help me save my daughter from whatever was to come, then that would be an added bonus to keeping him around.

But did I really want to put the burden of protecting Edie on someone I barely knew?

3
Edie

'Are you OK?' said Josh, pulling me to him. The skin on his chest was soft against my cheek, and he smelled like Calvin Klein aftershave. Mmm. 'Is your back OK?'

'I'm OK. Really.'

Josh had been patient and kind with me. He hadn't pressured me to have sex, and he was always checking in about my back injury. It twinged sometimes, like if I stood or sat down for too long, but I was mostly OK.

We chose a time when our families were out and we could have some real alone time. It was a Saturday afternoon, when our mums were out for lunch, and Harry was out with Josh's little sister, Abigail.

I didn't want to make a big deal out of it, but Josh had insisted on lighting candles and cooking a nice meal. I was pretty sure it was just an excuse for him to cook in his mum's kitchen, which was usually off-limits as she was a chef. I wasn't complaining. He'd inherited her cooking skills. And he was *definitely* romantic.

'Are you OK?' I draped my arm over his bare torso.

He kissed the top of my head. 'Yeah.'

Mum had always taught me that boys were selfish, and some of them never grew out of it. But Josh was different. During our first time together, he kept asking if

I was OK. And it just made me want him more. He was focused on my enjoyment and my pleasure, and it went against all the stories I'd read it magazines and overheard on public transport about anyone with a penis only caring about themselves. He was different. He was gentle and kind, mindful of my back injury, and really listened when I told him what I wanted. I hastened to sound gushy and like my first time was perfect, but... Josh was.

We lay quietly, a tangle of limbs. I never thought Josh would be interested in me; the weird kid. Turned out, he was. He'd even told Tessa, who kept throwing herself at him, where to go in favour of being with me. We'd spent as much time as possible together since then, and that had been over a month.

'Do you want dessert?' he asked.

'Didn't we just have that?' I said with a giggle.

He pulled me close, sending shivers up my arm and down my spine.

'I just want to stay here.' It was too perfect of a moment. I wanted to enjoy it for as long as I could; to capture it in my mind like a photo.

I looked up and gazed into his blue eyes. A cheeky grin crept over his handsome face. He leaned down and kissed my lips. They tingled at his touch. 'We can do that.'

*

I practically skipped as Josh and I walked, hand-in-hand, across the field to the local primary school. The sun was setting over the horizon, giving the muddy field an eerie glow. Occasional ghosts floated past us, roaming the barren landscape.

'Excited?' said Josh, laughing at me.

I nudged him. 'Don't you think this is cool? When does anything cool ever happen around here?'

He shrugged.

'We've got a real life – well, sort of – mummy in town!'

'I guess I'm not as into history as you,' he said. 'But it's kinda cool. I'm surprised they're opening up the school for everyone to visit it.'

'Why not? It's a good way for them to make money and do more stuff like this,' I said as we reached the edge of the grounds.

'True,' he said.

We climbed over the muddy hill. There was a queue outside, which a bored-looking receptionist was working her way through, taking payments.

'Wow, she hasn't changed a bit,' said Josh.

'You know her?'

He nodded. 'She started when I was here, not long after you left. Same bored, sullen expression and everything.'

'She looks like she's going to stab you in your sleep,' I said.

He suppressed a laugh. 'I mean, there were rumours…'

'*Really*?' I said.

Now he *was* laughing at me. 'No, silly. You're so gullible.'

'Am not!'

'If you say so, french fry,' he said, patting my head.

I tried to pull my hand out of his, but his grip was iron. Damn him for being stronger than me.

The queue went down quickly, so we paid the grumpy receptionist then went inside. The hallway was pretty crowded. The atmosphere was close; almost suppressive.

The faded white walls were littered with details of the history of Ancient Egypt and the mummy. What did they eat? How did they pay for stuff? What was a day in the life like? What *didn't* we know? What did we know about the mummy so far? How could we tell all of that? It was like stepping into the research notes for a historical documentary. I was in heaven.

The amount of people crammed into the school hall meant it was hard to move. The wooden floor was barely visible through the crowds. It was a great money maker for them, that was for sure.

It was easy to figure out where the mummy was – we just followed the crowds. The human crowds, that was. There didn't seem to be a ghost in sight, which was odd, because I saw ghosts pretty much everywhere. And in a room full of so many people, it didn't make sense there wouldn't be at least a couple, following whomever they haunted to the exhibit. They didn't exactly have a choice.

The mummy was in the centre of the hall, surrounded by so many people you could hardly see it. There was no chance of getting a good photo.

It wasn't just the crowds that told me where the mummy was, though. I could sense a buzzing coming from the mummy that was permeating my body. It was a strange sensation that made me uncomfortable as I'd never experienced it before.

But I also wasn't going to let it stop me from exploring the exhibition. I loved history too much.

The mummy was on tour from a museum, and would be travelling to a couple of other places in Nottinghamshire before moving to other parts of the UK. The school was super lucky to be housing it on the tour.

Cool, historical stuff usually just went to places like Wollaton Hall or Nottingham Castle. Not a school in a Nottingham suburb.

'Pretty cool, huh?' I said, gesturing to the direction of the crowds.

'A crowd of people? Yeah, I've never seen one of those before.'

I glared at him.

'I jest, I jest.'

Still holding my hand, he guided me through the crowd and to the front. It almost seemed like the crowd parted for him as he walked through, but I was pretty sure I imagined it. Crowds didn't actually make way for attractive people, did they? Oh, to be a part of his world…

The stone sarcophagus was encased in a glass box, with a rope fence keeping people at least a foot away from the glass. That hadn't stopped people from trying to touch it, though – the glass was covered in fingerprints.

In another glass case beside him were his four canopic jars – where his internal organs were stored. They were removed as part of the mummification process to help preserve the body, but kept nearby and stored in jars. These ones had the heads of different Egyptian gods on them. I recognised one, a jackal, as the head of Anubis, the god of the death and mummification.

The mummy's death mask was scarier than I thought it'd be. It looked different to the ones I'd seen in photos – nowhere near as shiny or ornate. The red paint was faded, appearing in flecks that didn't really bring out any detail in particular. I could still make out the face engraved into it, but as he didn't appear to be royalty, it was made from stone instead of gold. That didn't make it any less eerie. Especially with half the paint missing on his facial features.

The buzzing I sensed from it was stronger so close, too. What was it? What was I sensing?

I shuddered, stepping away and backing into Josh.

'Something wrong?' he said, putting his arms around my waist.

'It's creepier than I thought it'd be,' I said. I didn't want to mention anything possibly supernatural in a room full of people.

He leaned into me, whispering in my ear in a spooky voice: 'At least it's not open!'

'Oh my god! Can you imagine? It'd scar these poor kids for life!'

A couple who were with a young girl turned to glare at me, before shuffling away. Oops. I mean, if you didn't want to risk your kid seeing a dead person, maybe don't take them to a mummy exhibit? People sometimes. Common sense was so rare.

'Oh look, you offended someone,' said Josh flatly.

I shrugged. 'Pretty standard. It's a rare day when I don't pi—upset someone.' Thankfully, I hadn't sworn at the primary school, but if my experience was anything to go by, the kids all knew far worse words by now. It was just the parents who were in denial about it.

'I'm gonna go pee. Back in a minute.' Josh kissed my cheek then made his way back through the crowd. I resisted the urge to check him out as he walked away. That felt wrong in our old school. Mostly his, since I'd left when I was about eight, but still.

'Does that look like a pot or a loaf of bread to you?' said a guy leaning over the sarcophagus.

I looked down. A guy with dark brown hair, wearing a leather jacket and jeans, was talking to *me*. Who did I know who looked like that? 'Dominic?'

'Edie!' he said, standing up and smiling. 'How's your back?'

I gritted my teeth. 'Mostly fine. How are you?'

'I'm good, thanks. Excited we have something cool around here, you know?'

'Totally! Nothing this interesting ever happens around here.'

'Tell me about it,' he said with an eye roll. 'Are you interested in history?'

'It's my favourite subject,' I said. 'Although I prefer ancient history to modern history. I find it painful to study modern history and see it repeat itself.'

Dominic nodded in agreement. 'Yeah, I know what you mean. I find it crazy that ancient civilisations could do so much more than we thought they could, and so much of it was lost until recently.'

'It's fascinating, isn't it?'

'Yeah.'

'So what were you asking about the sarcophagus?'

'Just here. Does it look like a pot or a loaf of bread?'

We leaned forwards to examine it. There was a straight line, with two angular lines coming from either end, pointing upwards. The top of the symbol was faded, so it was hard to tell what shape it formed.

'Um…'

He crouched down, narrowing his eyes as he studied the sarcophagus again.

'Are you trying to read the hieroglyphics?' I asked.

'Hieroglyphs. Hieroglyphic is an adjective. Hieroglyph is Ancient Greek for "sacred carving". But yeah. This word is escaping me.'

'What have you got so far? Can you make it out from the rest of the sentence?' I suggested.

'So far I have…whether that's a pot or a loaf of bread.'

'Oh.'

'But I only started this morning, so I guess it's not much time.'

'Why did you decide to try to read it?'

'I want to study Egyptology at uni,' he said, his eyes on the mummy again.

'That's so cool!' I said.

'What's so cool?' said Josh, walking up to me and putting his hand on the small of my back. I naturally leaned into him.

'He wants to study Egyptology,' I informed Josh.

Dominic pocketed his pen and paper, wiped his hands on his jeans, then held a hand out for Josh to shake. 'Dominic.'

'Josh,' he said, shaking Dominic's hand.

'I was just asking Edie what she thinks this is,' Dominic said, pointing to the mysterious image on the sarcophagus.

Josh leaned forwards. 'Looks like a cup to me.'

Dominic gasped. 'I didn't think of that! That's brilliant!' He took a tiny notebook and pen from his back pocket and scribbled something down. 'Genius. Excuse me, I have some deciphering to do.' He nodded, then walked off.

'That guy was odd,' said Josh, guiding me in the opposite direction.

'Yeah,' I agreed. Inside, though, I wanted him to stay so that I could talk to him more. There was something about him…

*

While it was cold out, it was that horrible, sticky weather that was common in England no matter what the temperature was outside. Josh and I got back to his from the school with our clothes sticking to us and refusing to budge.

Josh pulled his T-shirt away from his torso. He cringed as the damp fabric fell back and touched his belly again. 'I feel gross. I'm going for a shower.'

'OK,' I said, kissing him lightly. He pulled me closer, wrapping his body around mine. He was so close I could smell his Josh scent, and I needed more of it. I pulled his wet T-shirt over his head as his lips peppered my face with butterfly kisses. My body tingled at his touch, sending me to a place completely absent of all thoughts but his touch on me. A low moan escaped my lips. I covered my mouth, worried someone had heard me. We were standing together, frozen, but nobody made a sound or came in. Phew.

We met each other's gazes and giggled.

He had a way of taking my mind off everything bad that was happening, and forcing me to focus on the positives. Even when Abigail had been trying to hurt him and his parents, he'd still focused on the positives and trying to save everyone. It was an attitude I admired and wanted to spend more time around. He was magical to me, and I needed more of that in my life. More proper magic, not the nonsense stuff that meant that I could see ghosts. Being able to see ghosts didn't matter to me; what mattered to me was Josh.

We fell back onto his bed, our arms still tangled together.

'We really shouldn't. Mum is home now,' said Josh.

I sighed. 'Yeah. You're right.' It took all the strength I had not to kiss him again. Dammit, I really wanted him. 'Later?' I said with a smirk.

'Always,' he said, kissing me one last time then walking towards his bathroom.

I sat upright on the bed and flicked through my phone. More news of the world falling apart; what a surprise. When would people stop voting in the same old stupid politicians?

Thud.

'Josh?' I ran into his bathroom. Luckily he hadn't locked the door, because he was lying in a heap on the floor.

4
Niamh

'Mum! MUUUUUUM!' screamed Edie.

'Just a minute, Edie. Maggie needs me!'

Needed was an understatement. She was unconscious on her kitchen floor. If I hadn't caught her, those tiles could've done serious damage. I put her into the recovery position as I shouted at Edie. 'What happened?'

'Josh passed out!'

'What? So did Maggie!'

'At the exact same time?' said Edie.

'Apparently.'

What the hell was going on? I was out of my depth and I knew it. As much as I hated to admit it, there was only one person who could help me. He answered after the second ring.

'Hey Niamh. I can't really talk right now.'

In the background, I could hear music and talking. Where was he? Was he on the date he and Jaya had discussed yesterday? I should probably feel less smug about crashing it.

'Sorry, are you busy? I wouldn't have called on a Saturday night but it's an emergency.'

'What kind of emergency?'

'Two people just passed out at the same time. Call an ambulance or a healer?'

'Who?' he said.

'Maggie and Josh. What should we do?'

'Can you call that doctor friend of yours? I'll bring a healer,' said Ben. It went noisier, then his voice grew distant. It sounded like he was apologising to someone. He definitely said 'Jaya' while he was talking, so I was pretty sure he *was* on a date with her. Why did it bother me so much?

'Good idea.'

'Are they both breathing?' he asked. The background noise changed from music and chatter to the whistling of the wind. It sounded like he was walking down the street based on that and the cars I could hear driving past.

'I think so,' I said. I checked Maggie's pulse. Yep, still breathing. Thank god. 'Edie, is Josh still breathing?' I called, hoping she'd hear me.

'Yeah. Mum, what's going on?'

'I don't know. Do you see anything dodgy?'

'Like what?'

'Like a ghost!'

'I thought you warded their house last month?'

'Not the point! Do you see anything?'

There was a pause, where I imagined she was inspecting their surroundings. I did the same, but it looked the same as it always did. Dining table in the corner. Worktops everywhere. Nothing dodgy or antagonistic attached to the table or hidden in cupboards as far as I could tell.

'No! Do you?' said Edie.

'No.' I sighed.

I crouched down and checked around Maggie's neck. I'd given her a protective amulet when Abigail had been possessed, but it looked like she'd stopped wearing it. Wasn't that just great timing?

'Doesn't mean it isn't something dodgy. Even if they caught the same bug, the odds of them passing out at the same time are pretty damn slim,' said Ben through the phone. I'd forgotten he was still on the line. 'I'm going to pick up a healer. I'll be there soon as I can.'

'You don't even know where I am.'

'Maggie's. You're always at hers or yours.'

Was I really so predictable that a guy I'd known a few weeks knew my movements? Yeah, I probably was.

*

It felt like an age that Edie and I sat with Maggie and Josh, waiting for them to wake up. We spoke to each other through our phones so that we didn't risk leaving them alone, or straining our voices, just in case anything happened.

But nothing did. Breathing was the only movement they made. What had happened that would cause them to become so ill so fast? What was I supposed to say to Harry? To Abigail? They'd already been through so much. For them to come home from their father/daughter day and find the other half of their family comatose…I had no idea how Harry would react.

I was pretty sure he thought I was a charlatan, which was charming. It said a lot about what he thought about me, when he still thought I was a con artist despite having known me for over twenty years.

But I'd worry about that when they got home. I had more pressing things on my mind.

Like what the hell to do with Maggie and Josh.

There was a knock at the front door, and I figured it had to be Ben as Harry wouldn't have knocked.

'Mum, who's that?' called Edie.

'Wait there,' I told her. You could never be too careful.

'Stay there, Mags,' I said, stroking her deep brown hair before jogging to the front door. It was Ben, with Doc and another woman I didn't recognise behind him.

'Thanks for coming,' I said.

'What did you do this time?' said Doc.

'It's not me,' I said. I so wasn't in the mood for his jokes.

'Niamh, this is Alanis. She's a healer. Alanis, Niamh is a ghost hunter.'

A reluctant one, but I supposed he was right. 'Lovely to meet you, Alanis. I'm sorry it isn't in better circumstances.'

'Thank you,' she said in a soft voice that was almost meditative.

'Ben, if you and Alanis go upstairs to Edie and Josh, I'll take Doc to Maggie.'

Ben nodded, then went upstairs while I guided the doctor into the kitchen.

'Can you tell me what happened?' he said as he opened his medical bag and took out a stethoscope.

'One minute we were talking, the next she was falling. Luckily I caught her before she head butted the floor.'

'That is lucky.' He knelt down and pressed the stethoscope to her chest. I curled my sweaty palms into fists as I watched him check her heart rate. What was he looking for? What would he find?

'Heart rate is good,' he said. He returned the stethoscope to his bag, then took out a blood pressure machine.

After an agonising half an hour examination, he said as far as he could tell, Maggie was perfectly healthy. There was no reason for her to have passed out. Or for her to not be waking up.

Was she in a coma? Was Josh?

No. That wasn't possible.

Was it?

I leaned against the kitchen counter, my head lowered.

He went into his bag and took out a needle and a sharps bin. 'I'll do a blood test and see what I can find, too.'

'Thank you.'

'Is this because of one of your supernatural friends?' he asked as he put the needle into the crux of her elbow and drew blood.

I looked away, cringing. 'I'm going to hazard a guess, but anyone who's done this to one of our friends isn't on my side.'

'No, I imagine not. I'm sorry I can't do more,' he said, looking genuinely sorry. It was a rare show of emotion from a guy whose default was sarcasm.

'Thank you for trying.'

He put the lid on the vial, the needle into the sharps bin, then returned everything to his bag and closed it. 'Perhaps we should relocate her to somewhere more comfortable? If we put her and Josh on the bed, it will look like they're sleeping when her husband comes home. It buys you some time to figure out what's going on.'

'Yes, you're right. That's a good idea. Thank you.'

He put down his bag and picked up Maggie's shoulders, while I lifted her by her feet. The two of us carried her up to her bedroom, where we placed her on the bed.

Edie, Ben, and Alanis walked in as we lowered her on to the bed.

'How is she?' asked Edie.

I shook my head. If I spoke, I might start crying, and that wouldn't help anyone.

Edie lowered her head. Josh was just as bad too, then.

She walked over to me and wrapped her arms around my waist. I rested my head on top of hers, inhaling the chemical smell of her recently dyed black hair. We'd redone it a couple of days ago, and I was surprised how comforting I found the smell.

'Where would you like me to put Josh?' asked Doc.

'In here, please,' I told him. 'That way we can keep an eye on both of them at the same time.'

Doc nodded, then followed Ben out to Josh's room. Alanis walked in a moment later. She had on baggy jeans and gigantic earrings the size of her head. They were very nineties. I kind of liked them.

'Did you find anything?' I asked her.

'I want to look at both patients before making an assessment,' she said.

Edie and I stepped away from the bed so that she could get a better look at Maggie. Still hugging, we watched as she waved seemingly random objects over Maggie's body, mumbling and chanting things. I'd never seen anything like it before, but I guess I'd never not known what was wrong with someone before.

She carried on when the two men brought Josh into the room. Then, when they were together, she examined them both at the same time.

When she was done, she turned to Edie and me. 'Your friends?'

'Yes?' chorused Edie and I, leaning towards her, desperate to find out what was happening.

'I cannot heal them. They have been cursed.'

*

'I'm sorry, did you say "cursed"?' repeated Edie.

Alanis nodded. 'I am afraid so.'

'But…how? Why? They were here when it happened. And the house is warded!' I said.

Had Javi been right? Were my warding spells really that inadequate that they couldn't even protect my friends from a curse?

She shrugged. 'I cannot tell you anything about the curse itself, only that it is present.'

'How can you tell?' asked Ben, ever the curious academic.

Doc was standing beside him, his eyes narrowed in curiosity. While he'd dealt with many ghost-related injuries, he had no idea about how the supernatural actually worked. It was no doubt like watching a real-life horror film unfold before his eyes.

'Their auras. Their auras are blood red and black. I've never seen auras this dark on people before. Only on demons.'

'*Demons*?' squeaked Doc.

Well, at least I knew where his line was.

She nodded. 'Demons have dark auras. Cursed people have dark auras. No one else.'

'Not even serial killers?' asked Edie.

Alanis shook her head. 'Serial killers don't feel for others. A lack of compassion or empathy for other people are different to this. An absence, rather than a darkness. This is pure darkness.'

I let go of Edie and sank onto the floor. I couldn't support myself anymore. This was bad, and I was pretty sure it was related to the warning from Maggie's dad. He'd visited Edie before crossing over, asking her to protect his children. Was this it? Fiddlesticks.

I needed to talk to a ghost and get answers. But would someone hear me if I called?

Edie crouched down beside me, her hands resting on my arm. 'What does that mean? Will it hurt them?'

Alanis pursed her lips. 'I cannot say.'

'You can't say? You *can't say*? That's *it*?' I said.

'Niamh, she's trying her best,' said Ben.

I sighed. 'I know. I'm sorry.' She wasn't the person to be angry at. Whoever was responsible I would destroy in this life and the next.

Edie squeezed my shoulder. I had no idea what to say to her. Or anyone else. What were we supposed to do?

5
Edie

Cursed. Who'd curse Josh and Maggie? They'd done *nothing* wrong! They were good people! Who'd want to hurt such good people?

Unable to help any further, Doc and Alanis left not long after their diagnosis.

Ben began to move the furniture in Josh's room so that we could do a seance. Moving furniture was a big part of the process, regardless of who we were summoning, just in case the ghost could muster up enough power to throw something at us. If they were angry or powerful enough to do it, it could result in serious injury. Mum had seen it happen a couple of times, so it was a risk she wasn't willing to take.

It helped to have a personal object that belonged to the ghost being summoned, but it wasn't always necessary. Sometimes a personal connection was enough. They were far more likely to respond to someone they knew.

I wasn't sure if Mum planned to summon Nathan or my dad. I hoped it was my dad, but I also knew that even if I did see him, it wasn't about me. Even if I hadn't seen him in forever.

We stood in a circle in Josh's room – well, more of a triangle, since there were three of us – then began to chant. 'We call upon the spirits, to commune with us tonight, grant us your presence, come join us in the light.'

A faint figure appeared in the middle. Blue eyes came into focus, followed by white hair. And a hospital gown. It was Josh's granddad, Nathan. 'I asked you to protect them!' He flew at me. I jerked back, almost stumbling into Josh's dresser. I clung to it to keep myself upright.

Mum got in front of me, staring Nathan down. She looked *fierce*. 'This isn't her fault.'

He turned on her: 'Isn't it?'

'How were we supposed to know what we were protecting them from? And besides, we've done everything we can.'

'It isn't enough!'

A gust of wind flew through the room, blowing the closed curtains and slamming Josh's door. I jumped.

'Javi!' Mum called. 'Javi!'

Dad appeared in a pop. It was the first time I'd seen him since his death ten years ago. He looked just like I remembered. Obviously. Ghosts didn't age.

His hair skimmed his chin, framing his face. He had on jeans and a black T-shirt, just like he always wore. And like he'd died in. He had the same fun, playful air that I remembered, too. Mum had always been the disciplinarian, while Dad had always been the rule breaker.

After Dad had died, I'd begged Mum to let me do a seance so that I could speak to him, but she'd said no.

Something about seeing him all the time making it harder for us to move on.

I was pretty sure it was because losing him had made her terrified of ghosts, but I couldn't prove it. And that didn't really make sense, since he'd died in a car accident, but whatever. Logic wasn't my mum's strong point.

'Nathan, it isn't their fault. We talked about this,' said Dad. My heart filled with love. Dad was right there. In front of me. For the first time in a decade. And he'd come to protect us! Was Nathan going to go rogue and turn into a poltergeist? Could ghosts who'd crossed over do that?

Nathan's nostrils flared. 'Who's going to protect my family if the people who know about all this supernatural malarkey don't?'

'They *are* protecting them. But they're not miracle workers. Or psychics.'

Nathan disappeared in a pop. Everyone alive exhaled.

'Why'd you summon him and not me?' Dad asked Mum.

'He was the one who sent the warning,' Mum replied. 'It seemed like a logical idea at the time.'

'He's pretty angry,' said Dad. He floated in a circle. Spotting me for the first time, he drifted over to me. 'You've grown! You never used to be this tall!'

I tried to be annoyed at his lame joke, but I couldn't hide my grin. 'Shut up.'

Dad grinned back. 'You look so good. My little rocker.'

My grin grew as I showed off my Foo Fighters T-shirt. Mum had given me a pop culture education Dad would be proud of, I knew that much. I'd inherited all his favourite CDs and would play them on repeat, falling asleep listening to them for years after he'd crossed over.

'I keep trying to get tickets to see them, but I'm never fast enough,' I said with a pout.

'Keep trying. It's worth it!' he said.

Mum cleared her throat. 'At the risk of breaking up the party, we have two people who are quite possibly in supernatural comas in the next room. Can we focus, please?'

'Right. Yes. Sorry Neevie,' said Dad. I suppressed a giggle at his use of Mum's nickname. Mum rolled her eyes.

'Do you know what happened to Josh and Maggie?' I asked him.

'Beyond what you already know?' His face fell. 'No. I'm sorry.'

Spirits existed outside of time on the Other Side, which meant that they could see past, present, and future events. They weren't allowed to interfere, but some did anyway. And apparently didn't face repercussions, since both my dad and Nathan had done it, and they seemed the same.

'We're not supposed to see stuff related to loved ones. Just in case, you know?' said Dad.

Mum nodded. 'That's why you only have fragments of information.'

He nodded, dejected.

*

Mum paced Maggie and Josh's living room. If she went any faster, she was going to dig a hole in the ground. Harry and Abigail were due home any minute. How the hell were we going to tell them what had happened?

'Just tell him the truth,' said Ben as he came downstairs.

'What are you doing down here? You're supposed to be watching them!' Mum snapped.

Ben put his hands up. 'I needed some water and you didn't reply when I called you.'

'She was busy marking the floor with her pacing,' I said.

Mum glared at me but didn't say anything.

Giving Mum a wide berth, Ben went into the kitchen. I followed him in.

'Do you know where the glasses are?' asked Ben.

I went into a cupboard and took one out, then passed it to him. 'Thanks,' he said as he filled it with tap water. 'Do you think Harry will be as bad as your mum is making out?'

'He's a sceptic, I can tell you that much. And a grump. And—'

The front door opened. Both us of jumped. We went into the living room, where Mum was stood in position, frozen like a deer. I put my hand on her arm. She rubbed her face, shaking her head. Thinking on her feet had never been her thing, and this was the ultimate test of that. Especially since we couldn't lie, either.

'Niamh, Edie. Ben, is it? What are you all doing here?' Harry asked as he walked in.

Abigail saw us and ran over, hugging Mum and me. Something pulled at my heart. We were about to break this family, and who knew if it would ever be repaired?

'You should sit down. We need to tell you something,' said Mum.

'I'll decide if and when I sit down. Abigail, come here,' said Harry. So he was in *that* kind of mood. Great.

Reluctantly, Abigail returned to her dad. They stood in the doorway, watching us expectantly.

'I'm really not sure this is something Abigail should hear,' said Mum.

'I can take her into the garden—'

'No, Ben. That won't be necessary,' said Harry. 'Where are my wife and son?'

Mum stared at the floor and rocked on her heels. 'They've been cursed.'

Harry's face went crimson. 'Meaning *what*?'

'They're in comas.'

'What? Where are they?'

'Mum? Josh?' said Abigail, her eyes filling with tears.

I went over to her and crouched down to her height. She leaned into me, her snotty tears going all over the side of my T-shirt. I didn't care. I'd do whatever I could to look after this little girl who'd already been through so much.

As far as we could tell, she'd had no physical after effects from the possession, but she was definitely much more withdrawn since it'd happened. I wouldn't have been surprised if she was traumatised. Which made it all the more important to get Josh and Maggie fixed for her. 'We're going to do everything we can to fix this.'

'Where are they?' growled Harry.

Mum's eyes betrayed her. She glanced upstairs.

Harry took the stairs two at a time, the rest of us behind him. He went into the room, saw the two figures on the bed and started shaking them. 'Maggie, wake up. Wake up!'

Abigail still holding on to me, I leaned into Mum. 'Well, at least he believed you.'

'One less hurdle. But not by much,' said Mum. She reached out to Harry and tried to touch his arm as he shook the unreactive figures in front of him. He jerked it away, glaring at her. 'What did you *do*?'

'It wasn't me! Edie and I were here, and Maggie and Josh passed out at the same time. They've been checked over by a doctor and a healer—'

'A *healer*? What can one of your so-called healers possibly do that a doctor can't?'

'Sense that they've been cursed,' mumbled Mum.

I glanced over my shoulder. Ben was hanging back, looking anywhere but in front of him, where the situation was unfolding. It was probably weird for him, being in a house where he was trying to help a family who were basically strangers to him. He'd met the Morgans a few times, but not enough to call them friends.

Harry shook his head. 'What is this? Some kind of prank?'

Ah. There it was. The denial.

'I wish it was,' said Mum. 'We've already started researching, although so far we haven't found much.'

'Then we need to get them to a hospital,' said Harry.

'No!' said Mum. 'There's nothing a hospital can do for them.'

'A hospital can keep them stable,' said Harry.

'With all due respect,' said Ben, stepping forwards, 'a hospital would be out of its depth with a condition this complex.'

'Complex? You said they were in comas,' said Harry.

'They are,' said Ben. 'But they're in supernatural ones. It's not the same thing. We have no idea what's going on right now other than that they're stable and still breathing.'

'Is that supposed to reassure me?'

'No. It's just the facts,' said Ben.

I suppressed a snigger.

'What am I supposed to tell their jobs in the meantime?' said Harry.

'That they're contagious?' I suggested. 'Nobody will question that. They'll be too afraid of catching something. They won't even need to know the details if you say that.'

Ben nodded. 'She's right. That's a good idea.'

Harry ground his teeth together, clearly trying not to rage in front of his five-year-old. He squared up to my mum. Ben and I stepped forwards, ready to protect her. Abigail tensed beside me. 'You have forty-eight hours to fix this, then I don't care what you say. I'm taking them to the hospital.'

6
Niamh

Forty-eight hours to figure out what the hell was wrong with Maggie and Josh. No problem. No problem at all.

No, it was a Jupiter-sized challenge I wasn't sure I could solve in that amount of time. Which of course made me feel worse, because I didn't want to see my friends suffering.

After Harry's threat, Ben went home to reach out to his connections and raid his book stash to see what he could find out. Edie and I took turns watching Maggie and Josh, but there wasn't much to watch: nothing changed.

We had to move them every so often to make sure they didn't get bedsores. Harry at least helped with that, since they were too heavy for Edie to move on her own.

If I'd remembered to bring the stupid gargoyle over sooner, would it have made a difference? Would it have protected them? I'd never know, and that made me even more annoyed at myself.

To give Harry some alone time, Edie and I went home to get food and feed Tilly. We left him to monitor Maggie and Josh, hoping he wouldn't do anything stupid.

'Mum?' said Edie as we walked home. There was something in the way she said it that suggested she was nervous. About what, though?

'What?' I said.

Edie balled her hands into fists. She glanced around us, to check if anyone was nearby. Aside from a couple of ghosts on the other side of the road, we were alone.

'When the demon was inside Abigail, before you and Ben got there, it…it said something.'

I stopped walking. 'What did it say?'

'It said it wanted me.'

I tried to hide my shock and horror, but it was hard. 'Are you sure?'

'Yes I'm sure!'

'OK, sorry. Why didn't you tell me sooner?'

'I knew you'd freak,' she said. 'And I was distracted with the Josh thing. I was just glad everyone was OK. But now…'

'Now it looks like it might be related,' I finished.

'Do you really think someone would target them as a way to get to me?' she asked as we walked down the hill back to our place. I could feel the anxiety radiating from her as she sped up her pace.

'I hope not. But that's how you get to people, right? Through the ones they love.'

Edie tensed, digging her nails into her palms. 'I really hope we're wrong.'

'Me too.'

*

After feeding Tilly and Edie – I didn't eat as I wasn't hungry – I went back to the Morgans' place. Harry was in the same seat he'd been in when we'd left, leaning over his wife and holding her hand. It was a rare show of affection from a man I'd always known to be very stoic.

When he looked up at me, his eyes were glassy from tears.

'Why don't you go for a walk, get some fresh air?' I suggested. 'I can keep an eye on stuff here.'

Everything was quiet. Abigail was watching TV in her room, and it wasn't like Maggie or Josh were going anywhere. There was nothing he could do sitting in the same chair all day other than make his joints go stiff.

He narrowed his eyes at me. I waited. It was on him to accept or reject my offer. I wasn't going to justify myself or offer again. He didn't have anyone else that could help and he knew it.

Sighing, he stood up and walked out without saying anything. A few minutes later, I heard the front door slam.

My body relaxed. Harry's anger was palpable and it didn't help my nerves.

I sat on the armchair he'd placed by Maggie's bedside. It was still warm from the hours he'd spent sitting in it. I held Maggie's hand. 'I'm so, so sorry Mags. But don't worry. I'm going to fix it. I'll fix it if it's the last thing I —'

Before I could finish my promise, my phone rang. I ignored it, letting it go to answerphone. It wasn't Edie or Ben – they had special ringtones – and they were the only people I wanted to hear from.

But whoever it was, was persistent. They rang me again.

Letting go of Maggie's hand, I took my phone from my bag. It was Manju, an old friend from school. She was now headteacher of the very same school we'd studied at, and which was currently home to an Ancient Egyptian mummy. We didn't speak much anymore because life and proximity had forced us apart, but she knew my secret, and I knew she'd be there for me if I needed her. Why would she be calling me now?

'Oh my god thank god you answered!' said Manju's frantic voice as soon as I picked up. 'I have the kind of problem only you can fix!'

Another ghost? Great. Perfect timing. Honestly, utterly brilliant.

Could it be a ghost related to the mines, or was it one tied to the mummy she'd brought in? The latter seemed more likely given the timing of the activity. Edie had been excited to see the exhibit, but historical objects were far safer in museums – who often employed supernatural experts in case of something going awry – than in a school, where nobody had any experience of dealing with supernatural occurrences.

Ghosts that were thousands of years old weren't impossible, but unlikely. By that age, most were too weak to do anything malicious and couldn't manifest as anything more than a glowing blob. At that point, there was nothing that could be done other than encouraging them to cross over.

I stood up and walked the length of the double bed while I spoke to her. There was far too much furniture in

Maggie's bedroom for me to pace satisfyingly. 'I want to help, but I'm really tied up right now—'

'Please! I can't have the parents finding out! They'll either think I'm mad or burn the place down to get rid of the evil spirit! I'm begging you! I'll pay you anything!'

I sighed. What could I do? I'd warned her against bringing historical objects into the school, but she'd insisted in the name of education. Education for her on the supernatural, it seemed.

'I'll be there tonight at eight,' I said.

'Eight?'

'Do you want me hovering around talking to ghosts when there are other people there?'

'Right. Yes. Of course. Yes. I'll see you then.'

*

I pulled up at the school just before eight. Manju ran out and dove towards the car. Her tanned skin was flushed, her black hair stuck to her sweaty skin.

'Quick…please…music…room…'

I put my hand on her arm, then followed her through the school. We cut through the hall, where the Ancient Egyptian display was still intact. Aside from the inevitable dirty fingerprints on the glass case around the sarcophagus, that was.

A security guard lingered on the edge of the hall, his eyes never moving from the mummy.

We arrived at the music room, just off the school hall. I opened the door, a shaking Manju stood behind me. But there was nobody else – human or ghost – in there.

'He was just in here!'

'You *saw* him?'

She nodded. 'Is that normal?'

'No.'

Her eyes went wide. 'Wh-what?'

'Are you sure?'

'Yes! I saw him!'

'I believe you. I just don't get how.'

I'd gone to school with Manju. She knew I could see ghosts, since most of the people I went to school with did, thanks to something that had happened that I preferred to forget. Many of my old school peers had long since moved away, but a few remained, Manju included.

Why did everything seem to make no sense ever since I'd moved back to my hometown, hoping things would make *more* sense?

'Could he be invisible?' she asked.

I clicked my tongue. 'Maybe. I doubt it, though. I don't sense anything. Usually the room would feel cold or suppressed or something, but it doesn't.'

'Oh.'

'Wait here.'

The corridor outside the music room led in two directions. To the right was the hall, which we'd walked through to get there. Straight in front was the cloakroom.

'Are you sure it's safe?' she asked, clinging to my sleeve.

'You'll be fine,' I reassured her, patting her arm.

I instructed Manju to stay there and shout me if anything happened, then I walked through the cloakroom. All I could hear was the sound of my breathing. There was no chill; no suffocation. No glowing. No whispering. None of the usual signs of ghost activity.

I flicked on the cloakroom light.

'ARGH!'

I turned. Behind me was a guy. Partially wrapped in bandages.

*

He ran at me, gesticulating wildly and shouting stuff, but I couldn't understand what he was saying. Bits of bandage clung to his leather-like skin, flapping about as he ran towards me. He had a thick head of cropped black hair on his head, with sunken, yellowing eyes. They were the most animated part of him, and they conveyed he was old beyond the young features of his dehydrated face.

His skin looked like an old leather jacket that hadn't been treated properly in, well, thousands of years. It was wrinkly, dry, and angry looking. Aside from the handful of bandages left on his skin, he was pretty much standing in front of me, totally naked.

I held my hands out. 'Whoa, whoa. Stay there. Personal space.'

He seemed to get the message as he stopped walking, then lowered his head and shoulders as if deflated. Dammit, he was trying to tell me something, but we didn't speak the same language. Of course not. He was thousands of years old. How was he even still moving about?

While Ben had suggested there were more supernatural creatures out there than I knew of, mummies hadn't been one I'd ever considered. They weren't supernatural creatures; they were dead people with no internal organs and wrapped in linen. If they were from Egypt, anyway, which I knew this guy was from what Edie had told me about the exhibit. What the hell was going on?

I smacked my lips together. What could I do? What spell could I cast? I didn't have any resources with me. Think, woman, think!

Could I make up my own spell? I'd never done that before, but all spells started in someone's head, right?

Please work, brain. 'Spirits I ask you: translate the words, spoken by a man who's cursed, so I can find out why he's on this earth.'

I doubted that would work, but it was worth a shot. It was a total stab in the dark. I didn't even know if he *was* cursed. But, I mean, a reanimated mummy seemed like a good candidate for a curse of some kind.

'What did you just do?' His voice came out garbled and deep, but it was pretty clear he was speaking in English. He seemed just as surprised by it as I did.

'Oh my god! It worked!'

'What worked? Wait, you can understand me?' said the mummy.

'And you can understand me?'

'Yeah. What did you do?'

'I cast a spell.'

'You must be a daughter of Isis,' he said.

'I'm not a witch,' I said. 'I'm a ghost hunter.'

'A daughter of Osiris! Fascinating,' he said. If my memory served me rightly, Osiris was the God of the Dead in Ancient Egypt. So I supposed, if you were into that sort of thing, I *was* affiliated with Osiris. 'Did you free me, Daughter of Osiris?'

'No,' I said, suppressing my chuckle at his nickname for me. 'You don't know who did?'

He shook his head. 'There was no one around when I woke up. I was on the floor in the hall, with my sarcophagus closed as if it had never been touched.'

Whoa. How the hell had that happened?

'What year is it?' he asked, his look of confusion growing deeper.

'2021.'

He let out a low whistle. 'I was in there for four thousand years.'

'WHAT?'

'Niamh, is everything OK?' called Manju from the music room.

'Yeah, sorry. Just figuring something out.'

'Is it safe to come out?'

I looked at my new mummy friend.

Before I could respond, Manju was beside me. And screaming.

I clamped my hand over her mouth. 'Sorry,' I said to the mummy. 'She's never seen anything like you before.'

'You mean she's never seen a cursed guy wrapped in bandages before? I wonder why.'

So apparently my spell had not only allowed him to speak twenty-first century English, but also given him my sense of humour. I was so going to regret inventing my own spell.

Slowly, I removed my hand from Manju's mouth. 'He's a mummy. He's been spelled to speak English. Seems pretty competent. Please don't scream.'

The mummy stood up. It wasn't as imposing as he wanted it to be. 'I *seem* competent to you? What does *that* mean?'

'I mean, you were in a glorified coffin for four thousand years. Lack of stimuli for that long would fry most people's brains.'

Manju let out a noise that sounded like a cross between a laugh and a sob. I patted her back.

He huffed. 'Part of my curse was that I remained compos mentis the whole. Damn. Time.'

'Dear lord, that's awful,' said Manju, clutching her heart.

I nodded my head in agreement. 'People suck. So, what are you? Human? Ghost? Zombie?'

He gestured to himself. 'I'm a person! Isn't that blindingly obvious?'

'But are you…*alive*?' asked Manju.

He harrumphed. As if to make a point, he put his hand to his chest to check for a heartbeat. Then placed the other in front of his face and breathed into see. 'See? I'm alive! How dare you?' His tone turned from jovial to angry; like he was going to lash out. Although what he could do when he was naked, skeletal, and barely taller than Tilly was beyond me.

Manju cowered. 'Sorry. New to this.'

'Didn't believe until you saw me in the music room?'

She shook her head. 'Why did you bang all the drums in there?'

'To get your attention. Obviously.' He gestured to me. 'Figured if I made enough noise, you'd come find me. Or find someone I could talk to. And you did! Well done you.'

I rolled my eyes. Would he always be so unnecessarily sarcastic?

'So, uh, how can we help you?' I said.

Manju had started to move behind me, as if she were hiding. I let it go. It was making her feel better in what was a weird situation. I'd let her have it.

'How should I know? I've been dead four thousand years! Everyone I knew has been six feet under for millenia!'

I sighed. Right. So it wasn't because he had unfinished business. But there had to be a reason why he'd woken up right now. Out of all the times he could've woken up, why this one?

'So, I hate to ask, but do you know how you were cursed?' I asked.

He glowered at me.

'Look, I know you don't want to relive it. If you even can. But it might help us to figure out what to do with you.'

'What to do with me? I'm not a prop!'

I rubbed my face. His defensiveness was making things harder than they had to be. Then again, it wasn't like I could blame him. He had been trapped for millenia. I'd be fuming after that, too. 'I didn't mean it like that. How much do you remember?'

He shook his head. 'All of it. It's played inside my head over and over for millenia. All my other memories have faded, but that one? That one I remember like it happened right before we met.'

'I'm so sorry,' said Manju, peeking out from my shoulder. Tears were running down her cheeks. 'That's horrible. How could anyone curse someone like that!'

Apparently my heart was made of stone because his story hadn't stirred me in the slightest. Maybe I'd heard too many stories like his in all my years of dealing with ghosts. So far, though, he didn't seem like he was going to be a massive arse because of his backstory. That was something.

'People suck,' my mummy friend and I chorused. We met eyes and laughed. Well, at least we agreed on something.

'Breaking the curse couldn't have been an accident,' he said.

'What do you mean?'

'To do the curse, you need a person's hair, teeth, or bone. And some blood. The people who cursed me were pretty confident nobody would ever find the spell to break the curse, no matter how hard they tried. You can't accidentally break it. It's why I've been trapped so long.'

'So you're saying someone broke you out on purpose?'

He nodded.

Fiddlesticks. As if I didn't have enough to worry about already.

7
Edie

'Harry, you can't—'

'Are you seriously telling me I can't take my sick wife and son to the hospital when *they're in comas*?' he said, his tone as if I was a stupid child. I hated him so much. 'Make yourself useful and look after Abigail while I pack a bag, would you?' He flitted around the room, muttering to himself as if I wasn't there. Abigail and I stood in the door, watching him.

Abigail tugged on my sleeve and looked up at me with big, doe-eyes. She was so cute, but that made it all the more unnerving that she'd been possessed by a demon just a few weeks ago. You never expect it to be the cute ones. Which is probably why it'd taken ages for anyone to work out she was possessed, too. Was it really Abigail standing next to me? What if Josh and Maggie getting sick was a sign Mum's wards didn't work?

'Will Mum and Josh be OK?' she asked me, a pleading note in her voice. Something tugged at my heart. She sounded so much like the Abigail I remembered. How could it *not* be her standing next to me?

'Of course they will!' said Harry, answering a question that wasn't meant for him. Not the first time.

Swallowing down any thought of her possibly still being a demon, I gave her my sweetest smile. 'We'll make sure of it, don't you worry.'

Harry scoffed. 'What, like you have so far?'

Did he really have to be so antagonistic? This wasn't the time for it.

'We're looking into it. And we had them checked over. As far as we can tell, they're perfectly fine.'

'Those hippy dippy freaks your mum works with don't count.'

I crossed my arms, resisting the urge to lose my temper in front of Abigail. I wanted to set a good example for her. 'Just because they do things differently to you, that doesn't make them freaks.'

He stopped emptying out a drawer and turned to face me: 'You mean people who don't follow real, empirical evidence, don't deserve to be called idiots?'

He was trying to intimidate me, and I wasn't going to let him.

'Does that make Aunt Niamh and Edie idiots, Dad?' asked Abigail.

Score one for the five-year-old. I met Harry's gaze, challenging him to insult us in front of his daughter, whom he knew adored both of us. 'No, of course not.'

'But you just said—'

'I said it didn't!' he snapped.

Abigail sniffled. Way to comfort the traumatised child. I glared at Harry, and he at least had the nerve to look sheepish. I really hoped that whatever was going on with Josh and Maggie, they could hear this conversation and how rude Harry was being.

'Come on, Abigail. Why don't we go get you some ice cream?'

'Are you sure they'll be OK?'

'Don't worry,' I said, still glaring at Harry. 'Your dad's got it all covered.'

*

Of course Harry called an ambulance to take Josh and Maggie to the hospital, traumatising his young daughter for life. Arse. He took her with him to the hospital, too. I offered to babysit, but it seemed that without Maggie around, his true feelings for me – and Mum – came through. And wow were they hostile.

I mean, I didn't like the old grump either, but that didn't mean I'd be outwardly mean to him without provocation.

He was worried about them and I understood that. Mum and I were worried, too, but we knew that the doctors couldn't help. He was still in denial. He seemed to think that science and magic couldn't work together. But why couldn't they? Not everything needed to make perfect sense to exist. Scientists couldn't explain love, but that didn't make it any less real. Like they'd never be able to explain what Maggie saw in Harry and his grumpy face.

He even made me walk home in the dark, at night, something that Mum, Maggie, or Josh – heck, even Abigail – *never* would've allowed me to do. You could never be too careful about who – or what – was out there. It wasn't like it was far. But him doing that and practically shoving me out of the door showed his true feelings towards me in a way I'd never expected.

The town took on an eerie atmosphere as I walked home on my own. I heard every door slam; noticed every light flicker. At least half the street lights were out because the council were too cheap to replace them, which meant most of the light that lit my way came through closed curtains.

It was cold, too. So cold I could see my breath as I wrapped my arms around myself and walked a little faster to get home.

I jumped at every shadow; every sound. Weirdly, there were no ghosts about. I was so used to seeing them everywhere, absent ghosts made things creepier for me. As if something was wrong and was repelling them.

Since it was around nine at night, there were only really dog walkers out. Most people wouldn't be out that late unless they had to be.

I kept my fist wrapped around my keys, just in case I needed a weapon and so that I could get into the house as quickly as possible. Tilly couldn't do anything if someone attacked me, but her presence would reassure me. Her barking would no doubt scare any weirdos off if they came too close. They didn't know they'd get licked to death if they stepped through the front door. All they heard was a dog who wouldn't stop barking. With the curtains closed, she could've been any shape, size, and temperament.

My heart thudded in my chest as I walked faster. Just one more corner and I'd be on my street. It really wasn't that far. Why did it feel so much farther in the dark?

A shadow appeared out of the corner of my eye, highlighted by a streetlamp as I walked past it. It wasn't mine; it was bigger. And it was close. Instinctually, I walked faster, my power walk almost turning into a jog.

There weren't even any ghosts around for me to ask for help. There were *always* ghosts around. What was going on? Was I completely alone? Well, except for the person gaining ground on me. They were so close their shadow almost covered mine, but still, I daren't turn around. What if they had a knife on them? Or a gun? I'd never seen a gun before, but that didn't mean someone in town didn't own one. I wasn't *that* naive. Was this how things were going to end for me? Before I could save Josh and Maggie?

'Fancy seeing you around here.'

I jumped a mile. The person who'd been behind me was Dominic, out walking his dog.

'Dominic!'

He chuckled, revealing dimples alongside his chiseled cheeks. 'Sorry, I didn't mean to scare you. You all right?'

I knelt down to fuss his border terrier, hoping stroking the dog would calm me down. I could apologise to Tilly later. 'Just a rough day, that's all.'

'Sorry to hear that,' he said. 'Anything I can do to help?'

I stood up. His dog looked put out and stared at me, as if to say, 'You're not done yet, human.'

'I wish,' I said with a sigh.

'Come on. I'll walk you home.'

'You don't have to do that,' I said, although I did want him to. I'd never felt more alone.

'Nonsense. Dave and I don't mind.'

'Who's Dave?'

'My dog,' he said, gesturing to the terrier still glaring at me.

I stuffed my hands into my pockets, still clutching my keys, just in case. 'Your dog is called Dave?'

'Yeah. Way better than some of these dog-specific names. I mean, come on. Fido? Who'd shout that in the park?'

'But you shout Dave?' I said as we carried on down the street. Having him walk with me made me feel better. I didn't even flinch when a car drove past.

He shrugged. 'Yeah. For all they know, I'm calling a kid.'

'True,' I said as we reached the front drive. 'Thanks for walking with me. Sorry it wasn't farther.'

What the hell had made me say that? That was so not me. Did that qualify as flirting? What would Josh think? Frazzle. I'd have to tell him when he woke up.

If he woke up.

I shoved that thought to the back of my mind and turned back to Dominic.

He pointed to Moonie. 'Nice gnome.'

'Thanks,' I said, grinning. 'He's called Moonie.'

Dominic chuckled, studying the gnome – sorry, gargoyle – for a moment, then looked back up at me. 'Hopefully we can do this again some time,' he said with a smile before walking off. He was an interesting one, that Dominic. I couldn't figure him out.

Tilly greeted me as soon as I walked inside, jumping up and barking and asking me in her doggy way how dare I leave her? I felt awful she'd been on her own for most of the weekend, but it wasn't like we'd expected Josh and Maggie to collapse.

I let her out while putting her dinner together, along with some extra coconut oil as a treat. It was her favourite and the least I could do for leaving her. I'd put some peanut butter in her Kong for her supper. She'd soon forget that I'd abandoned her.

Tilly came in at the smell of tripe and offal and happily munched away on it. When I went to close the back door, I spotted the local ghosts floating around. Where had they been on my walk home?

'Hey, Arthur!' I whispered to one of them, gesturing for him to come over. He haunted the street behind ours, having lived there in the 1950s. He had no interest in moving on and we left him to it, but if something happened in our area, he knew about it.

'How can I help you, young Edie?' he asked as he floated over and hovered in front of me.

While most ghosts – Dad not included – couldn't get into the house, our garden wasn't warded. We'd warded the garden at an old house and had to explain the symbols on the fence to our neighbours. It hadn't gone well. So we didn't bother anymore.

Mum did ward her greenhouse, though. Especially as she grew herbs in there that could be used for spells or potions. Or cooking.

'Where'd you go before?' I asked Arthur.

'What do you mean?'

'I was walking home and there were no ghosts. Like, anywhere. I always see you. Well, not you specifically, but you know what I mean.'

Arthur tilted his head, as if in thought. He looked up to the left, then to the right. 'I don't know.'

'What do you mean?' I said.

'I mean I don't know. I was here and the sun was up. The next thing I knew, I was here and it was dark.'

Well if that wasn't weird, I didn't know what was.

8
Niamh

'Edie, I can't—'

'Harry lied. He took them to the hospital. I'm really sorry! I tried to stop him!'

The temptation to bang my head against a wall was strong.

Instead, I carried on talking to Edie on the phone. Manju watched me with a concerned expression on her face. The mummy just watched me, his expression curious. Of course. He'd never seen a phone before.

'I'm really really sorry! I tried to stop him!'

'It's not your fault,' I reassured her. And it wasn't. Harry had always been an idiot that didn't listen.

'I really tried, but he just got meaner. I didn't want him to cause a scene in front of Abigail, but he didn't seem to care.'

'Of course he didn't,' I mumbled.

'What's wrong?' asked Manju.

I sighed. She was such a teacher. 'Where are you now?' I asked Edie.

'Home. He wouldn't let me go to the hospital.'

'All right. Stay there. I'll be back as soon as I can.'

'Mum?'

'Yeah?'

'Be careful. Something weird is happening,' said Edie.

A chill went down my spine. Something weird was happening, all right.

'Another mummy?' teased our new friend as soon as I'd hung up.

I glared at him. 'No.'

'No need to be such a grump,' he said.

Oh, that was it. I squared up to him. He was shorter than me by about a foot. '*I'm* the grump? You've been nothing but sarcastic since we met and all I've tried to do is help you. I should leave you to fend for yourself, see how long you survive as a real-life not-mummy in a society that likes to dissect people and things it doesn't understand all in the name of science!'

'What's science?'

I rubbed my forehead. How had I gotten into this situation? What the hell even was my life?

'*That's* your answer?'

'Lady, I've lived through worse than you can possibly imagine. After the horrific things I've had done to me, don't you think I deserve to be a little grumpy?'

'Enough!' shouted Manju, walking up to us and pushing us apart. 'You *both* have the right to be angry. But that doesn't mean you have to take it out on each other. You can help one another if you learn to cooperate, and you both know it.'

I sighed. 'You're right. I'm sorry.'

The mummy nodded. 'I'm sorry too. I truly do need your help.'

Damn right he did. Most people wouldn't believe he was real, and as soon as they did, he'd be either exhibited or dissected. Or both.

'Can you give me a minute to make a phone call?' I asked them.

They both nodded.

We didn't have room at our place for the mummy to stay. He'd end up sleeping on the sofa. In his current state, he looked too frail – mentally and physically – to be able to handle a hyperactive westie. I also didn't want to risk leaving them alone, but that would've been an inevitability. Somehow I didn't think Spectre would be a good referee. There wasn't much a ghost could do, let alone a ghost cat.

Ben picked up right before his phone went to voice mail. Phew. I could hear someone laughing in the background, and the faint sounds of music. 'Hey, Niamh. I'm kind of busy right now. I'm with Jaya.'

I swallowed down the dread that that statement filled me with and focused on what was going on. 'I'm sorry for interrupting again, but, uh, I have a situation.'

'What do you mean?'

I lowered my voice. 'I have a mummy.'

'A mummy?'

'The Ancient Egyptian kind.'

'If you're joking right now…'

'Why would I make something like that up?' I said.

'Fair point. So what do you need me for?'

'He has nowhere to stay.'

'And I live alone,' he finished for me.

I nodded, then realised he couldn't see me. 'Could you…babysit him?'

'Babysit!' echoed the mummy. 'I don't need a babysitter!'

'But you *do* need somewhere to stay,' said Manju. 'We can't have you staying around the school, sorry. Unless you want to remain perfectly still in your sarcophagus again…'

The mummy's shoulders slumped. He looked like he'd miss the place. God only knew why; I'd always thought school was the worst place ever.

'Can you give me half an hour?' he said.

'Sure. See you in a bit.'

I hung up then turned to Manju: 'Do you have anything for him to wear? At least to get him out of here without it looking too weird.'

A smile crept across her face.

*

'A black cloak? How is that inconspicuous?' I asked, studying the outfit Manju was holding out for the mummy to wear.

'It's the only thing we've got that's big enough.' She shrugged. 'Downside to teaching primary school.'

'You're telling me that your drama department doesn't have any outfits for adults or absurdly tall kids?'

'We don't have adults in our performances and the tall kids just bring their own stuff.'

Of course they did.

I held the wool-blend cloak out for our mummy friend. He wasn't quite naked anymore, but he sure wasn't inconspicuous, either.

While Halloween was nearing, that didn't mean someone small and fragile like him wouldn't still attract attention for all the wrong reasons. Society had a habit of 'othering' people it didn't understand, then treating them like science experiments.

He stared at the scratchy cloak.

'It's this or go naked,' I told him.

He snatched it out of my hand and wrapped it around himself.

*

'How long do I have to wear this awful piece of fabric?' the mummy asked, fidgeting in his seat and pulling at the cloak as we drove to Ben's.

'I'm sure Ben will have something better when we get there,' I said, even though I wasn't sure. He was a lot shorter and slimmer than Ben, for obvious reasons. We might have to raid the children's section. Or raid a charity shop. Or even make something.

Wait. I couldn't sew. Did I know anyone who could?

The mummy sighed, settling for staring out of the window as we drove. 'So this is how you get around everywhere?'

'This or walking. There are also bikes, but I hate those.'

'Why? What are they?'

'They have two wheels on, and you move them using your leg muscles. It's a lot of work.' I also couldn't ride one, but that was besides the point.

'That sounds interesting,' he said. 'So much has changed.'

'It has been a few years,' I said.

'Really? I had no idea,' he said.

Yeah, he definitely got my sense of humour from that spell.

He reached over and stroked the plastic dashboard. A hint of embarrassment surged through me. My car was cheap, old, and not that good. But then, to him, it was probably still a marvel. His fingers carried on to the door, then over the glass in the window. 'It's all so different.'

'How much were you aware of in your sarcophagus?'

He sighed. 'I couldn't hear anything. When they found me in the pyramid, I felt vibrations. Sometimes heard muffled voices. But never much more. They tried to open the sarcophagus at some point, but I think they damaged the foot, because I heard something snap. Then they stopped trying to open it. At another point, they put me through some sort of tunnel that made loud, whirring noises. I was moved about a lot after that.'

'If they damaged your sarcophagus, they'll have put you through a machine that can see inside to the contents. To you.'

Edie had made me watch so many historical and archaeological documentaries, I was pretty sure I could direct one myself from everything I'd learned.

'What's a machine?'

Oh fiddlesticks. How did I explain that?

'Um…it's a mechanical device that does different things.'

'That…didn't clear anything up.'

'I'll find you a dictionary that will explain things better,' I said.

'What's a dictionary?'

It was going to be a long evening.

*

The mummy and I arrived at Ben's place right after he'd told us to. He was stood at the door, talking to someone. She kissed him. I flinched.

'Something I should know before I go in?' said the mummy, his eyes narrowed at me.

'No. Nothing to know,' I said a little too quickly. Nothing except that I was apparently jealous of whomever was standing on Ben's front porch, anyway. Jaya?

He sighed. 'If you say so.'

The woman turned around. It was Jaya. Why did I feel so jealous that she'd been at Ben's when I'd rang him?

Didn't matter. There were more pressing matters to deal with.

I waited until Jaya had driven off, then the mummy and I got out of the car.

'Truly a fascinating contraption,' he said as we walked up the drive, still staring at my car. He couldn't keep his eyes off it, which meant I had to guide him up the drive so that he didn't walk into Ben's Ford Fiesta. Idiot.

'You'll get used to them,' I told him.

Ben spotted us and smiled. 'Miraculous.'

'Why thank you,' said the mummy.

Ben jumped back. 'He *talks*?'

'I cast a spell to help him speak English,' I said to Ben. When I'd cast it, I wasn't sure how effective it'd be. But so far, it seemed to work on everyone the mummy came into contact with. I was impressed.

Ben smiled. 'Nice spell.'

Butterflies filled my stomach at his compliment. I tried very hard to kill them as I said, 'Thanks.'

'He has a name, too,' said the mummy, shooting me a look that suggested I should've asked for it. Oops. 'Fadil,' he said, glaring at me.

Ben smiled at his new houseguest, tilting his head in curiosity. 'Ben.'

The three of us stepped inside. Once we were in the privacy of Ben's place, Fadil shrugged off the cloak.

'The clothes you wear in these times are so itchy.' He shivered, as if trying to get rid of the itches. 'How do you wear such horrible things?'

'We don't. That's a costume, usually worn over the top of other clothes. You don't feel the fabric usually,' I said.

'That explains a lot,' said Fadil, rubbing his arms with his mangled hands.

Ben's eyes went wider than saucers. I was starting to wonder if Ben would treat him like a science experiment, but then I knew that if he did, it would be to help Fadil. Any academic understanding would be a bonus to him.

'What? Never seen a mummy before?' said Fadil.

I bit my lip. It was too easy to laugh. Did he even know he'd made a joke?

Ben's lips were pursed and his eyes narrowed, as if he were studying Fadil and trying to work out what to make of him. Which, to be fair, he probably was.

'Do you have anything to drink?' asked Fadil. 'I'm parched.'

The inside of his mouth looked as dry as the outside of his body. It was a miracle he could even talk. Did it hurt him to?

'Of course,' said Ben. He returned a minute later with some pyjama bottoms, a T-shirt, and a glass of water.

'They might be a bit big, but it should keep you a bit warmer,' Ben said as he handed him the clothes.

'Thanks,' said Fadil, staring at them. 'These are much nicer than that cloak was.'

I scowled. Ben laughed. Our options had been limited. It was better than him catching pneumonia hours after being reanimated.

Ben and I looked away as he pulled on the clothes, although it wasn't like we hadn't already seen him naked. It didn't seem to bother him outside of the odd shiver that he elicited, no doubt from the English weather he wasn't used to.

We turned back around, and he was wearing Ben's black pyjama bottoms with a white T-shirt. He sat back down.

Fadil took the water from Ben with hands that barely looked big enough to hold the glass. Ben and I watched as he lifted the glass to his lips with shaking hands. He stopped before taking a sip and glared at us. 'I'm not on display, you know.'

'Sorry,' we chorused, looking away sheepishly.

He sipped his water, then swallowed. And coughed. It was the sound of someone whose throat was dry. Which, of course, it was. He started chugging the water.

Ben held his hands out and reached for the glass. 'Whoa, whoa, whoa. Slow down there. You'll make yourself ill.'

Fadil paused, holding the glass halfway to his lips. He'd already drank more than half of its contents. 'What?'

'You haven't drank anything in a long time. Going from nothing to a lot in a short space of time, when your body isn't used to it, could make you sick.'

Fadil put the glass on the coffee table. 'You're right. I do feel strange.'

I shifted from foot to foot.

'What's wrong?' said Ben.

'As if I don't have enough to deal with already, Edie called me while I was at the school: Harry took Maggie and Josh to the hospital.'

'I thought he said he'd give us forty-eight hours?' he said.

'I thought he was a nice guy, albeit a little boring and a non-believer. Turns out I was wrong,' I grumbled.

'I'm sorry, Niamh. Why don't you go home to Edie? I can handle this.'

'This? *This*? I'm not a this!' protested Fadil.

'Sorry,' said Ben.

I leaned into him, barely moving my lips as I spoke: 'he's very easily offended.'

Ben snorted. 'Noted.'

'What are you laughing about?' asked Fadil.

'Nothing important,' I said. 'Are you sure you'll be all right?'

'Yeah, I got this. You go see Edie. She needs you.'

'Wait. Is he the mummy who was in the sarcophagus that's on display at the school?'

'Yup. Someone broke into the glass case, then his sarcophagus – which is damaged, by the way – and broke *him* out. The best part? The sarcophagus and glass casing are still intact.'

I couldn't even. Why would someone do that? How would they even know that he was cursed to break him out? Especially a guy that old? It didn't make sense.

Was that why I'd sensed the buzzing coming from him? Was that because he was still alive? How would I be able to sense it, though?

'So they used magic to get him out?'

'They must've done. Even if there were several of them to lift the lid, there's no way they couldn't have exacerbated the damage to the sarcophagus's foot without magic. It's too fragile,' said Mum.

'None of this makes sense,' I said.

Mum shook her head.

No wonder she seemed on edge. Someone had just added to our problems.

'Could that be why I could feel something coming from him?'

Mum narrowed her eyes at me. 'What do you mean?'

'When we visited, I could feel this, like, *buzzing* coming from him. It's hard to explain.'

Mum opened her mouth to reply, but didn't get the chance to say what she was thinking. Her phone rang. She closed her eyes and tensed her jaw. So much had happened already; what could someone want *now*?

She took her phone from her handbag and answered. 'What is it?' she said, trying to keep her tone even, but she sounded frustrated.

I tried to listen in, but her sound was too low, so I could only hear her end.

'What do you mean, smashed?'

She sighed. 'One minute,' she said to the person who was on the phone. She turned to me: 'could you order that pizza ASAP please? I'm about to chew my arm off.'

'Sure,' I said. I picked up my phone and opened the website for our local pizza place. We always ordered the same thing, so it was easy enough to do. I carried on listening as I ordered.

'Can you put what you can find in a bag? And make sure they don't empty the dumpster? I mean, I don't know how we can stop that, but—' Pause. 'Oh. That would work. I'll be there after school. I can't do anything in the meantime.' Another pause. 'All right. Talk to you tomorrow.'

'What was that about?' I asked.

'Manju said the cleaner found parts of a broken jar in the dumpster when emptying the hoover. She thinks it might be one of the canopic jars, since a couple of them have gone missing.'

'They found the mummy's insides in the bin?' I said.

'No. His insides are intact, as far as we know. Whoever cursed him put the spell ingredients in a canopic jar, along with some empty ones since mummies usually had four, disguised it with another spell, and left it with him so that he was treated like an actual mummy.'

'Doesn't that mean someone would have to know he wasn't a real mummy to break it?'

'Sorry, did I wake you up?'

'Sort of,' he said.

'Sorry.'

'It's OK. I need to get up anyway,' said Ben.

My phone buzzed. I moved it from my ear for a minute. It was a text from Doc. He had the blood test results for Maggie and Josh already. And they were clear. I texted him a quick thank you, then resumed my phone call with Ben.

'Doc says their bloods are fine,' I informed Ben.

'There's no way their comas aren't supernatural,' he said.

I sighed. He was right. But that just made things even more complicated, especially now that Harry had taken them to hospital.

'How's Fadil? Did he settle in?' I asked, needing a change of subject.

'Yeah. So far, he's enjoyed tea, toast, and CBeebies.'

'You put kids' TV on for him?'

'Fun but educational. It seemed like a good way to help him adjust to modern life while leaving out the scary bits.'

'Supernatural, historical, or modern?'

'All of the above?' Ben said with a laugh.

'Well it was a good idea anyway. I'm sorry for dumping him on you. With everything else going on—'

'There's nothing to apologise for. Have you heard any more about Maggie and Josh?'

'Harry won't even answer my phone calls.'

'What a charmer.' I pictured him rolling his eyes, even though I couldn't see him. That seemed like a Ben reaction.

'He's started rejecting them now.'

'Why? There's no need.'

Rustling came through the microphone. Getting his clothes out ready for work? I tried to picture what he'd sleep in. Pyjamas? Bottoms? Boxers? Nothing…?

Head, get out of gutter. There were bigger things to worry about.

'He's always been a non-believer,' I said, still trying to shake the image of a shirtless Ben from my head.

'This feels more like he blames you.'

I hesitated. Was he right? Did Harry blame us? Then again, I blamed us. 'I never thought of it like that, but you might be right. Fiddlesticks.'

'I'm sure we can get him to see things differently,' said Ben.

'But what if he's right?' I said. 'What if it is all my fault?' I cut through the graveyard. I enjoyed how slow it was in there, compared to everywhere else I seemed to frequent.

Thomas, the Victorian boy who haunted it, saw me and kicked his football in my direction. I kicked it back and smiled. He chased after it, giggling.

'We don't know that. There's no point jumping to conclusions yet. We still don't know enough.'

'Yeah, about that.' I sat on one of the nearby benches, which looked across at the church. I could just make out Lord Byron's book-shaped memorial in front of me. Someone had laid a rose in the centre.

'What? What happened?'

'Edie's been talking in her sleep. To the demon who possessed Abigail.'

Thomas sat beside me. He didn't interrupt my phone call, but I had a feeling sitting with someone who could see him made him happy.

'How do you know that's who it is?'

'She tells it to leave Abigail alone, says she's just a kid. Then there's a pause…and she asks the demon what she wants from her.'

'Her as in Abigail?'

'No. Her as in Edie.'

Ben didn't answer. There was a worrying silence on the other end of the line. I glanced over at Thomas, who gave me a supportive smile.

'Ben? You still there?'

'Yeah, sorry. Just thinking.'

I leaned back on the wooden bench, sinking farther down towards the ground. Thomas watched me, giggling. At least my situation was funny for someone.

'We'll figure this out,' Ben promised. I wished I shared his confidence. 'I need to go check on Fadil and get ready for work. Talk to you later?'

'Yeah. Bye.' Sighing, I hung up and turned to Thomas. 'Have you heard anything lately?'

'About what?'

'Our comatose friends. Or demons. Or the mine ghosts.'

Thomas adjusted his newsboy cap. 'I don't know anything about your friends or demons, I'm sorry. But I have seen and spoken to some of the ghosts from the mines. They seem harmless. They've just been floating around town, commenting on how much it's changed.'

'That's good. That's reassuring. Could you get their names, please? Then we can cross them off our list of ones to track down.'

'What list?' said Thomas.

'We found a list of everyone who worked at the mines, so we can track them down and make sure they're not causing any trouble or in any pain,' I said.

Thomas stood up straight and grinned. 'I shall do my best!'

'Thanks,' I said, pulling myself up and off the bench. 'Right. I'd better get to work.'

'Have fun!' said Thomas.

*

I arrived at the building site just before eight. They checked everyone's bags when we got there, although the only thing they'd find in mine was my phone and purse. I hadn't even taken lunch because I fully intended to leave the site and go into town to get something. I got stir crazy when I stayed in the same place all day, even if it was for work. It was part of why I liked being self-employed.

So much had changed there in such a short amount of time. So many more houses had cropped up in just over a month. They were almost ready for new homeowners to move in, which is why they needed someone to come in and help them paint. The more people they had on hand, the faster they could finish and get their money from house sales.

I met Eamon, the foreman, in his office. The last time I'd seen him, it had been because they'd opened a sinkhole in the middle of the site, and unleashed a bunch of ghosts as a consequence. Ghosts I was supposed to be investigating.

As if my to-do list wasn't long enough already.

'Niamh, welcome back,' said Eamon.

'Thanks,' I said.

He explained the rules of the site, introduced me to a few people, then took me to the house I'd be working on for the next few days.

There were footsteps on the dusty wooden floorboards, leading upstairs. I figured that was messy builders coming and going. Even if they'd worn shoe protectors, there'd still be footprints in the dust. Although why they hadn't hoovered all that up after plastering was beyond me. Some people really didn't take any pride in their work.

As much as I wanted to clean up, I ignored the mess and pulled on the overalls I'd brought with me. I was there to paint, not clean.

'Need any help, or ya happy to get on with things?' asked Eamon.

'I'm good,' I said, already starting to set up. My predecessor had left some equipment behind, and apparently had gone off sick without even bothering to put the lid on one of the tins of paint. By some miracle, it hadn't completely dried out.

'All righ'. You know where I am if you need anythin'.' He gave the house one more cursory examination, then left.

It wasn't very often I had somewhere to myself. Usually there was a person, or a dog, or a ghost, to keep my company. This time, it was just me. It felt like I'd be able to make better progress that way.

Humming to myself, I studied what my predecessor left behind. He hadn't even cleaned the roller after finishing for the day, the day he'd left. Ugh.

I removed the roller head and went into the kitchen. It was already fitted, but most of it was covered in sheets, the sink aside. Every wall was plastered, but not painted in the magnolia the homeowner had requested. The floorboards were covered in a thin layer of dust.

After cleaning the roller with some white spirit, and leaving it to dry on the sink, I wandered through the rest of the house. I wanted to get an idea of how much my predecessor had done, and if it was worth me redoing any of it. I hadn't asked Eamon because he probably would've said it was fine, but if it wasn't done to my standards, I was redoing it. Someone who left without putting the lid on a tin of paint didn't seem like the kind of guy who paid a lot of attention to detail.

The downstairs toilet was tucked away under the stairs. It had been plumbed in, and was the only room so far that seemed to be finished.

The fresh floorboards on the stairs creaked as I went upstairs. The sound echoed through the empty house. It was weird. I couldn't remember the last time I'd been in a house so empty.

Aside from the paint, the bathroom was done, which would be useful. Beyond that, the rest of the house had barely been touched. There were a couple of rooms with half-finished base coats. Why would he start a room and not finish it before moving on? It didn't make sense. It just meant that rooms would take longer to do. Some people's logic would always confuse me.

Shrugging it off, I returned downstairs. A couple of steps below the bottom, I slipped. Grabbing on to the handrail, I managed to right myself before hitting the stairs. That could've been painful.

When I was at the bottom, I turned back to see what I'd slipped on, but I couldn't see anything. Maybe I'd just lost my footing. Edie would blame my old age.

I laughed to myself, returning to the living room. The opened paint tin was a few feet away from where I'd left it. Had I moved it and forgotten? Had someone crept in and moved it while I was upstairs, as a hazing thing? God, I hoped not. I hated hazing. It was another reason I preferred to work alone.

Using my house key, I lifted the lid from another tin. The smell of fresh paint filled my nostrils, taking me back to when I was younger and used to help my mum redecorate. It was one of the few happy mother/ daughter memories I had.

'Ooooooo.'

I jumped, falling back onto my arse. What was that noise?

I couldn't sense any ghosts. That was what I didn't get. I'd always been able to sense ghosts in a house, so if someone else was there, I'd know. It had to be other people talking outside, or the wind. Maybe they hadn't finished sealing the windows properly yet. Idiots doing half-arsed jobs.

Ignoring it, I picked up the masking tape and started sealing around the skirting board. Half the room was done, but the other half wasn't. And I figured some of it would have started to come off after having been left over the weekend, so it couldn't hurt to go back over it. I preferred to know it was lines I'd laid myself rather than someone else.

The masking tape done, I stood up, pleased at a job well done. I could get the base coat done in the morning, then move on to another room after lunch. Probably somewhere upstairs. The exercise would do me good.

After stretching, I went to the window. Even though it was cold out, the house felt stuffy. It was hot work painting, and I wanted to cool the house off before I started properly. I could see a few people on another house in the distance, hear the faint sound of drilling, but mostly, it was quiet. And I was alone.

Until a silhouette appeared in the window.

11
Niamh

I jumped back. The silhouette disappeared.

What the hell? Was I going mad? I could've sworn I heard someone laughing as I backed away from the window, but I couldn't see anyone.

Hazing. It had to be hazing.

Forcing myself to shrug it off, I began painting the edges and corners. Some of my lines were wobbly, showing how much I was shaking.

But it couldn't be a ghost. I'd have sensed it. It *had* to be a person.

Didn't it?

I kept worrying for the rest of the morning, until I could go on lunch and get some fresh air. I'd made fairly good progress, having finished the base coat in the living room. I'd been determined not to go on lunch until it was done, using that as my incentive to finish it.

I pulled off my overalls so I wasn't walking around town covered in paint, then headed to my favourite sandwich shop. I'd earned it.

It was so small there was only room for a couple of people inside, so I joined the queue outside. It was worth the wait with their fresh ham from the local butchers and homemade bread.

Cars drove down the busy main road; people walked their dogs past the old Co-Op building opposite. It was part charity shop, part empty building nowadays. Remembering what it'd been like to wander around as a kid reminded me of how old I was. I shuddered.

'Cold?' said a voice.

I turned to see Jaya, joining me in the queue. What was she doing here? She wasn't local. I didn't mind her, but it felt like a long way to come just for a sandwich. 'Little bit. You?'

'Yeah,' she said, pulling her red scarf tighter around herself. 'But Ben says I need to try a sandwich from here, so here I am.'

'Where is he?'

'He's still at work. I said I'd pick up the sandwiches so he wasn't wasting his lunch in a queue,' she said.

'Yeah, that makes sense.'

Why was she meeting him for lunch? What was going on between them? Were they dating? I mean, they did kiss the other day. It wasn't a massive stretch. But why did it bother me so much?

The teenagers in the shop left, leaving room for Jaya and me to step inside.

'Afternoon,' said the man behind the counter. He was retired, using the sandwich shop as a hobby in his retirement. It sounded like a stressful way to spend your retirement, but who was I to judge?

'Can I get a ham salad cob please? With a bottle of Sprite?'

'What salad would you like?' he asked.

'Lettuce, tomato, cucumber, mayo,' I recited on autopilot.

I paid, then waited by the window as he gave my order to his wife, who hid in the back making the sandwiches.

'I'm sorry to hear about your friends,' said Jaya.

My back stiffened. How did she know?

'It must be awful, them being so sick and you still having to work.'

Had Ben told her? How dare he! It wasn't his story to tell. What if she told someone else? What if word got out? I barely knew her; I had no idea if I could trust her.

'Mmm,' I said, biting my tongue. Being a cow to her wouldn't get me anywhere, much as I wanted to be. And I didn't have the energy to really talk to her anyway. She didn't feel the same way.

'Do the doctors know what's wrong with them?'

'No,' I said. And they never would.

'Wow. With all the things modern medicine can do, you'd have expected them to have figured something out by now,' she said.

Please stop talking. For the love of sandwiches, please stop talking.

'I'm sure they'll figure something out,' she added, after I didn't respond.

'Yeah,' I said. Where was my sandwich? I really needed it. And maybe a sausage roll from Birds, too. Painting was hot work. And nothing was better than fresh, crumbly pastry.

The shop owner returned from the back and held out two sandwiches. One to me, and one to Jaya.

'Thanks,' we both said.

I practically snatched it out of his hand and started to power walk to Birds, but, unfortunately, Jaya was going in the same direction.

'Are you all right, Niamh?' she asked. 'You seem skittish.'

'Just got a lot on my mind and don't have long for lunch,' I said. 'Downside to working for someone else.'

'Oh yeah. Ben said you were working on that new building site for a few weeks. How's that going?'

'I'll let you know. I only started today.'

'No wonder you're in such a hurry! You must want to make a good impression!'

What was she talking about? I *always* made a good impression. Hmph.

We reached the zebra crossing that would take me to Birds. The library, where Ben worked, was on the side of road we were already on, so she didn't need to follow me. And I really hoped she wouldn't.

A part of me wanted to go see Ben, but it would've felt too much like I was crashing their lunch date. If he wanted to date Jaya, it was none of my business.

'Well, I'll see you later,' I said as I scurried over the road while there were no cars coming.

'Take care,' said Jaya.

My body relaxed as we went our separate ways. It released tension I hadn't even known I was carrying. Why did she make me so uneasy? Was it her questioning, or was it something to do with Ben?

Whatever. I didn't have time to worry about it.

*

I got back from lunch to find my painting equipment had moved again. The roller was standing upright on the living room floor, flanked by my open paint tin on one side and the tray on another. The roller had still been drying in the kitchen when I'd left. There *had* to be a ghost about that I wasn't sensing.

'Come out, come out, wherever you are,' I said, creeping through the house. 'I know you're here, ghostie. And I can see you. So let's cut the games, shall we?'

My hands were curled into fists. I should've known better than to come unprepared to the site of an old, haunted mine. But then, I'd figured all the ghosts would've moved on to somewhere more interesting. Oh, how wrong I'd been.

I explored the whole house, looking for something amiss, but, aside from my painting stuff, everything was exactly as I'd left it.

Maybe I really was going senile.

*

First days at any new job were stressful, but when you weren't sure if you were being haunted or going senile, it added just a tiny bit to your stress levels.

At the end of the day, I washed my rollers and brushes, closed the windows, then headed for the door.

I could've sworn I felt a pair of hands push me out of the front door, but before I could turn around to see anything, it slammed behind me.

*

It was not a ghost. It was *not* a ghost who'd slammed the door behind me. I would've sensed it. It was just the wind. Or some sort of weird prank they'd set up to haze me. It was definitely not a ghost.

And it didn't matter if it was, because it was tomorrow's problem. It was time to check on Maggie and Josh. I wanted to see them before going to the school to find out more about the canopic jar. They were still my priority. They were in good hands, but the poor hospital staff had no idea what they were dealing with.

Bright side, if they had the same curse put on them that Fadil had, they weren't going to deteriorate any time soon.

Given the timing of when Fadil had woken up, and when Maggie and Josh had been cursed, it felt too coincidental for them not to be related somehow. Curses that strong and that long-term were rare from what Ben, Edie, and I had researched. Why else would someone break Fadil's curse, if not to study it?

I knew the hospital wouldn't let them have visitors while they were finding them a bed in a ward, so I'd held off and struggled through a day at work before going to check on them.

I pulled up outside the hospital at four o'clock. Harry didn't finish work until six, so I was hoping I could avoid seeing him. At least then I couldn't actually punch him.

The smell of disinfectant hit me as I walked through the doors. Some things never changed. Partially holding my breath, I walked towards the hospital receptionist, who was playing on her phone.

Given their complex situation, I wasn't sure where in the hospital they'd be. And Harry hadn't been returning my calls. So, my best bet was to ask someone who worked there.

'Hi, can you tell me where Maggie and Josh Morgan are please?' I said to the hospital receptionist. The receptionist looked up at me, staring down her nose at me through her rimless glasses. 'Your relation to the them?'

'Family friend.'

'The Morgans are family only.'

'I've known Maggie my whole life. I couldn't be much closer to family!'

'Family. Only.'

Wow. What the hell?

'Since when?'

'Since the family requested it.'

Harry. Of course it was bloody Harry.

'Can you at least tell me how they are?' I begged. '*Please*?'

She sighed. 'I can give you the extension number of the ward they're in. It's up to them if they share any updates with you.'

It would have to do.

'Yes. Thank you,' I said through gritted teeth. I wanted to shout at her, but it wasn't her fault. No, I'd save that wrath for Harry.

The receptionist wrote down the hospital's phone number and the ward's extension number on a Post-it Note, then handed it to me without another word. Snooty old woman.

*

In no mood for other people's bullshit, I confronted Harry at work. I knew it would be the perfect place to embarrass him, since he wouldn't want his wife's weird friend causing a scene in front of his colleagues.

I told the receptionist to pass on a message to Harry that I had an update on his wife. I knew that would get his attention. I conveniently didn't mention my name, and the receptionist didn't ask.

But when he came down the stairs and saw me, his face fell.

'Niamh,' he said, trying to usher me into a corner.

I stood my ground. 'What do you think you're doing?'

'Pardon?'

'Stopping Edie and me from seeing Maggie and Josh! Don't you think we care about them too?'

I didn't even try to lower my voice to so-called normal levels, but Harry spoke in a loud whisper. The receptionist was looking at her computer screen, but glanced up every so often. She was definitely listening.

Harry crossed his arms over his suited-up chest. 'Don't you think you've done enough damage?'

I waved my arms around, almost hitting him a couple of times as I spoke. Oops. '*I've* done enough damage? Do you seriously still think this is my fault? I've been there for Maggie a lot longer than you, and I'll be there long after you're gone.'

'Who are you kidding, Niamh? Face it: all you and your daughter do is hold my family back. You're nothing but trouble, and that's all you've ever been. It's all you'll ever be.'

'You're unbelievable, you know that?'

mum and brother had been targeted by more magic, I had a feeling they were definitely on someone's radar. And I was determined to stop anything else from happening to them.

'What about Maggie? How's she getting on?'

I stared into my tea.

'She's sick. So's her son, Josh.'

Mr Brightman reached out to touch my arm. I couldn't feel his touch, but knowing he understood made me feel better.

Mrs Brightman stared at me, wide-eyed. 'What happened?'

'They're both in hospital. Comas.'

'Oh my. I'm so sorry. If there's anything I can do, please let me know. Myself and the church will be happy to help. We'll pray for them.'

'I hope they're OK,' said Mr Brightman.

I smiled meekly. 'Thanks.' With total strangers out to get them, they needed all the prayers they could get.

*

Tired after a long day, I still wasn't done. We needed to find out about Fadil's canopic jars. He'd said they weren't really filled with his internal organs like normal canopic jars were. Instead, they were filled with the objects needed to complete the curse.

If we could find his, maybe we could find out who'd broken it. Or more about the curse. Or some other information we didn't have. It was a small thread of hope, but we had to try. I found it hard to believe that even someone who'd freed Fadil for nefarious reasons would destroy such a historical object. There were still two left, but that wasn't the point. Manju would still get into trouble for two going missing. Hopefully we could find them.

Or something that resembled them so that we could enchant them to replace the originals.

I met Manju at the back of the school, where the dumpsters were. She was staring at them, a grossed out expression on her face.

In her hand was the bag containing what the janitor had found. I was there to see if we could find anything else.

'What am I supposed to say to people? I'm two canopic jars down. I'm lucky the security guard hasn't noticed! How he gets paid I'll never know,' she said.

'Tell them they've gone for cleaning,' I suggested. 'That takes forever on historical objects.'

She grinned. 'Yes! Thank you.' Her grin turned into a frown as she eyed the dumpster before us. 'Are you sure about this?'

'No. Not in the slightest.'

Without any magical way to find out where they were, we only had one solution: go through the rubbish. And, as bin day was tomorrow, we didn't have long to do it.

I pulled on some overalls, gloves, and a face mask. 'Best get to it.'

12
Edie

Mum told me to meet her at the primary school where she'd discovered Fadil, so I did. What I didn't expect was to find her in a dumpster. Searching for a historical object. I was both proud and grossed out.

Manju, who I vaguely knew from Mum's birthday parties, hovered nearby, anxiously shifting from foot to foot as she watched Mum dumpster dive.

What would they say if someone found her?

Oh, who cared? If it could get us answers, that was all that mattered. Most people were too wrapped up in themselves to care what other people were doing anyway.

'I can't believe Harry wouldn't let you in!' I said.

Mum poked her head out of the bin. 'I can't believe he broke the forty-eight hours he'd given us. Because he's such a lovely person.' She chucked a black bag over the side. 'This one came from the hall.'

'How can you tell?' asked Manju.

'It's bigger than the others. The hall has a bigger bin.' Mum hopped over the side and landed on the ground, then pulled open the bin with her gloved hands. The remains of what looked like ceramics and ash fell onto to concrete playground. Along with the remains of students' lunches. Gross.

Mum, Manju, and I leaned in. Could it be what we were looking for? Was it that easy?

Mum picked up a piece of the ceramics, held it up to the light, and studied it. 'It looks old.'

'But is it old enough?' I said.

She shrugged, putting it into a plastic bag she'd pulled out from her pocket. 'We'll see if Fadil recognises it.'

'Would he recognise his own canopic jars if he's been in a coma?'

'I'm more thinking he'll recognise the style and materials,' said Mum.

'Oh. That makes sense.'

She leaned in to the ash that had fallen on to the ground. 'Do you smell that?'

Manju and I leaned in. The ash smelled like, well, ash, but there was a hint of something else, too. The texture of it wasn't just black ash, either. There were different shaped bits that almost looked like part of a plant, but I couldn't tell what they were. I'd never paid much attention in biology, especially not when it involved plants. Yawn.

'What is that?' I asked.

'I'm not sure,' Mum said.

'Could it be mixed with someone's leftover lunch?'

Mum wrinkled her nose. 'Maybe, but I don't think so. I've never met anyone at primary school who likes such fragrant food. Whoever burned this used some sort of essential oils or herbs or something.'

Manju picked some ash up and rolled it between her fingers, then sniffed it. 'The way it's clumped together, that feels like either someone threw a drink in the bin, or some sort of oil was used.'

'Thanks, Manju. I wonder if we can test it somehow, see if there are remnants of something,' said Mum.

'Ben must have something,' I said. 'He has all sorts.' And hopefully he'd have a way to separate out spell ingredients and lunch leftovers. Was there a way to tell somehow? Could he cross-reference it with his library? I really wanted to raid his science kit.

And call it something better than a science kit.

'We'll soon find out,' said Mum. She collected what she could of the jar and ash in the little bag, taped the black bag back together, then threw it back into the bin. 'I feel disgusting.'

'But you did a good thing,' said Manju. 'You're helping a man who can't help himself, and who's been helpless for millenia.'

'Yeah, it's kinda cool,' I said.

Mum smiled.

'It's mad to think he looks so different now to back then.' That's when an idea hit me. 'I could wear a disguise to go see Josh and Maggie!'

Mum narrowed her eyes at me.

'That way I look more like one of the Morgans and nobody gets freaked out by my all-black ensemble. I can play up the sweet and innocent angle.'

She narrowed her eyes further. Fine, I wasn't so good at playing sweet and innocent. But I saw the looks people gave me because I wore a lot of black clothes and make-up. They never tried to hide their judgment from me. If I wanted to get someone on my side, I had to look like one of them. I'd do whatever it took to help Josh and Maggie.

'What? As if you haven't lied before for ghost stuff,' I said.

She sighed. 'I don't do it willingly. I do it to save people. And don't call it "ghost stuff". It trivialises it.'

'Well then what should I call it? And isn't this to save people? To save *our* people?'

Mum closed her eyes and took a deep breath. She knew she was losing the argument but didn't want to admit it. Ha. 'Just…I don't know. Not "ghost stuff". And fine. Do what you need to do. Just keep it legal!'

'Mum, come on. What do you think I'm going to do? Scale the wall and break in through a window?'

She snorted. It was one of the few times I'd seen her smile since Dumb Dan had left. 'You don't have long. Harry only works until six. Visiting time is three until five, then six until eight.'

Frazzle. It was already half five. That wouldn't give me long, since it took fifteen minutes to get to the hospital.

'Can you drive me there? I'll get the bus back.'

'Sure.'

'Just let me grab some things.'

*

'I'm not sure about this,' said Mum, glancing at me out of the corner of her eye as we drove to the hospital.

Before we'd left, I'd put on a chestnut brown wig and shoved in some blue contacts, leftover from a Halloween costume. It was weird seeing myself with lighter hair, but I kind of liked it.

I'd also borrowed some of Mum's clothes so that I looked more 'normal'. I'd even washed off my black eye make-up. I was taking this gig seriously.

'Relax, would you? I'll fit right in.' Staring at my reflection in the tiny mirror, I sat upright and smiled. I really did look like one of the Morgans. What would it be like to be a part of a normal family like that?

'If things look like they're going wrong, I'll get out of there,' I said.

Harry wouldn't give up work for anything and he regularly worked late, so I really hoped that today was one of those days.

'And if you can't?'

'I'll figure something out. Mum, you've got to give me more credit. I'm not stupid.'

We stopped at some traffic lights and she turned to face me. 'It's not that I think you're stupid or that I don't trust you. It's that I don't trust other people. You never know what they'll do.'

'Am I not good at thinking on my feet?'

The lights turned green and we pulled away, now only a couple of minutes from the hospital. I drummed my fingers along the door handle, adrenaline coursing through me.

Mum lowered her shoulders. 'Yes, you are.' It sounded like she added, 'better than me,' but it wasn't loud enough for me to tell for definite.

She checked her rearview mirror and indicated left, then turned into the car park. It looked like she wanted to say something else, but changed her mind.

She pulled up outside the front doors. 'Do you want me to wait for you?'

'No, thanks. It'll cost a fortune. I'll text you when I'm on my way home.'

'OK, if you're sure. Good luck.'

I checked my wig one last time, then got out of the car. Mum waited until I was inside to drive away. What did she think would happen in the ten-second walk between the car and the doors? That was the easy part.

It had been a long time since I'd been in a hospital. Mum had written down which ward they were in, so I bypassed the reception desk and studied the sign to the right. Navigating the labyrinth of corridors could get interesting. I didn't have a bad sense of direction, but the place was so big and had about a dozen buildings to it that it was impossible not to get at least a little lost. At least it wasn't raining, so I wouldn't get wet trying to find where I was going.

I took my phone from my messenger bag and opened the map I'd downloaded. I was in the right building, according to that. Now I just needed to find the right ward.

They didn't have a nice, easy-to-remember naming system, either. Everything was a weird combination of letters and numbers, as if they'd done it for admin purposes without thinking about how much nicer it'd be for patients if they named them after local celebrities or writers or something.

According to the map and the directions in front of me, the ward they were in was upstairs and to the right. I was pleasantly surprised they'd kept them together and not put Josh in the kids' ward, but then he was only a couple of weeks shy of eighteen. He'd be out of place in a kids' ward, comatose or not.

Reaching the lift, I noticed there was already a group of people waiting to go up in it. And it was taking forever. Sighing, I turned to the left and went up the stairs instead. It'd help me burn off some of my nervous energy, at least.

I took the stairs two at a time, reaching the glass doors for the first floor and pushing them open with more force than necessary. Everything smelled so clinical that it made me want to gag, but I forced the urge from my mind.

That wasn't the worst part. There were ghosts everywhere. Some floated around, looking lost. Others followed staff members, desperately trying to talk to them. Some floated alongside patients being transported from one place to the next.

I was used to seeing a lot of ghosts around, but part of the reason I avoided hospitals was because of how damn haunted they were. And, with so many ghosts trying to communicate with the living, they were noisy, too. Why hadn't I thought to take my headphones with me?

None of it mattered, though. I was on a mission. I *had* to see Josh and Maggie, to reassure Mum and myself that they were OK.

I reached the door to their ward, but it was shut. Unusual, given that it was visiting time. Weren't they meant to keep them open so that people could come and go during visiting times? Wasn't that a thing?

I pressed the communication button, then gelled my hands.

'Hello?'

'Hi. I'm here to see the Morgans,' I said, keeping my tone as bright and even as possible.

'What's your relation to them?'

'I'm a cousin,' I lied. It came out of my mouth so easily it unnerved me.

'I'm sorry, it's immediate family only to see the Morgans.'

'But I came all this way! Can't I at least see them?'

'Sorry.' The line clicked. She was done talking to me.

'What an old bat,' said a voice.

I turned to see a middle-aged woman dressed in modern hospital scrubs, looking at me. I figured she couldn't have been dead for more than a few years. Her eyes went wide when she realised I was looking right at her. Thank god the corridor was quiet.

'You can see me?' she said. Her voice was deep and gravelly, as if she were a chain smoker.

I nodded, just in case anyone could hear me, then I leaned against the wall, trying to look casual. You could never be too careful with all the cameras hospitals had around for protection these days.

I grabbed my phone again and pretended to be talking to someone, while actually talking to the ghost nurse.

'I'm Edie. And yes, I can see you.'

'Wow, we haven't had someone like you around for a while. I'm Anna. I used to work here until—never mind. You say you're related to the Morgans?'

I lowered my voice just in case, shifting away from the intercom. 'Family friend. I knew they were only letting relatives in. Why is the door shut during visiting time?'

'The Morgans. Something weird is going on around here, and I can't put my finger on it.'

'Can you get in to see them? To tell me how they are?'

'Psht, I can do better than that. Type 4365 on the keypad.'

I did as she asked and the door clicked open. I looked over my shoulder at her and grinned. 'Thank you, Anna. If there's anything I can do—'

'I'll keep an eye out for you.' She floated away as I walked into the ward. The nurses behind the reception desk barely glanced up when I walked past, nor did they question how I'd gotten in without them opening the door. Showed how much attention they actually paid.

I had no idea which room Josh and Maggie were in. Trying not to linger and look suspicious, as I walked past the reception desk, I studied the whiteboard behind it out of the corner of my eye. It said that Josh and Maggie had a room to themselves, tucked away in a far corner of the ward.

When I reached Josh and Maggie's room, the door was pulled to. I pushed it open. There was no one in there, and the blinds on the window were shut. Josh and Maggie lay in parallel beds, Maggie by the window, Josh to her right. They had their own bathroom, too, but it wasn't like they'd need it. The blue paper curtains were pulled all the way back, meaning if one woke up before the other, they could see them. Not that that would happen without my help if they really were cursed.

Machines beside each of them beeped to signal that their conditions were stable, but they didn't need them. If Fadil was anything to go by, they'd be stable for a *really* long time. And they could hear everything I said.

Much like when Fadil was in the sarcophagus, I could feel a buzzing emanating from them. It was stronger than what I'd felt from Fadil. Maybe because they were younger? I still didn't know what the buzzing meant, but I took it as a sign they were still alive.

I sat down between them, reaching out to hold Josh's hand. It felt cold against my touch, so I rubbed it to try to give him some warmth.

They looked so pale and fragile. Like they'd already started to lose fat and muscle from not eating or moving about. Was that a thing? Or was it just the curse taking its toll on their bodies?

What should I do? If they could hear me, how could I reassure them? What could I say that would help?

Ever since Harry had sent them to hospital, I'd tried to plan what I'd say to Josh and Maggie when I saw them again. But now that I was there, it all felt inconsequential. Like none of it mattered.

'Hi Josh. Maggie. It's me, Edie. I know you can hear me. And I'm really sorry about what's happened to you. I don't know everything yet, but Mum and I are looking into it. I promise you we'll fix it. We know what's causing it now, so we just need to find a solution. Mum's met an Egyptian mummy, believe it or not, and he seems to know a lot about this stuff, so we're going to find out what else he can help us figure out to help us get you better. And I promise you, we won't stop until you wake up.'

The door flung open and a nurse burst in, her cheeks red. 'Who are you?'

Anna floated in through the wall. 'That's the bitch nurse that wouldn't let you in.'

Great.

The bitch nurse's eyes fell to my hands, which was still clinging to Josh's. Her expression softened. 'You his girlfriend?'

I nodded.

'Daddy Dearest doesn't like you?'

I shook my head, my eyes welling with tears. Was all this because he didn't want Mum or me near Josh and Maggie? I was pretty sure it was.

'Oh, girl. You stay here as long as you need. If the dad comes along, I'll stall him and send one of the other nurses to get you out of here the back way.'

'Well bugger me. She does have a heart after all,' said Anna.

I suppressed a laugh, turning it into another sob. It wasn't hard, given how badly I wanted to cry. 'Why? You wouldn't let me in before.'

'Rules are rules. But…love is love. No one should tell you who you can have a relationship with, whether they're your parent or the government or some supernatural overlord. Take whatever time you need.'

I smiled, warming to the woman. 'Thank you.'

She smiled back, then walked out of the room and closed the door behind her.

'I never saw that one coming,' said Anna. 'I'll keep an eye out for Daddy Dearest, too.'

'Thank you,' I said as Anna floated back through the wall.

What else could I say to Josh and Maggie? It was eerie knowing they could hear everything but couldn't respond.

'I know you know what's happened with Harry,' I told them. 'Ever since you passed out, he's had it in for Mum and me. But I swear, this isn't our fault! It's like he's blaming us or something.' I wiped at my face with the back of my fist, my other hand still holding onto Josh's. I wasn't letting go until I left. I didn't know if he could feel as well as hear, but I took comfort in feeling his touch.

Knowing Mum would have something to say as well, I grabbed my phone and video called her. It was the closest she'd get to coming inside, but it was better than nothing.

'Edie? You got in?' she said.

I nodded. 'I had some supernatural assistance.'

Mum smiled. 'You can tell me about it later. How are they?'

I spanned the room with the camera, starting with the bathroom, then moving on to Maggie, the useless TV that wasn't even turned on, the door, then Josh.

'It's so cold,' said Mum.

'Literally and metaphorically,' I said, putting my phone down a minute to zip up my hoody.

'What's the atmosphere like?'

I picked my phone back up. 'Normal. I mean, it's a cold room, but that's because it's a hospital in November. The atmosphere is nothing like it was with Abigail.'

Mum pursed her lips.

'Does that mean anything?'

'Honestly? I don't know. I'm going to go see Fadil in a bit to see if he can tell me anything else.'

'Do you want me to meet you at Ben's?'

'Do you want to meet the mummy?' she said, seeing right through me.

'Yes. Yes I do.'

'All right, I'll—'

Anna floated through the door. 'The bastard is here early! Get out of here, Edie!'

'Frazzle. Mum, I've got to go. Harry is here. I'll meet you at Ben's and update you there.' I hung up and stuffed my phone back into my bag. After kissing Josh and Maggie on the cheeks, I said goodbye and promised to see them again soon.

A nurse I didn't recognise came in as I reached the door. 'Follow me,' she said.

Out of the corner of my eye I saw the nurse that had let me stay talking to Harry.

'She's giving him a so-called update,' Anna informed me as I followed the other nurse. 'Not that there's much to update.'

I nodded, unable to speak to her with so many people around. She smiled at me, though, so I knew she understood what I was doing.

The living nurse took me to another exit. 'Here you go. You should be able to find your way out from here. I'm sorry you couldn't stay longer with your boyfriend.'

'Thank you for helping me,' I said.

She smiled. 'Of course. It's what we're here for.' She closed the door behind her, leaving Anna and I alone in the corridor. I leaned against the wall, overwhelm washing over me. Maggie and Josh looked so awful. Almost inhuman with how pale and withdrawn they were.

My scalp began to itch from the wig. I reached to rip it off.

'I have to go,' said Anna, her voice turning panicked. Before I could respond, she'd gone. That was odd. What was wrong? Had something happened?

A door farther along the corridor opened, and who should walk out, but a teary eyed Dominic.

'Dominic?' I said, straightening up and pretending I didn't feel as bad as I did.

'Edie?' he said, his voice wobbling. He wiped at his red and puffy eyes, but it was obvious he'd been full-on bawling his eyes out.

'What are you doing here?' I asked, walking over to him.

We were standing in the middle of the empty corridor. It was made all the more eerie by the absence of ghosts. Not every corridor was haunted. Some were quieter than others. We'd obviously stumbled on a quiet one. Not a bad thing when my friend was crying.

That's what he was, wasn't it?

'My grandmother just died.'

'Oh, Dominic,' I said, pulling him into a hug without even thinking about it. He leaned into me, resting his head on my shoulder. That gesture must've been too much for him, because he began to cry again.

'I'm sorry,' he said in between sobs. 'We were so close.'

I rubbed his back. 'It's OK. I understand.'

'Are you close to your grandmother?'

'I never really knew her. She didn't get along with Mum so I didn't see her much. She had a very…militant way of doing things.'

He pulled away, snivelling and wiping at his face with his hands. 'I'm sorry to hear that.'

I shrugged. 'It is what it is.' And was related to ghost hunting so it wasn't like I could explain why they didn't get along. 'Do you want to go get a drink downstairs?'

'If you don't have time—'

'You helped me after Tessa pushed me over and wrecked my back. It's the least I can do.'

We turned around and began walking towards the cafe, where we could sit down and get a drink. I was starving anyway, so taking a few minutes to eat wouldn't hurt.

'Is that why you're here?'

'No. I mean, it still hurts sometimes – usually if I sit for too long – but no. I'm not here for me. One of my friends is sick, so I was checking on them.'

I didn't want to go into details. So far, news of their comas had avoided the town gossip. I wanted to keep it that way. If we drew attention to Josh and Maggie, it would make it harder to fix them. People would want photos of them and to poke and prod at them as if they were zoo exhibits or science experiments. I wasn't letting that happen.

'I'm sorry to hear that. I hope they get better soon,' he said.

'Thanks.'

We walked in silence the rest of the way to the cafe, but it wasn't an awkward silence. It was a calming, friendly one that I appreciated given the current situation. It was the calmest I'd felt since Josh had passed out. The image of him lying, semi-naked, comatose, on his bathroom floor, still haunted me. As far as we knew his fall onto the tiled floor hadn't caused any damage, but we wouldn't know until he woke up. *If* he woke up.

No, not if. When.

I'd fix Josh and Maggie if it took me the rest of my life.

*

'So what's with the wig?' said Dominic as we sat eating sandwiches and drinking tea. It felt so normal, as if our lives hadn't completely changed within the walls we were sitting in.

The cafe was near the entrance to the hospital, serving a variety of old-school sandwiches with fillings like like egg and cress, tuna mayo, and chicken salad.

It was run by volunteers, most of whom were retired. They made all the food by hand, so I liked that we were supporting it.

It was pretty busy, with barely a vacant table in the small space, but not so busy that we couldn't hear each other speak. We'd managed to find a spot by the window, which looked out on to the empty courtyard.

I chuckled, touching the wig self-consciously. How natural did it look? I really should've checked that before I left, but there hadn't been enough time. 'Trying out a new look.' Not a total lie. Just mostly one.

'I like it.' He looked across the table at me, his dark gaze meeting mine. A shiver went down my spine. Did Dominic like me? Was that why I kept running into him? Was that why his presence gave me goosebumps?

No. That wasn't allowed. I was with *Josh.* I'd crushed on Josh for years. Was I really going to throw that away as soon as things got difficult? It was a level of difficult most people would never comprehend, but still.

Josh was it for me. Dominic was just a friend. If he was even that.

'Are you all right?' said Dominic.

How did he know something was wrong? Was I making it obvious I might like him? It was too complicated and I couldn't handle it. I had to get out of there.

'I have to go,' I said, gathering my things. My egg and cress sandwich wasn't so appetising anymore, so I left the other half and grabbed my takeaway cup of tea. 'See you around.'

'Edie—'

I scurried off before he could say anything else. What was I *doing*? I had to stay focused, whatever it took.

13
Niamh

'I hope Edie got out OK,' I said as I sat on Ben's sofa. After showering the smell of refuse from me and putting on clean jeans and a jumper, I'd gone over to his place to wait for Edie. Since Tilly had spent a lot of time on her own the last couple of days, I brought her with me, but kept her on the lead. I wasn't sure how she'd respond around Fadil, or how he'd respond around her. So far, since I'd walked in, she was staring at him but keeping a wide berth. She hopped onto the sofa beside me, settling with her head on my lap and her eyes on Fadil.

Ben sat beside me, hugging a mug of coffee to him, and Fadil sat in the armchair perpendicular to us. Was it weird, a mummy sitting on a leather sofa? Especially when his skin didn't look that different to aged, poorly cared for leather? Was there anything we could do about that, to help him? It couldn't be fun for him knowing he'd been trapped for millenia and now he still couldn't go anywhere in case he got chopped up like a science experiment and treated less-than-human. In the name of science, my arse. They just liked playing with old toys.

'It sounded like she had a pretty good plan going on,' said Ben. 'The wig and contacts were a great touch.'

I shifted in my seat. Tilly adjusted herself accordingly. 'You don't think it was a little over the top?'

'She was trying to sell herself as family and they were only letting family in. It must've worked or she wouldn't have called you from their room.'

I sighed. He was right. But that didn't mean I wasn't worried about her. I hadn't heard from her in over an hour, and she'd had to rush out because Harry was there. What was she doing? Had something happened? Even if she'd gotten the bus that took the long route, she still would've arrived by now.

'Maybe she went to get some food or a drink,' suggested Fadil, his eyes on Tilly, who was still watching him. 'All that adrenaline is enough to make anyone hungry.'

'Yeah, you're right.' I fiddled with the sleeve of my coat. Where *was* Edie? Was she all right? If Harry hurt her—

'Did you find anything at the school?' Ben asked, interrupting my violent thoughts.

'Yes! Thank you!' I'd been so distracted I'd forgotten about it. I got up and grabbed my bag from behind the door, then took out the remnants of what I hoped was a canopic jar. Tilly stole my spot on the sofa.

I handed what the janitor had found to Fadil. He took the bag from me, opening it gently. He froze when he saw it.

'What? Is this it?' I said.

'I can't be sure, but I think so. It's the same style, same materials. You found it at the school, you said?'

'Yeah,' I said. 'How Manju is going to explain to the exhibit that it's missing, I don't know.'

'I'm sure we can come up with a fix or an enchantment or something,' said Ben. I hoped so. Manju didn't deserve to get into trouble for something that wasn't her fault. I could see the headlines already: *Headteacher loses priceless Ancient Egyptian canopic jars.* Shudder.

'Thanks,' I said.

Fadil turned the bag around in his hand. 'Was this all you found?'

'That and some ash. Why?' I took out the second bag and passed it to Ben.

'There should be more than one.'

My back stiffened. 'More than one?'

Fadil lowered the bag to his lap. 'Well, I doubt the curse ingredients were in all of them, but most mummies had four. They wouldn't have needed four, but they would've used four anyway to make me look like a real mummy. I'm lucky grave robbers didn't steal one of them. It would've been impossible to break the curse without them.'

'Fiddlesticks.'

'Maybe you missed it?' suggested Ben. He lifted the bag with the ash in to his face and sniffed it. 'Smells potent.'

'Lunch potent?' I said.

Ben shook his head. 'No. Way to fragrant for a kid's lunch.'

'Good. Hopefully it's a starting point. I'm not going back in that bin. It was nasty,' I said. 'Do you have any tech to break down what could be in the ash? We think it must've been burnt with something else. If we can find out what it is, we might be able to find out how to free Maggie and Josh.'

'Leave it with me,' said Ben. He closed the bag and put it on the TV unit in front of him.

'Do you know how many jars were at the exhibit?' I asked as I lifted Tilly and returned to my spot on the sofa.

Ben shook his head. 'Haven't had time to go yet. And now it feels wrong, somehow.'

'Don't like the thought of your squatter being on display?' said Fadil.

'Something like that,' said Ben.

Knock knock.

Tilly and I dove out of the chair and to the front door. Edie stood on Ben's front porch, still wearing her wig and contacts. I hugged her. Tilly jumped up at her legs. 'Are you all right? I was so worried!'

'Sorry. I ran into a friend so we had food.' She picked Tilly up, scratched her behind the ears, then lowered her down again. I put my foot on the end of her lead so that she couldn't run off.

'Told you,' said Fadil from the living room.

I rolled my eyes. He could be such an insensitive know-it-all sometimes.

I ushered Edie into the hallway. Once she was safely through the door, she started to unfasten her wig.

'These things are so itchy,' she said, tugging at it. Part of her hair had gotten stuck on her wig cap, so I helped her to untangle it since she couldn't see what she was doing.

'What are you doing out there?' said Fadil.

'Why? Want to meet another ghost hunter?' I teased him.

Edie's face lit up. 'Is that what I am?'

I yanked her wig cap off and her head jerked back. 'Ow!'

'Sorry.' No, she wasn't a ghost hunter. And I shouldn't have encouraged her by saying that.

'I was helping her take her wig off,' I said as Edie, Tilly, and I went into the living room.

'Hey Edie,' said Ben.

'Hey,' she replied absently. Her eyes were glued to Fadil. I mean, I didn't blame her.

'Hi,' said Fadil. His face was so worn and wrinkly it was hard to read his facial expressions, but if I had to guess, Edie's scrutiny made him uncomfortable. It made me uncomfortable, too. He wasn't a museum exhibit or someone from one of those Victorian freak shows.

I nudged her. She shook her head, looking around, as if staring at Fadil had put her into a trance.

'Sorry! I'm so sorry!' she said, now unable to look at Fadil at all. Her pale cheeks turned crimson, contrasting with her black hair.

Fadil gave her a forced smile. 'It's OK. I've been staring at everything that's new to me, too.'

I hadn't expected him to react like that. It was the calmest and kindest I'd seen him since we'd met. Had Ben been some sort of good influence over him?

'Can I get you a drink, Edie?' offered Ben.

'Tea would be great, thanks,' she said.

'Anyone else?' said Ben.

'Same, please,' I said.

'No thank you,' said Fadil. 'My body is still building up a tolerance to modern-day foods.'

'Have you eaten at all?' I asked, sitting back on the sofa with Tilly.

'A little. I'm still adjusting. My body went so long without food I don't have much of an appetite. And I struggle to sleep, too. When I try to sleep I…see things.'

'What things?' asked Edie.

'Flashbacks of what happened to me. It sounds so stupid, remembering what happened millenia ago, but to me, it feels like yesterday.'

'That doesn't sound stupid to me,' said Edie. 'It's the last thing you saw. You probably replayed it in your head millions of times, right?'

Fadil nodded, a solemn expression on his face.

'Do you want to talk about it?' offered Edie. She was being so calm and compassionate towards a stranger. Pride washed over me.

Fadil shook his head. 'What difference would it make?'

'It can help to talk through what you experienced,' said Ben, walking back in with a tray carrying our drinks.

He handed one to me, one to Edie, then took one for himself and rested the empty drinks tray on the coffee table.

Edie sat on the floor beside the tray and near Fadil, while Ben and I returned to our spots on the sofa. Having him close made everything that was going on seem less scary and intimidating, somehow. Like between us, we could figure it all out. I really hoped my instincts were right.

'Thanks, but I'm not ready yet,' said Fadil.

We all stayed silent, allowing him to lead the conversation.

'Maybe one day.'

'Whenever you're ready,' said Edie.

Fadil nodded. He was wearing jeans and a hoody that hung off him. They'd no doubt come from Ben. We really needed to get him something that fitted him better, but then, it was probably hard to find something that fitted an adult male that slim. And short. Kids' clothes would've been *too* short, but adult men's clothes would've drowned him. Women's clothes, maybe?

Ben shifted in his seat, staring into his tea. 'At the risk of asking you to tread uncomfortable ground—'

'You want to know more about the curse they cast on me,' said Fadil.

'Yes. It might help us stop other people from going through what you have.'

'OK. I don't know how much help I'll be, but I'll try.'

'You will?' I found myself saying.

Fadil looked up and met my eyes. 'I have to believe there was a reason someone woke me up now. Whoever that person was, I'll always be grateful to them, even if their motives were wrong, because they gave me back my life. Believing there's a reason I was woken up now is the only thing keeping me going. Maybe that reason is to help your friends.'

'Thank you,' I said.

He nodded.

'One thing I don't get,' said Edie, 'if you were still alive, how did everyone think you were a mummy?'

'It's part of the curse. As time goes on, your vital signs slow down until they're untraceable,' said Fadil.

'Even with modern technology?' asked Edie.

'I wouldn't be surprised if the curse blocked modern technology. Obviously it wasn't around back then, but time operates differently for the spirit world.'

'What do you mean?' said Edie.

'Don't ask. Your head will hurt,' said Ben.

'Now I *really* want to know.'

'Most spells channel spirit energy. Potions attract it. That's why many spells reference spirits or ask for their help. And time doesn't actually exist – humans invented it. Consistent times were only invented just over a hundred years ago, when we needed them for trains. Before that it was measured using things like the sun. But the spirits can come and go as they please. They're not always here, but when they're in purgatory, they can go pretty much anywhere they want.'

'Purgatory is a thing?'

'Yes,' said Ben. 'That's where spirits live when they're not here but haven't crossed over. Purgatory exists on a different plane to ours. It doesn't run parallel, though. The spirits have a lot of control over how it looks, which means they can make it resemble pretty much any time zone, then visit in our plane, too.'

'Now I get why you told me not to ask.'

'Sorry. Personally, I wouldn't choose to be a ghost. It's a horrible fate, if you ask me. But we're not supposed to be talking about ghosts. Fadil, what do you remember about the curse?' asked Ben.

'They cut some of my hair off and took some of my blood, then mixed it with some stuff in a bag.'

Ben jumped out of his chair and scurried into his library. We waited, listening to him pulling books off shelves and putting them back as he grumbled in frustration. He returned ten minutes later with a book in his hand.

'Did it look like this?' he asked, putting a book in front of Fadil. Edie and I went over to study the page they were discussing. It was from an old book, and the page in question mentioned a blood curse. It talked about needing a person's hair, nails, or teeth to make it.

'Yes,' said Fadil.

'You can read that?' said Edie.

'It's only Latin,' said Ben.

'Only,' said Edie, looking at me. Both of us started laughing.

'What's so funny?' said Ben.

'Never mind,' I said. 'What does the book say?'

'To cast a blood curse, you need someone's blood, and either their hair or a fingernail. You also need something that's important to them. Add a few herbs, say an incantation, and put everything into a vessel of some sort. The cursed person will black out and never wake up. Unless…'

'Unless what?' said Edie, craning her neck to look at the page, despite not speaking Latin.

'Unless you destroy the vessel holding everything.'

Edie sat on the floor with a thud. 'Frazzle!'

'What?' said Fadil.

'My back. Shouldn't have fell back that hard.'

I knelt down beside her. 'Do you need anything?'

'A new coccyx?'

I rubbed her upper back. She leaned into me, her expression tight. If I ever saw Tessa again, I was going to give her an even more painful and lifelong injury. So long as it didn't put me in prison. Maybe I could get a ghost to injure her for me?

'What did you do?' said Fadil.

'I got pushed to the ground by some bitch and since then I've had back problems,' she told him.

'Who'd do that?' said Fadil.

'Bitches,' I grumbled.

Fadil sighed. 'People make out like this world has made so much progress. Seems more like people are just as cruel, but they express it differently.'

'In a nutshell,' I agreed.

'It's not that bad,' said Ben.

The three of us turned to look at him. Well, at least one of us was an optimist. Someone had to be.

'What kind of vessel do the ingredients have to be stored in?' I asked Ben, bringing us back on topic.

'Pretty much anything, I think. If it has ties to the person, all the better, but it doesn't have to.'

'Does it say if everyone ends up like me?' asked Fadil.

Ben reread the page then looked up at him. 'No, I'm sorry.'

Fadil shrugged. 'Had to try.'

'We'll find answers for you, too,' I promised him.

Fadil gave me a wan smile, but it didn't meet his sunken eyes. He didn't seem to believe there was any hope for him, but I was adamant I'd prove him wrong.

'Do the Morgans have any vessel-type items that ingredients could be stored in?' Ben asked.

'Crockery?' suggested Edie.

'Do they have favourite mugs?' said Ben.

'No. Maggie is adamant they're all white Denby,' I said.

'Yawn,' said Edie.

I looked down at the Wonder Woman mug I was drinking from and laughed. Edie had an X-Men one, and Ben's was Batman. Had he chosen those intentionally? I wouldn't have put it past him.

'So it probably isn't a form of crockery,' said Ben.

'No,' I said. 'She'd know the second something was missing.'

I sipped my tea, frustrated at our lack of progress. It had been two days and it felt like all we knew was that someone had broken Fadil out to use a similar curse on Maggie and Josh. Did they do that to study his curse? We didn't even know that for definite, we were just going based on assumptions.

Leaning back in my seat, I hugged my tea to me, wishing it would offer me some comfort.

'On another topic, which I know you probably don't want to think about right now, but I might have an idea of how we can ensure all the ghosts from the mine have either crossed over or aren't causing any problems,' said Ben.

'What mine? What list of ghosts?' said Fadil.

We filled him in on the recent earthquake, which had caused a surge in ghost activity, then waited for Ben to tell us his idea.

'We could ask your husband to help,' said Ben.

I sat upright, my body tensing. 'No. We can't drag him into this.'

'Who else can we ask? We need someone on the Other Side we can trust,' said Ben. 'Who better to trust than—'

'No. It's not fair on him.'

'Isn't that his decision to make?'

'I agree,' said Edie. 'Why don't we at least ask Dad what he thinks?'

She was just looking for an excuse to see her dad again. I hadn't let her summon him, and I knew she resented me for it. I hoped one day she'd understand. Grief was part of being human, and it wasn't fair she got to be spared that, just because she could communicate with ghosts.

'Will I be able to see him?' Fadil asked.

'Depends on if he makes himself visible or not,' said Ben. 'He seems to have enough power to be able to, so I don't see why not.'

When did everyone start ganging up on me?

Knowing I wasn't going to win, I stormed into the kitchen. It wasn't like there were many places for me to go when I was in someone else's house. Ben followed me anyway.

'I know, I know. We need to ask him. I shouldn't answer questions for him.' I gripped the edge of the counter, grinding my teeth together. Why did we have to bring Javi into this?

He'd been killed by a poltergeist. He didn't deserve to get dragged into more ghost problems from the Other Side.

Ben didn't say anything. He waited for my cue. I went back into the living room and began arranging the furniture for a seance. Tilly kept trying to interfere, so I put her in the kitchen out of the way.

When the furniture had been moved, the four of us sat in a circle. My palms were sweaty at the thought of seeing Javi again. Especially around Ben again. My head was a mess. I hated burdening Javi in the afterlife with the problems of the living, too.

'We call upon the spirits, to commune with us tonight, grant us your presence, come join us in the light,' Edie, Ben, and I chorused.

Javi appeared instantly.

Fadil gasped, so I took that as a sign he could see Javi.

'Dad!' Edie said with a grin.

'Twice in one week? To what do I owe the honour?' he said, looking at me. I narrowed my eyes at him.

He ignored me, turning his attention to Edie and looking her up and down. 'What happened to my little rocker?'

'I needed a disguise to get into the hospital and see Josh and Maggie,' I said.

'Did you learn anything useful?' he asked.

'Not really,' she said with a sigh. 'But at least I know they're OK.'

'We'll figure this out,' he promised.

Edie smiled, but it didn't reach her eyes. I could tell it took her everything to put on a positive facade and hope for the best. It killed me that she felt she had to do it, but then, didn't I do the same thing with her?

Sensing something was going on, Tilly entered the room.

I frowned. 'Tilly, how did you get out?'

Tilly waddled over to Javi and barked. He grinned. Of course he'd opened the door. 'Shh, little westie.'

She shushed.

'How do you *do* that?' I asked.

He shrugged. 'Just call me the Doctor Doolittle.'

'As well as Super Ghost?' I teased.

He winked. For a moment, I saw a glimmer of the man I fell in love with so long ago. And I missed him. I missed him so badly.

'I heard what you were arguing about,' he said, changing the subject.

My body tensed. How often did he eavesdrop on our conversations?

'I was only eavesdropping because you were talking about me,' he said, reading my mind. Could ghosts do that? I really hoped ghosts couldn't do that. 'And I'll do it.'

'Javi—'

'Ben's right. You need someone you can trust on the Other Side. Who can you trust more than me?'

I didn't have an answer for that and he knew it.

'The more of us who are working on this, the sooner we can get through all the names on the list,' he added.

'What's that supposed to mean?' I asked.

Another figure began to appear beside him.

No. For the love of ghosts no. Just bloody no.

But there she was. My mother.

'Niamh,' she said, giving me a curt nod.

She noticed Fadil and eyed him judgmentally. 'And *who* are *you*?'

'He's a friend, Mum. They both are.'

My mother floated closer to inspect Fadil. '*This*?'

'Who are you talking to?' said Fadil.

'You can see me but not Nika?' Javi asked, floating closer to Fadil. It was the first time I'd heard someone call my mother by the shortened version of Veronica for a long time. Actually by any name. Most of the people who knew me knew not to mention her.

'Yeah,' said Fadil.

My mother rolled her eyes. She clicked her fingers. '*Now* can you see me?'

Drama queen. She'd done the clicking thing for dramatic effect. There was no magical reason to need to do it.

Fadil gasped. 'This is your mum? You don't look alike.'

Phew. I didn't *want* to look like her.

'So who are you, exactly?' my mother repeated, studying his cracking skin and yellowed eyes. She still hadn't even acknowledged her granddaughter. What a charmer.

Not that Edie seemed bothered. She mostly knew about my mum from stories I'd told her, which hadn't exactly endeared her to her grandmother. Her focus was on her dad, whom she hadn't seen in so long, then seen twice in a week.

He floated over to her, watching her and studying her while the rest of us focused on my mother.

Fadil glared. 'I'm four thousand years old. You try looking good after being alive for that long.'

My mother gasped again. 'You found it!'

'Found what?' I said.

'The secret to immortality!' She looked Fadil up and down, further taking in his dry skin, wrinkles, and withering frame. 'Although, there are obviously some kinks to work out.'

'You mean like how his body was frozen but his mind was still active for four thousand years?' I said.

My mother's eyes went so wide they almost bugged out of her head. 'A blood curse?'

'Yes,' said Fadil. 'I heard them talking about it after casting it, but I don't think they knew I could hear them.'

'Well. It's not like they're alive anymore for you to get revenge, is it?'

Fadil's jaw tensed. Edie reached out and held his hand, giving it a squeeze. I loved how supportive she was of a guy who was basically a total stranger.

Her curiosity abated, my mother turned back to me: 'If Javier and I search for the ghosts on this side, it will make the list a lot faster to get through. We can find who's already crossed over, then you can cross them off, safe in the knowledge they're not causing any harm.'

'No,' I said.

'Niamh.' The way my mother said my name made me feel like a naughty fifteen-year-old again. Why was she agreeing to work with Javi, someone she'd hated when they were alive?

'I don't trust you,' I said.

'Well isn't that just lovely, turning down the offer of help from your own mother because of your silly vendetta.'

'It's not a *vendetta*. You were controlling, selfish, and rude. Why would I work with you?'

'You're not a child anymore, Niamh. This isn't about you.'

She'd never get it, would she? As far as she was concerned, she was always right.

I left the room, unable to handle being in her presence. It might break the seance, it might not. Since my mum and Javi seemed to have enough power to visit even without a seance, there was a chance they'd choose to stick around anyway. I didn't care.

It was childish, but I was done feeling ganged up on. Bringing Javi into it was one thing, but my mother? It sounded harsh to say I was glad she'd crossed over, but her being on the Other Side meant she wasn't in my ear every day. It had been a relief. The last thing I wanted was her back in my ear and wearing her 'I'm just trying to save the world' hat.

I went into the kitchen and leaned back in one of the chairs.

Maggie. Why couldn't I talk to Maggie? Other than Javi, she was the only one who really knew what my mother had been like. She'd seen it all. She might've even heard more of it, growing up next door to me. Our arguments had been so loud, Maggie had heard them from the bottom of her garden when we were in the front room.

It wasn't something I was proud of, but it was something that had always confused me. My mother had picked pointless arguments with me when I was growing up, and there'd been nobody around to protect me. Just the prospect of having to work with her again made me feel sick. Anyone but her. *Anyone.*

'Are you OK?' Ben asked.

I sighed, staring up at the ceiling. He closed the door behind him, then sat in one of the chairs next to me.

'I'm sorry. I didn't know she'd want to get involved. Or that…'

'That our history was that bad?'

He lowered his head.

'It's not like we've known each other long enough for you to know my life story,' I said, sitting up. 'And it's not like I talk about it much.'

'Tell me.' His voice was so gentle, but so curious and pleading, I couldn't say no.

'My dad passed away when I was maybe four or five. For as long as I remember, it was always my mum and me. And for just as long, she tried to control me. She tried to tell me what to do. But it was like she resented me at the same time and I never understood why. One minute she'd put loads of pressure on me to get me to do something, the next she didn't bother at all. It didn't matter what I did, I couldn't please her. Javi and I left and got our own place as soon as we were old enough. I just couldn't handle feeling like a total failure. It ruined me.' I wiped a tear from the corner of my eye. I was too upset to hide that I was crying from him. If he didn't like seeing me cry, he wasn't the good guy he made himself out to be.

To my surprise, he gestured for me to get closer to him. I shuffled my chair towards him and he put his arm around my shoulder. I leaned on him, soothed by his proximity. 'I'm sorry she put you through that. Nobody deserves that.'

I clung to his blue shirt, trying not to cry any more than I already was.

'We can find someone else who can help if you like. I'm not sure who. We need someone with an understanding of—'

I pulled away from him and looked at him. 'Are you trying to talk me into using her?'

'No!' He put his hands up in a surrender gesture. 'No. I wouldn't do that. You or Javier must have some other relatives who could help us.'

'Javi was adopted. We don't know anything about his birth family,' I said. 'My mother was too busy judging him to try to help him explore what he could or couldn't do.'

'That explains a lot,' said Ben. 'Judgment always clouds the greater good.'

I glared at him.

'I hadn't meant for that to sound like a dig, I swear.'

I sighed. 'No, but you know you're right. Whether I like it or not, she's the second best person to help us get through the damn list of miners. And the longer we take, the more people who are at risk. Which means we have to use her offer of help, because if I say no, anyone who dies because of it is on me.'

Ben didn't say anything. What could he say? Agreeing with me that we needed my mother would annoy me. Disagreeing would be a lie. He was stuck.

I sat up and rubbed his hand. 'Thank you.'

'For what?'

'Listening.'

14
Edie

Josh and Maggie had only been in their comas four days, but Mum and I were already exhausted. It felt like it was one thing on top of another. As I was eating my breakfast Tuesday morning, someone knocked on the front door. As far as I knew, we weren't expecting anyone. I opened the door to find Melanie on our doorstep. Her hair was down, framing her face and drawing your attention to her golden brown eyes. They were further accentuated by teal eyeshadow. She wasn't traditionally pretty like Tessa, but she could've been a great model with her unusual look.

'Can we talk?' said Melanie.

I didn't even think she knew where we lived. But, after everything she'd been through, I couldn't really say no. It wasn't like she had anyone else to talk to about being possessed by a ghost. And after an ordeal like that, having someone to talk to probably helped a lot.

I stepped aside to let her in.

She wasn't at college yesterday. I figured it was because she'd needed some time to rest. Understandable after everything she'd been through.

Tilly, who was asleep in the kitchen, ran over and started jumping up at Melanie's legs as we walked in there.

'Sorry,' I said. 'Tilly!'

'It's OK,' said Melanie, crouching down and rubbing Tilly behind her ears. Tilly stopped jumping up and sat nicely, enjoying the attention she'd demanded. 'Tilly's a cute name.'

'Thanks. She's named after my great aunt Tallulah.'

'Cool.' Melanie stood up, shoving her hands into her pockets and rocking on her heels. 'Is your mum about? I wanted to talk to you both, if possible.'

'Yeah, she's just in the greenhouse. I'll get her. Tea?' I said as I walked past the kettle.

'Please,' she said, rubbing her hands together. It was freezing outside, and Mum was a lunatic for gardening in that weather. She said she found it relaxing and a mindful way to start the day, so I left her to it.

I put the kettle on, then went to get Mum. She was fiddling with some herbs I didn't know the names of, bobbing her head along to the music playing through her headphones. 'Mum!'

She jumped, chopped something off a plant, then put her headphones around her neck. 'What's up?'

'Melanie's here.'

'Why?'

I shrugged. 'She wants to talk to both of us.'

Mum stood up and took her gloves off. 'All right, let me pack this stuff up. I'll be right in.'

I left her to wrap her gardening up, then went back into the kitchen. Melanie was fussing Tilly.

'Your dog is really cute,' she said.

I smiled. 'Thanks. She'll let you do that all day if you're not careful.'

She smiled. 'I don't mind. We had a dog until last year. He was fifteen when we lost him.'

'Sorry to hear that. Losing a dog is always hard when they're a part of the family,' I said as I made three cups of tea. 'Fifteen, though. That's impressive.'

'Yeah. He was a good dog. I miss him.'

'Are you going to get another?'

She shrugged. 'My parents don't want to get one with me going to uni soon. Something about me getting too attached and not wanting to leave. If I didn't know any better, I'd think they wanted rid of me.' Her smile lowered and she looked sad. There was a hint in her tone and body language that there was a lot more to her than just being Tessa's bitchy sidekick.

'Milk?' I asked, holding it up.

'Please. One sugar.'

'Coming up.'

Mum came in as I finished making the drinks. She picked hers up from her favourite mug. 'Thanks.' Remembering her manners, she faced Melanie. 'Hi, Melanie.'

'Hi, Mrs Porter.'

'Please, call me Niamh. Mrs Porter makes me feel about a hundred.'

'You shouldn't act like it then,' I said, giving her a wry smile.

'Does that make you my carer? You'll have to do more around the house if that's the case,' said Mum.

Melanie watched our exchange and laughed. Tilly wasn't impressed she'd stopped fussing her, and started jumping up again.

'Tilly! Pack it in!' said Mum.

Tilly, ever the westie, ignored her.

Mum sighed. 'Bloody westitude.'

'What's that?' said Melanie.

Mum put her tea down and picked up Tilly. 'Westie attitude. They're stroppy little buggers when they want to be. Cute, but mardy.'

I walked over to them and rubbed Tilly behind the ears. 'Part of their charm.'

'If you say so,' said Mum.

'You wouldn't change her and you know it.'

'Mmm.' She kissed Tilly's head then put her in the living room and shut the door. Tilly cried a couple of times, then went silent. 'There we go. So, Melanie, what brings you here?'

'Well, uh, actually,' she sipped her tea in an effort to delay whatever it was she wanted to say. 'I did some research into my ghost. Well, not mine. You know what I mean.'

'The ghost who possessed you,' said Mum.

'Yeah. Her.'

'Did you find anything out?' I asked. Nobody we'd worked with had ever done that before. I guess because they were too young to know what was going on, and their parents just wanted to move on. But Melanie's ghost had a history, that much was evident.

'Yeah, actually, I did. Her name was Ashley Hall. She wasn't much older than us, but she had three children. Two died in the mines with her and her husband, Roger.

They were barely five or six. The last one was stillborn, not long before the accident. The grave we walked to every night belonged to their stillborn child. And the ghost with me was Roger.'

'That's horrible,' I said. I hugged my tea to me, sinking into one of the chairs at the breakfast bar.

'Yeah. Now I get why I felt so much pain from her. I'd say I can't imagine what she was going through, but now, well…'

Mum rubbed Melanie's back. 'How are you doing after everything?'

Melanie sighed. 'It's so weird. Everything just carries on as normal around you, doesn't it? Your whole world has shifted on its axis, and you're a totally different person with all this new knowledge and this new experience. And you can't talk to anyone about it because they'll think you're a mad person.' She shook her head, tears filling her eyes. 'I'm sorry. I didn't mean to bother you. I've just been feeling really lost and needed someone to talk to.'

'It's OK. We understand,' said Mum.

We knew all too well what it was like when people thought you were a nutter for believing in ghosts, let alone actually having seen one.

I'd never been possessed, so I couldn't relate to that bit, but your world shifting on its axis from one event? I was going through that right now with Josh and Maggie, and it terrified me that we didn't know when – or even if – it would all be over.

Josh had finally let me in, and we'd lasted less than a month before something supernatural had intervened in our relationship. It was my first relationship. It didn't exactly give me high hopes for my future. Or Josh's.

'Edie? Are you all right?' said Mum. Both her and Melanie's gazes were on me.

I straightened up, looking away from them to hide the tears forming in my eyes. 'Uh-huh. Fine.'

'If you ever need someone to talk to, we're here,' I told Melanie.

She flashed me a fragile smile. 'Thank you. I don't deserve everything you've done for me.'

'It's not about what you deserve. It's about doing the right thing, and making you feel like you're less alone,' I said.

Mum rubbed my shoulder, a proud smile on her face.

15
Niamh

Even though I couldn't sense a ghost in the house I was painting, I was convinced there was one. I'd seen a couple of ghosts hanging around the building site, some floating around, minding their business, others haunting a builder or two. They all seemed pretty harmless, but it wasn't a big stretch to think one could be doing something in the house when there'd been accidents on the site, even before I'd arrived. Eamon had mentioned them when we'd come to check out the sinkhole, and the accidents had started around then. As far as I knew, there hadn't been any recently, but that didn't mean all the First Pit ghosts had gone. Sometimes ghosts just got bored and stopped hanging around for a while.

While I could see the ghosts floating around the site, I couldn't sense their presence. They were too far away. That's what I told myself, anyway. It had nothing to do with my possibly wonky powers.

I took solace in the fact that I couldn't sense anything at the house, either. Maybe I really was being paranoid and there were no ghosts about. I really hoped I was right. Because otherwise, it meant that the few powers I did have were wonky and I had no idea why.

My whole life, I'd been able to sense the presence of ghosts. So why couldn't I now? What had gone wrong? Sod's bloody law.

I carried on as normal, convincing myself over and over that there were no ghosts about. Even when my stuff moved an inch this way, or an inch that way, I told myself I was losing it. That was a better option than losing my powers.

Why had I agreed to work on the building site again?

Oh yeah. Money. Bills. Food. Ugh.

After a morning tea break, I returned to the back bedroom to find my paintbrush upright, stirring the paint in the pot. I couldn't see anything or anyone nearby. I couldn't sense a ghost, but I was damn sure there was one.

'All right, show yourself. I'm tired of this.'

The paintbrush stopped moving. I waited for the ghost to reveal itself. Would it be a friendly ghost? One from the mines? Someone who'd want me to help them cross over, *Ghost Whisperer*-style?

'Hello?' I called out.

There was nothing. As far as I could tell, I was alone again.

Sighing, I resumed painting the bedroom. I was almost done with the base coat in there, then I could move on to the next bedroom. I wouldn't get the chance to paint anything interesting – the occupants wanted magnolia throughout – but at least it allowed me to turn my brain off.

Which actually wasn't a good thing, because my brain chose to panic when it didn't have to think about anything. Panic about the house being haunted. Panic about Maggie and Josh. Panic about Ben and Jaya. Panic about Edie. And Fadil. It was a never-ending stream of anxiety going through my head, and I couldn't turn the damn thing off.

Frustrated, I rested my roller on the tray and sat down for a minute. I wiped my brow with the back of my hand, probably getting paint all over myself. It wouldn't be the first time.

From the back bedroom, I couldn't hear much. It faced away from the rest of the estate, looking out on to fields. It was a pretty view, one that would no doubt cost someone more.

I stood up and walked over to the window so that I could get a better look. Trees and fields, as far as I could see. It really was pretty. But it would be a nightmare for anyone who suffered from hay fever, like me. Thank god it was November.

I chuckled to myself, picturing Edie, Tilly, and me living in the house, snivelling nonstop as the pollen ransacked our allergies. We could practically open our own pharmacy with all the hay fever remedies we'd tried over the years.

Thud.

I turned around. My paint tin had flown across the room and smacked into the wall. Leaving a massive dent in it.

*

How was I supposed to explain a dent in the wall to Eamon? My second day, and someone had to come in and do a repair job. Wasn't that just great?

Better to get it over with, I supposed.

'Niamh, wha's up?' said Eamon after I knocked on his front door.

'There was an, um, accident in the house I'm painting. I tripped over the paint and it hit the wall.'

'Tha' explains why you look like you've been paintin' yourself instead of the wall.'

I looked down at my overalls. He was right. I was covered in fresh paint. I guess I'd been so anxious to get out of there – and away from the maybe-ghost – I hadn't even thought about how much of it I was covered in.

'What room was it? I'll send someone in to assess the damage. Can you do a differen' room in the meantime?'

'Yeah, but I need more paint.'

'Jeez, how much did you spill?'

'A bit,' I said. Meaning a lot.

'Bugger. You'll have to go Wickes an' get some more. The delivery's late. You OK to expense it?'

'Yeah.'

'All righ'. Go get it whenever,' he said.

'Thanks.'

I left his office feeling like a massive idiot. He must've thought I was one, too. Tripping over a bloody paint tin. But what other reasoning could I give him? I couldn't even prove to him that we had a ghost.

Once I'd changed out of my overalls, I got in the car and called Ben over Bluetooth. I wasn't sure if he'd be able to answer, but I figured I'd leave a voicemail if he didn't. And he didn't. Fiddlesticks.

'Hey Ben, it's me. Quick question – ever heard of a haunting where someone who can see ghosts can't sense them? Or see them? Call me back,' I said. Did I sound panicky and anxious? I hoped so. I *felt* panicky and anxious.

As I pulled up at Wickes, my phone rang. It was Ben.

'Ben, hey. Did you get my message?' I said.

'No, sorry. I saw you left it but I haven't had a chance to listen to it yet. I came home for lunch and, uh, Fadil's panicking.'

I heard mumbling in the background, but I couldn't make out any words.

'What do you mean?'

'It seems like he's lost his ability to speak English.'

'What do you mean?'

There was a pause, then, Fadil came on the line. He was talking in the same way he had been at the school, before I'd cast the spell. What the hell?

'Do you remember what the spell you used was?' Ben asked.

'No, sorry.'

'All right, I'll do some research. Why did you ring? Not that I wasn't glad to hear from you.'

I smiled. Take that, Jaya. 'I think the house I'm painting is being haunted. But I can't sense any ghosts. Even when I've seen things happen.'

'What have you seen?'

'A paintbrush moving on its own. Stuff being relocated.'

'Oh. Wow. Erm. No. That's new. Look after yourself. Whatever it is, I doubt it's anything good.'

*

Ben's words echoed in my mind as I wandered around the DIY store and drove back to work. I took the long route, trying to think up ways I could defend myself against an unknown foe. Could I use the amulet I'd leant Maggie? It wasn't like she was using it. It also wasn't like it'd done her much good. Sigh.

In an effort to avoid going into the house even longer, I'd tried ringing the ward for an update. But they wouldn't tell me anything.

If I ever saw Harry again, he was getting a punch in the face. I'd take the prison time. He deserved it. Edie could look after herself and Tilly for a couple of months.

Ben texted me as I sat in the car, avoiding returning to work. Fadil could speak English again. Had the spell had a momentary lapse? Was that a thing? He was the one with the parapsychology degree, not me. My brain couldn't handle any more questions.

Eamon tapped on the passenger-side window. 'Did you get it?'

'Yeah,' I said, handing him the receipt, which I'd stashed on the centre console.

'Cheers.'

Knowing he was checking up on me, I got out of the car, took the paint from the boot, and walked towards the house. To my dismay, Eamon followed me.

'One of the lads looked at the damage while you were out. Said it wouldn' take much to fix. But he could've sworn he heard voices while he was there. Weird, huh?'

'Yeah, weird,' I agreed. Great. The ghost was making itself known around other people, too. Just so long as it didn't hurt anyone else.

I really, really hoped it was just a bored ghost on a powertrip and not a poltergeist. Poltergeists were nasty pieces of work that could do way more damage than your average ghost. They channelled all their negative energy into causing as much chaos as they could. It didn't matter who got hurt. It wasn't about hurting *someone*. It was about hurting *anyone*. They needed an outlet for their emotions, probably because they hadn't had one in real life, or they'd been a ghost for too long and were angry at their fate. They were still restrained to haunting people or places, like normal ghosts, but how far they could stray from where they haunted varied depending on their strength.

I hadn't faced a poltergeist since Javi had been killed. And I really didn't want to. I'd left the world of ghost hunting. Being a part of it again still made me nervous, sometimes.

'Niamh? You still with us?' said Eamon, chuckling to himself.

'Yeah, sorry. Just worried about my daughter,' I said. Not entirely untrue. Just an easier topic of conversation.

'Understandable. Mine have their GCSEs comin' up. I'm not sure who's more nervous – them or their mam and me. How old's yours?'

I lifted the paint I was carrying, hooking it under my arm instead of carrying it by the handle. 'Seventeen. Got her A Levels in the summer.'

'If she's 'alf as smart as you, I'm sure she'll do great.'

'Thanks,' I said, surprised by what seemed like a genuine compliment. I didn't get called intelligent very often. Edie had definitely inherited her smarts from her dad.

We reached the house and I put my hand on the handle, ready to open the door. 'I'm really sorry about what happened. Don't worry, it won't cause me to fall behind schedule.'

Eamon nodded and smiled, then walked off, humming to himself.

I put the paint on the floor, then pushed the door handle down. It didn't open. I pushed harder. It still wouldn't open. Fiddlesticks.

'Come on, you bugger!' I shouted.

'Niamh?' said Eamon.

Fiddlesticks. He'd heard me.

'Just having some issues with the door. Did someone lock it while I was gone?'

'Don't think so,' he said. 'Here, le' me try.'

I stepped aside. Eamon opened the door without any issue. I was pretty sure my cheeks went crimson. The ghost inside that house was going to be toast if I got my hands on it.

Eamon held the door open for me, and I stepped through it, utterly mortified. Way to make me look like even more of an idiot.

'New doors. Sometimes they get a bit stuck. There's a bit of a knack to it. You'll get there,' said Eamon. He was covering for me, trying to protect my ego. I appreciated it, but I knew he was talking nonsense.

'Thanks.'

'Well, I'll leave you to it.' He walked off again, whistling a song I didn't recognise.

I closed the door and leaned against it, exhaling. I still couldn't sense anything in the house, but there were too many things going on to suggest otherwise.

'All right, ghostie. I know you're here. Show yourself, or I'm exorcising you.'

'No! Please don't!' A female ghost appeared in front of me. She had long blonde hair floating around her, and wore a scruffy, ankle-length skirt with a baggy shirt. If I had to guess, I would've said she was about Edie's age, working class, and had worked in the mines.

'I'm really sorry. I was just curious. All of this is so new to me,' she said. 'The world has changed since I was last here.'

'You're from the mines?'

She nodded. 'I'm Gwendoline. Please don't exorcise me.'

An innocent ghost, curious about how the world had changed? That I could forgive.

'It's nice to meet you, Gwendoline. I'm Niamh. Please don't trash my paint or wall again.'

'Done!' she said.

She stuck around for the rest of the day, watching me as I painted one of the other bedrooms. We chatted occasionally about how the world had changed and what her life was like in the mines, but mostly, she watched me in silence. Usually it bothered me to be watched, but there was something about Gwendoline that put me at ease. She was a calming influence, and I really needed that after recent events.

I left work that day feeling triumphant. The ghost problem was solved, and I hadn't even needed to do an exorcism.

*

Mrs Brightman had invited me for dinner that evening. It'd been organised before Maggie and Josh had been taken ill, and I felt bad for letting her down as she didn't have many other friends. Not that I did, either.

If nothing else, I could ask her ghost husband if he'd heard any more about the ghosts around town.

So I stuck to our reservation, leaving Edie to hang out with Fadil, since Ben was also out. Was he with Jaya? I really needed to let it go. I wasn't even interested in him romantically.

Except it wasn't Mrs Brightman at the table when I sat down for our reservation.

'Hello, I'm Martin,' he said, standing up to shake my hand. He was a weedy looking guy, with thinning hair. Had she actually set me up? Even though I'd told her repeatedly not to?

Cursing her internally, I sat down. If I'd known this was a set up, I would've cancelled on it. It was Mrs Brightman I didn't want to cancel on, not a random stranger.

'Mrs Brightman told me your name is Niamh,' he said.

'That's right,' I said. 'My mother had a fondness for names people can either spell or pronounce, but not both.' It was only a half-joke. She always had had a twisted sense of humour.

Martin didn't find my joke funny. He sipped his water and looked around the restaurant.

Hucknall wasn't the kind of place to have many restaurants. It mostly had cafes, coffee shops, and charity shops. So we were sitting in one of the two Italian restaurants in town. It'd been a nightmare to park, and since I thought I was meeting a half-blind woman, I hadn't put any effort into my appearance.

Then again, it didn't look like Martin had. And it wasn't like I was interested in him anyway. My life was too complicated to drag anyone else who couldn't see ghosts into it. Maggie had proven that time and time again.

'So, what do you do?' asked Martin.

What a question. Yawn.

'I'm currently decorating houses on the new estate,' I said.

Martin wrinkled his nose. 'That place? That's such a waste of green space.'

Was that an out? That he hated what I did for a living?

'We need more houses, though. People have to go somewhere.'

'True,' he agreed. Fiddlesticks. I hadn't pushed hard enough on that angle. Could I backtrack?

We skipped starters and ordered mains. I hoped that was a sign he wanted to leave early, too.

'What is it you do?' I asked, trying to salvage the conversation. The least we could do was talk about something. Anything before my brain died of boredom.

'I'm a gardener,' he said.

Was that why Mrs Brightman had set us up? Did she think we'd connect over our love of gardening? Hold my hair while I throw up.

My phone rang. Desperate for an out, I excused myself and went to answer it outside. It was Edie.

'How's Mrs B?' asked Edie.

'She set me up,' I said.

'What?'

'I'm on a blind bloody date!'

Edie sniggered.

'It's not funny!'

'It so is,' she said.

'Whatever. I'm using you as an excuse to leave.'

'Why? Everything's fine. Well. Sort of. You know what I mean.'

'Don't care. See you at home.'

I stuffed my phone back into my pocket, then ran inside as if I was in a hurry. They were just putting our food on the table. 'Sorry, can I have mine in a doggy bag please? I've got to go.'

'Sure,' said the waiter. He carried my plate back to the kitchen to put it in a box.

'Everything OK?' said Martin. He sounded like he genuinely cared.

I rifled in my purse for some money and put it on the table, barely looking at Martin. 'Sorry. Family emergency. You know what it's like, having a teenage daughter.'

'No. I don't have children.'

'Oh. Well. They're high maintenance.'

Pulling on my coat, I scurried off. The waiter greeted me at the door with my takeaway box. 'Thanks,' I said, not even looking behind me as I ran out the restaurant door.

16
Edie

It had been a while since I'd checked the infrared cameras Josh and I had fitted to trees around town. They were there to track ghost activity and were how we'd found out about Melanie and her ghosts.

But since Josh's curse, I hadn't been able to open the app on my phone. It brought back too many memories of the evening when Josh and I had fitted them. It had been a cold and late night, but it had been time we'd spent together. And I was terrified we'd never have that again.

I'd been trying to will myself to open the app all day. Mum hated Gran, so if I could find more ghosts from First Pit myself, it would mean Gran wouldn't need to get involved as much. I just needed to work myself up to do it, first.

I figured if I could take a look at the camera footage, it might help us track some more ghosts and see what they were up to so that they couldn't hurt anyone else. Not that Melanie's ghost had really hurt her – beyond sleep deprivation – but there were bound to be far nastier ghosts out there than hers.

Plus, it was my duty to protect the rest of the town from ghosts wanting to hurt people. So, on my way to see Fadil from college, I opened the app. The screen was blank.

The cameras hadn't even been up for a couple of months. Surely they couldn't have ran out of battery already?

Technology wasn't my thing. I wouldn't know what I was looking for even if I could check. But I couldn't, because I was too short to reach where Josh and his six-foot frame had attached them.

Dejected, I returned my phone to my pocket and entered Ben's house. The TV played CBeebies in the background, while Fadil was tugging at something on his leg.

'What are you doing?' I said.

Fadil jumped. 'Why do you look like crap?'

It was so nice of him to use the language Mum had given him to insult me. His ability to speak English had intermittently stopped working, but for the most part, he spoke it just fine. Better than most native speakers, in fact.

'Technology problems and flashbacks of my comatose boyfriend. Your turn,' I said.

He looked surprised I'd been so frank with him. He probably hadn't expected me to give him an answer. Ha.

Fadil sighed. 'I have some linen attached to my leg still. It won't come off. I wanted to get rid of it before Doc got here.'

I dumped my bag on a chair, then gestured for him to follow me into the kitchen. He sat on one of the barstools, watching me.

Doc was coming over to give Fadil a health check. Mum had reluctantly filled him in on everything to get him to come over faster. Her theory was that if Fadil was fine, it meant that Maggie and Josh would be, too. It would buy us more time to fix them. Even though we didn't need more time, we needed more answers.

I searched Ben's cupboards for a cloth and some warm water, then sat beside Fadil. After soaking the cloth in the water, I held it on his leg. 'You should never rip a bandage off; you'll damage the skin. You should always soak them off.'

'That'll take forever.'

'As opposed to four thousand years in a stone sarcophagus?'

'Fine.'

I removed the cloth, soaked it again, and repeated the process.

'So, what are your technology problems?' said Fadil.

'Do you really care?' I said.

Fadil flinched. 'What do you take me for? Half-dead or heartless?'

'I'm sorry. I shouldn't have said that. It's just…Josh helped me put some cameras up before his coma. And now they're not working. But I can't fix them because I don't know technology and I'm too bloody short!'

'Why don't you ask Ben?'

'He has enough going on. I wouldn't want to bother him,' I said.

'I've only been living with the guy for two days and I already know he loves to play with technology. Have you seen this house?'

He had a point. Ben had every gadget you could think of, from a smart speaker to an air fryer to a milk frother. Most of them looked like they'd barely been used, but I guess that wasn't really the point for him. It seemed more like he collected them. Everyone had their interests.

'Maybe I will ask him. Thanks.'

Fadil smiled.

I removed the cloth and his bandage moved a little.

'Can I pull it off yet?' said Fadil.

'Let's soak it some more first, then you can,' I said. Although I was hoping it'd fall off on its own and do less damage to his skin.

After soaking for a little longer, to Fadil's disappointment, it fell off on its own. I handed him some kitchen roll and he patted it dry. 'That's much better. Thanks.'

I smiled at him. At least I could help someone.

*

Doc turned up not long after, while we were watching a show on CBeebies about numbers. It was weird seeing how different those kinds of shows were compared to when I was younger.

When I answered the front door, Doc had a big grin on his face. 'Where's the patient?'

'You're way too excited for this,' I said.

Doc grinned. 'I don't get the chance to do blood tests very often anymore, let alone on someone old enough to be my – how old is he again?'

'Too far back to count your relatives,' I said.

Fadil was sitting on the sofa, rubbing his hands together. He'd agreed the tests were a good idea, but I guess that didn't mean he had to like the concept. It was a seriously different type of health care to what he was used to.

Doc sat beside him. He didn't have any sort of judgment on his face, nor did he examine Fadil like there was anything unusual about him. 'My name's Doc. What should I call you?' He held out his hand to shake Fadil's. Fadil stared at it.

I leaned into him. 'You're supposed to shake it.'

'Oh! I'm Fadil.'

He reached out and clasped Doc's hand with both of his and shook it rapidly. Doc laughed.

'What I'm going to do today is a blood test and a biopsy. To take the blood, I'll put a needle into your arm. It might take a few attempts to find a vein, but I'll do my best to be gentle. You might bruise after it. For the biopsy, we'll cut off a small part of the top layer of your skin.'

'Why do both of those things sound terrifying?'

Because they were? Not that I was going to voice my fear of them to Fadil. We needed to do the tests to make sure he was healthy, and to give us further hope for Josh and Maggie. We couldn't do that if he was afraid of the equipment.

'They're not. You'll just feel a sharp scratch.'

I suppressed a laugh. Doc glared at me.

'Why don't I believe you?' said Fadil.

'Because Edie isn't helping?' said Doc, still glaring at me.

I curled into myself. 'Sorry. Not a huge fan of needles. But it'll be fine. It won't take long.' That much was true.

'What *is* a needle, exactly? And a biopsy?' said Fadil. 'All this modern equipment is...I'm not sure I trust it.'

'That's understandable,' said Doc, 'but I assure you, they're perfectly safe. They've been used for hundreds of years. Imagine how far medicine has come in that time!'

'That doesn't answer my question,' said Fadil.

Doc took the needle from his equipment case and held it up. It was still wrapped in plastic, showing it was sterilised. He also took out a purple tourniquet, which was covered in bats. 'Thought the tourniquet might help in case it's hard to find a vein,' he said. 'It'll help with blood flow. This is a needle. It goes into your vein, removes some blood, then we're done. With that part, anyway.'

'What will all these tests show you?' asked Fadil.

I shifted from foot to foot, anxious to get the tests over with. It was so annoying that I was the only one free to be there with him.

'Everything. Anything. I won't bore you with the details. We're doing all of this as a precaution. We don't think anything is wrong, but, well, when you've been prostrate for as many years as you have…it never hurts. I'll also do an assessment to check your heart rate, breathing – a full health check, basically.'

'Sounds…intense.' Fadil's hands shook. He sat on them. If Doc noticed, he didn't say anything. He kept his face and body relaxed, like it was no big deal. Which, I supposed it wasn't, for a GP who did things like that every day.

'If you need me to stop at any time, just say so. There's no rush and no pressure.'

Fadil smiled. 'Thank you.'

Doc opened his black leather bag and took out a stethoscope. 'This will measure your heart rate, check everything is ticking along nicely.'

'This is all so strange,' said Fadil as Doc put the stethoscope to his chest. 'We looked at the body very differently.'

'How so?' I asked.

'Well, I mean, we knew the basics of how internal organs worked. But we didn't do even a quarter of what you do now. I saw a medical documentary on TV last night.' He shuddered. 'You seem to have such a deep understanding of it all.'

'Modern medicine has come a long way in the last hundred years. We've still got a long way to go, though. Believe it or not,' said Doc. He lowered his stethoscope. 'Your heart sounds good. Perfectly healthy.'

Fadil beamed.

Over the next half an hour, Doc checked his breathing with a peak flow meter – it was better than mine – took blood, and took the biopsy. Fadil relaxed as soon as Doc said he was done. I didn't really blame him.

As Doc was packing up, he turned to me: 'How's your back been?'

'The pain comes and goes. It hurts more if I sit or stand for too long. Will it ever go away?'

Doc pursed his lips. 'I can't say. My best advice is to keep stretching and keep the muscles around that area strong. Yoga and cross trainers are particularly good for it.'

'Thanks,' I said. Did I really have to resort to exercise to make it better? Ugh. I hated exercise.

'I'll take this to the lab now and we should have results soon. Obviously it's dependent on how fast my friend can put things through, given she isn't doing this on an official basis.'

I nodded. 'Of course. We really appreciate your help.'

'Happy to help where I can. One thing I would suggest is a vitamin D supplement.'

'What's that?' said Fadil.

'Why?' I asked.

'Well,' said Doc as he zipped his bag, 'our main source of vitamin D is the sun. And you've been deprived of that for quite some time. And the UK isn't exactly known for having much of it, especially this time of year. Most people should take a vitamin D supplement, to be honest with you. A lack of it can cause depression, bone problems, all sorts.'

My eyes went wide. 'Do I need to take one?'

'With the amount of sunscreen a ginger needs to wear? Yes. Just because you dye your hair, doesn't make your skin less susceptible to the sun.'

'Thank you for the reminder of how easily I end up looking like Edie, the Red-Nosed Reindeer.'

'You're very welcome,' said Doc, smirking. 'Sun protection is no joke. Remember: a tan is damage!'

'We shall heed your words,' I teased. 'And I'll pick some vitamins up on the way home.'

Doc nodded approvingly. 'Then my job here is done, so I'll be off. You know where I am if you need me.'

I showed Doc out, then sat on the sofa with Fadil. 'You OK?' I asked him.

'I am now it's over,' he rubbed the plaster from the spot where the biopsy had been taken. 'Was that really necessary?'

'You want to make sure you're healthy, don't you? That there are no long-lasting effects from the curse?'

'Who's to say that if there are, part of the curse wouldn't cover it up anyway?'

'I doubt whomever cursed you would've had the forethought to conceal everything from modern medicine,' I said.

'It hid me from modern technology,' he pointed out. 'The scanners didn't pick up that I was alive.'

'This isn't technology, though. Not on the same level. It's one person and a microscope. Maybe some chemicals to separate out what's going on in your blood.' I was talking out of my arse. I had no idea what they actually did with the blood samples.

'I guess we'll have to wait and see,' said Fadil.

'Yeah, I guess we will.'

17
Niamh

Doc rang me early the next morning, as I was getting ready to head to work.

'As if you have test results this fast,' I said.

'Your lack of faith disappoints me,' he joked. 'When else can pro bono tests be done but out of hours?'

'Granted. What did you find?'

'Aside from some vitamin deficiencies, which are to be expected after thousands of years in a darkened sarcophagus, Fadil is perfectly healthy.'

'Pardon?'

'He's healthier than you.'

'I resent that,' I said.

'But you know I'm right.'

'No, I don't. I haven't seen the test results. And my health isn't *that* bad.'

'Judging from what I've seen, health-wise, he's not far off Edie's age.'

What had he just said? 'Are you saying he was still a teenager when he was cursed?'

'It's likely, yeah.'

'Bloody hell. That's rough,' I said.

'Yeah,' agreed Doc. 'Someone must've really hated him. We could do some scans to see what's going on internally, if you'd like. But that would take some more effort to organise,' said Doc.

'Do we have a reason to do them?'

'Scientific curiosity?' said Doc.

'Let's put it on hold for now. Then, when Maggie and Josh wake up, we can reassess.' We had enough going on as it was. I didn't want to add more to my plate. Especially when doing any sort of scan on a guy who looked like a walking mummy would have to be done late at night, and Edie and I were already sleep-deprived.

'All right. Look after yourself,' said Doc.

'You too.'

My hope renewed, I practically danced into Edie's room. She was choosing which band hoody to wear for the day.

'Fadil is healthy! The tests came back clear!'

'That's…good.'

'That's it? That's your reaction? Don't you get what that means for Maggie and Josh?'

'Nothing if we can't find answers,' she said. She settled on a Linkin Park hoody – I had a proud mum moment at that – then pulled it over her head.

I sat on the edge of her bed and patted the spot beside me. She sat down. Sensing we were together, Tilly ran into the room and jumped up. Edie picked her up and put her on the spot between us. Tilly licked her hand in thanks.

'I dreamt of them last night,' said Edie.

'What about them?'

'They came back, but they weren't the same. Their eyes were black and they spoke in funny voices and they wanted to hurt us.'

I rubbed her back. 'They're not going to come back like that.'

'Aren't they? You don't know that. We have no idea what's happening with them. We're just going on assumptions and hope.'

I pulled her to me, resting her head on my shoulder. 'Maggie and Josh will be OK.' They had to be.

*

I got to work and found paint everywhere but in the tin. The lid had been removed. The floor, walls, and skirting were splashed with magnolia. It was mostly in the living room, with a little in the kitchen and hallway. Thank god the kitchen units were covered in sheets so that they hadn't been covered in paint. That would've been a lot harder to fix.

'Gwendoline!' I shouted.

She appeared in front of me, her eyes wide. 'Oh my gosh.'

'Did you do this?'

'No! I swear!'

'Are you sure?'

'Yes! I promised you I wouldn't! I keep my promises!'

A malevolent chuckle filled the room. A broad, male figure appeared in front of me. His hands were crossed over his chest, and his face had an evil grin across it. 'What do you think to my redecorating?'

I didn't need powers to know he was a poltergeist.

Gwendoline stared at him like a frightened deer. She faded away, disappearing before he could acknowledge her. I didn't take that as a good sign.

I ran out of the house, barely able to breathe. No. Not another poltergeist. I couldn't do it. I *wouldn't* do it. I'd throw the job in.

But then…what about all the people who couldn't see ghosts, or do anything about them? How many of them would get hurt if I didn't do something?

I sat on a bench, far enough away from the house that I hoped the ghosts couldn't get to me, but also far enough from my colleagues that they wouldn't notice me, either. Burying my head between my knees, I tried to stop myself from hyperventilating. Breathe in. Breathe out. Don't panic. It's fine.

It's fine.

It's *fine*!

Oh my god I couldn't breathe.

Of course it wasn't fine. A poltergeist! The last time I'd encountered one, Javi had been killed. How had I gone ten years without seeing another one?

Well, I'd avoided ghosts. Then moved back into town just as the very building site I was working on had awakened a bunch of them that'd been trapped for nearly two hundred years. Great timing, I know.

Was it too soon to hand in my notice?

Yes. I needed the money.

But I couldn't work in a house with a poltergeist!

Why couldn't all ghosts be like Casper?

Actually, he was creepy too. I never understood why Edie insisted on watching that film every Halloween when she was little. She hadn't even been born when it was made. I guess it made her feel like less of a freak, since none of her school friends could see ghosts. I'd been lucky to grow up with Javi, who could. But that didn't make being away from him any easier.

'Sooooo a poltergeist, huh?'

I jumped. Javi had floated in and was sitting beside me on the bench.

As I lifted my head, my surroundings began to spin. I swallowed, closing my eyes while everything righted itself.

'Shouldn't you be up there watching people's lives unravel like movies or playing cards?' I said.

'I'd rather be with you.'

Something tugged at my heart. I'd have preferred him to be with me, too.

'I can't do it, Javi. I can't go back in there.'

'That's just what he wants. You know that, right?'

'Of course I know that! But it just brings back too much. I don't even know if I have it in me to get rid of him.'

'Why wouldn't you?'

'I couldn't even sense that there was one ghost haunting the place, let alone two. Even when they were interacting with objects I was right next to. My powers are wonky and I don't know why.' I rubbed my face with my hands.

Javi frowned. 'Hmm, that's odd.'

There was no one else around, so thankfully nobody to see me talking to air. I could hear voices in the distance, but they sounded like they were coming from the other side of the building site. I was safe talking to my dead husband. For now, anyway.

'This is the last thing I need. And I can't tell Edie. Not with everything else going on.'

'Let's focus on finding answers first,' said Javi. He reached out, resting his hand beside mine. God, I wished I could touch him. Hug him. Feel his comforting touch.

'I don't have time! With Maggie, and Josh, and Mrs Brightman trying to set me up, and Edie, and her exams, and money, and now all this with the poltergeist? I don't have time to worry about why my magic is wonky!'

'I'm so sorry, Neevie. I wish I could do more,' he said.

I sighed. 'I wish you could, too.'

*

Before going to tell Eamon what had happened, I wanted to talk to Gwendoline. Javi managed to locate her and bring her to me. Which made me worry that the poltergeist could follow us, too, but Gwendoline assured me that he was too drained from doing other things to travel that far.

'It takes energy, and he used a lot trying to cause trouble,' she said. She sat on the bench beside me.

Javi paced the small patch of grass in front of us.

'Who is he?' I asked.

'He's my old boss. His name was Peter. He was…' She shook her head. 'Bad. Very bad.'

'Like, Me Too bad?'

'What's that?'

'Right. Um…did he cross any boundaries?' I didn't want to be totally blunt about it, but I had to ask. I needed to know who I was dealing with.

'Like personal boundaries?'

I nodded.

So did Gwendoline.

'Bloody hell,' I said.

'And you couldn't sense him? At all?' said Javi.

'No. I already told you that,' I said.

'Can you normally?' said Gwendoline.

'Yeah. I should've been able to sense you both. You'd have different energies.'

Gwendoline wrinkled her nose. 'What was the last spell you cast?'

'Um, I don't remember. Why?'

'Maybe it's tied to that,' she suggested.

'Are you a ghost hunter?'

'No. Part witch. My paternal grandmother was one, although my mum was human, so not all the powers passed down.'

'I see,' I said.

Javi was still pacing, a sexy, pensive look over his face. Not going to lie, I was jealous that he was permanently thirty and I was ageing. And not like a fine wine, I might add. Javi had always been attractive. For him to stay that way for eternity was just cruel.

'To get rid of him, you'll have to exorcise the house, won't you?' said Gwendoline.

I nodded. I'd need to purify wherever he was attached to, and that seemed to be the house itself. The homeowners were due to move in within a couple of weeks. I didn't have long to finish painting it. Or to decide what to do about our poltergeist.

Purifying the house] meant it risked hurting *any* ghost within the vicinity. Which also meant it could hurt Gwendoline. I didn't want that. But she had a determined look on her face: 'If you have to exorcise me to stop him from hurting anyone else, then so be it.'

*

When I told Eamon I needed more paint, this time, I had no excuse. I didn't have the energy to come up with one. Bad, I know.

Eamon lowered a bushy eyebrow at me. 'So you need more paint, after havin' only bought some more yesterdee, and you can't tell me why?'

'You wouldn't believe me if I told you,' I said.

He shook his head. 'I'm gonna need to see the damage before I authorise any more.'

He was going to regret that, but I agreed anyway. It was the only way to get him to agree.

We walked back to the house in silence. As he walked through the front door, I hesitated.

'Aren' you gonna come in?'

'Nope. Not right now,' I said.

'Neevie!' Javi whispered in my ear. I couldn't see him, but I took that as a sign he was watching. Why didn't he watch at useful times instead? I ignored him, not wanting my employer to think I was any more of a nut job than he already did.

A gust of wind blew me through the front door. 'Javi!' I said through gritted teeth. He chuckled. Git.

'Did you say somethin'?' asked Eamon.

'Nope,' I said. 'Must've been the wind.'

More chuckling. If I could've strangled him, I would've.

'What's this? Where's the magnolia hallway the buyer wan'ed? This house is suppose' ta be finished this week!' Eamon went around the house, inspecting every room. Of course most of them weren't finished. I'd had to redo a bunch thanks to Peter.

Finishing his inspection at the top of the stairs, Eamon sighed. 'I don' wanna be 'arsh, Niamh, but you're gonna put us behind if ya work like this.' He gestured into the bedroom where Peter had splashed all the paint. 'An' wha' the 'ell am I suppose' ta do abou' tha' mess?' He growled, his accent coming out thicker as he got more annoyed with me. Wasn't that just great?

'I know. I'm sorry.' It wasn't like I could tell him the real reason I hadn't finished on time.

But the decision was taken out of my hands. Peter appeared behind Eamon and grinned. He reached out to him. 'No!' I said, jumping between them. Peter's eyes went wide, then he vanished.

'What was tha'?'

'Wasp,' I said.

'In November?'

I shrugged. 'Climate change.'

Eamon and I went downstairs. Every step, I had visions of Peter pushing him down them. But he didn't. He waited until we were at the bottom, then as Eamon went to leave, he locked the door to the downstairs loo. It was a subtle, clicking noise. The kind of thing most people would dismiss. But not Eamon.

'What was tha'?'

'What was what? I didn't hear anything,' I said.

Eamon narrowed his eyes, then went in the direction of the sound. The downstairs toilet, which was under the stairs, was locked from the inside. But there was nobody in the house but us.

'Did you do this?' said Eamon.

'No,' I said.

Eamon tried to unlock it from the outside, by turning the dial with his hands. It wouldn't budge. 'What the—'

Peter moaned. I couldn't see where he was, but he was clearly trying to play into the ghostly stereotype. And having fun doing it. Twat.

'There's somethin' really wrong with this place,' said Eamon. He went into the kitchen. I followed him, annoyed I hadn't brought anything more than the spells I'd memorised with me as a backup. But then, how could I have smuggled anything else in with the morning bag checks?

The downstairs toilet door unlocked. Then, it began to open. Slowly, it creaked out towards the hallway.

Eamon, braver than he looked, walked into the hallway and peered inside the downstairs toilet. And screamed.

I ran to his side. Peter stood in the tiny room, grinning. Then, he vanished.

'Wh-what was tha'? Did ya see tha'?' said Eamon, pointing to where the ghost had been moments earlier. His accent grew thicker as he shook with fear.

I sighed. Bastard poltergeist. I suppose I would've had to exorcise the house eventually. But I'd been hoping to put it off for as long as possible. Especially with my wonky powers. I needed to preserve what little energy I had for Maggie and Josh.

'Yeah. You've got a poltergeist.'

Not wanting to encourage Peter any further, I walked out of the house, hoping Eamon would follow me. Thankfully, he did. We relocated to the tarmacked front drive of the house.

He studied my face for signs I was joking. My blank face must've told him I wasn't. He ran his hand over what was left of his hair. 'Great. Isn't that just great?' He walked in circles a few times, then stopped and stared at me. 'Wait. How do you know we've go' a poltergeist? Why do I believe you?'

'Because you've seen it. He made himself visible to you. And I can see him even when he isn't visible to you. Most of the time.' Please don't let him ask about the technicalities of it. I was too tired to explain that how visible ghosts were was tied to energy, but also people like me could see them almost all the time. Unless they actively decided to make themselves invisible.

'Wait. Wha'? No, that can't be righ'. Ghosts don' exist.' He paced up and down the drive, rubbing his face. He looked up at me, those bushy eyebrows meeting in the middle as he frowned. 'So you can see ghosts?'

I nodded. 'And I get rid of them when they cause problems.'

'You a ghostbuster?' He laughed at his own joke.

'Something like that,' I said through gritted teeth. I *hated* the *Ghostbuster* joke, but it made it easier for people to process what I did.

'You gonna bring in one of those contraptions?' He mimicked using a proton pack.

'No. I use a spell.'

He doubled over, laughing. 'A *spell*? Wha' are you, Sabrina the Middle-Age' Witch?'

I glared at him. Did he want me to exorcise the house or not?

'You know what? I don't have time for this. My friends are in comas and I should be helping them instead of hanging around here.' Fed up his of ribbing, I started walking away.

'Wait! Wait!' He said, panting as he tried to catch up with me. I hadn't even walked that far ahead. I stopped, folding my arms.

Eamon sighed. 'Will ya be able to finish the house on time if I let you exorcise it?'

'"Let me"? "*Let me*?" You think I want to go back in there? My husband was killed by a poltergeist! The last thing I want to do is stay around here! But which is worse? Leaving it as it is, or having Peter learn how to use his powers more and more, ready for when the new family moves in and he can *really* have some fun?'

Eamon lowered his head. So wha' do you need? To get rid of it?'

'To get in without someone checking my bag in the morning?'

He wrinkled his nose. 'Can't skip corners like tha'. The lads'll notice and everyone'll expect special treatment. I'll check it in the mornin' instead. No judgment. How's tha'?'

It was better than nothing, I supposed. 'I'll bring the stuff tomorrow.'

'All righty then. Off to buy more paint you go.'

18
Edie

We still had no idea how to find the objects behind Josh and Maggie's curse. Without those, it was impossible to reverse it.

Not that we had the incantation to do that either. Ben needed to know exactly what the ingredients used to break the spell were before he could cross-reference it in his collection, since, while the type of curse was rare, there were a few possibilities. Which was very unhelpful.

I tapped my foot against the chair in Ben's kitchen, simultaneously drumming my finger against my Superman mug.

'Are you done yet?' said Fadil as he made himself some toast.

I stopped. 'Sorry. Agitated.'

He sat opposite me while his toast cooked. The smell of cooked bread filled the kitchen. 'Have you got a spell book of some kind you could look in?'

I tapped the mug again. He glared. I stopped. 'Yeah, but it's hard when you don't know what you're looking for.'

'What about your dog?'

'What about her?'

'Unless something has seriously changed about dogs in the last few thousand years, they have a better sense of smell than us. Ben said the curse ingredients were pretty potent. Maybe she could sniff them out? Or sniff out something that smells like Josh or Maggie?'

I dove out of my seat and hugged him. He froze, but I refused to let go. Why hadn't we thought of that before? We were such idiots!

Fadil relaxed, patting my arm with his. Satisfied he was getting used to people again, I ran into Ben's library, where he and Mum were researching.

'We could use Tilly!' I said.

Mum looked up from the ancient (ish, if you compared it to Fadil) book she was reading. 'For what?'

'To sniff out the curse stuff!'

Mum and Ben exchanged glances. I had no idea what they were silently communicating to each other.

'It's worth a shot,' said Ben.

Tilly the sniffer dog. Could solving everything really be as simple as Tilly sniffing out the curse?

We left Fadil at Ben's, then drove to ours. It was all very well and good using Tilly as a sniffer dog, but there was one big hurdle we needed to overcome first: how were we going to get inside their house when Harry hated us?

'Harry's never going to let us in,' I said on the drive home.

'He doesn't need to. I have a key,' said Mum.

'But what about any nosy neighbours? Or if he's home, since he left work early?'

Mum clicked her tongue. 'What time is it?'

'Five,' said Ben.

'Fiddlesticks,' said Mum as we pulled up on the front drive. 'We might have to wait until tomorrow.'

'But we don't have time!' I said.

'We can only do what we have the scope to do,' said Mum.

'What's that supposed to mean?' I said.

Mum clutched the steering wheel, her body tensing. 'With Harry blocking us from doing anything, there's nothing we can do right now.'

'But at what cost to Josh and Maggie?'

She ground her teeth. 'Take that up with Harry, not me.'

Oh, I wanted to. But I also knew that Harry would practically laugh me off his drive. I wouldn't put it past him to call the police on me.

We got home and I stomped into the living room and sat down. Tilly sat on the floor by the bookshelf, a bored expression on her face. Normally she was excited to see us. She didn't even look up when Mum and Ben walked in. Spectre came into view, an equally mardy expression on his face. Was Tilly turning into a cat?

Mum rolled her eyes at the dog, then went into the kitchen.

'We'll figure it out,' said Ben, sitting next to me.

'People keep saying that. But it's been four days. We still don't have any answers. Who can even begin to imagine what they're going through right now?' I said.

'Something this complicated takes time. And I know, it sucks,' said Ben. He was right there.

'I can't even make myself useful tracking down the rest of the ghosts around town,' I said. Fadil had mentioned I ask Ben for his help, but I didn't want to burden him with more to do. Mum relied on him loads already. But if he happened to offer…

'What do you mean?'

I took my phone from my pocket and showed him my blank infrared camera app. 'I don't know how long ago they stopped working. Seeing the heat signatures is how we found Melanie.'

'Do you want me to take a look?'

'Could you? That would be amazing!'

'I think I work nearby where you put them. I can go in early and take a look.'

*

Ben's offer of help reassured me a little. It was nice having someone on my side again, even if it was Mum's not-boyfriend instead of Josh.

I climbed into bed that night, my mind and body exhausted. Tilly curled up at the foot of my bed and dozed off straight away. I admired her ability to fall asleep so quickly. While she liked Josh and Maggie, she had no idea what had happened to them, so of course she wasn't as worried as the rest of us.

I snuggled farther into the duvet, pulling it up over my shoulders to keep the coldness away.

Mum's footsteps echoed around the house as she paced, probably trying to come up with other things we could do to help Josh and Maggie. It was becoming a routine for her to stay up and pace. I hadn't heard her do it this much since Dad had died.

The sounds of her pacing became like a clock ticking; a metronome that drifted me off to sleep.

I don't know how long I was asleep when I felt something. Like a small electric shock. I sat upright. Tilly dove off the bed, barking. My door was shut, so she couldn't get through. Instead, she jumped up at it, barking and scratching at it.

'Tilly, shh! You'll wake Mum up!' She was sleep-deprived enough as it was.

Too late. Mum's bedroom door opened and she knocked on my door. I opened it.

'What's wrong?'

Tilly pushed past Mum and ran to the front door. Surely someone wouldn't be at the front door in the middle of the night?

'I don't know. Did you feel it?' I said, following Tilly downstairs.

Mum rubbed at her eyes. 'Feel what?'

'It was like an electric shock. Then Tilly started barking.'

We reached the front door. Tilly was still barking. Mum picked her up, shushing her, as she unlocked the front door and peered out. The street was silent. No people. No cars. Nothing abnormal.

Mum passed Tilly to me, then bent down to pick up Moonie. He'd been living to the left of our front door for the last few days. 'Did he always have a bit missing from his foot?'

I rubbed Tilly behind the ears, trying to calm her. 'Not that I remember.'

'Do you think it worked?'

'You mean you think someone was trying to get in and Moonie stopped them?' I said.

Mum checked the street one last time, put Moonie back, then locked the front door. 'Yeah. Tilly going mad, you feeling the electricity, Moonie missing a bit of his foot…what else could it be?'

'I don't know,' I said. And that's what scared me.

*

True to his word, Ben went and checked on the cameras the next morning. It wasn't just that they weren't working. They were gone. Someone had taken them down. Which meant not only was Josh's money wasted, but if I put any more up, it was likely to happen again.

Having answers sucked sometimes.

Who would do that, though? And why?

Was it a good Samaritan who didn't want Big Brother monitoring everyone? Was it related to the ghosts from First Pit? Or the noise from last night? Or did it have something to do with Josh and Maggie's curses?

One day, I'd get more answers instead of more questions.

I went through the rest of the morning in a daze, hoping at least I could help when Tilly played sniffer dog later. Until Mum ruined that plan, too.

I went home at lunchtime, assuming I'd be joining her, Tilly, and Ben at Josh's house. I was very wrong.

'But why can't I come? Three heads are better than one,' I begged Mum. She shoved some more spell and potion stuff into her bag. It felt like she was only half listening to me. Ugh. 'It's not like I've been able to concentrate in class. I've been trying! And besides, I don't have any more lessons until last period.'

'You get to leave between lessons?' said Ben.

'Yeah. What's the point in me hanging around if I don't need to be there?'

Mum wrinkled her brow. 'What do you usually do during your free lessons?'

'Go for a coffee or to the library. Means I can concentrate somewhere away from everyone else.'

Mum sighed. My logic was solid and my grades were good. She couldn't argue and she knew it.

'Fine. But you're on lookout duty.'

I rolled my eyes, but agreed. It was better than not being involved at all.

*

After lunch, Mum, Ben, and I walked Tilly to Josh's house. To anyone not paying attention, we looked like any normal family out on a walk. Of course, we couldn't have been any further from normal if we'd tried.

All the curtains were shut and the lights were off at the Josh's house. Harry's car wasn't there, but that didn't mean anything.

Our cover was to send Ben over with a parcel, pretending that Maggie had ordered something, to double check nobody was home. It was just a candle that Mum had had lying around, repackaged in an old Amazon box. She had the snorkelling gnome in a separate bag, which she'd put in the hedge on her way in. How would things have turned out differently if she'd planted it before someone targeted Josh and Maggie? Would it have protected them? We'd never know.

'Know what you're doing?' said Mum.

'Yep,' said Ben, nodding. 'Let's do this.' He squared his shoulders, then walked across the road.

Mum and I hid around the corner, trying our best to listen in while kneeling down to Tilly, playing with her while we listened so that it didn't look weird that we were standing around in the street.

We heard him knock, then there was silence. A few seconds later, a door opened. Frazzle.

'You after the Morgans?' said their neighbour. I wasn't sure of her name.

'That's Mrs Lopez,' said Mum. 'She's lived there since before you were born.'

'Yeah,' said Ben.

'You'll struggle to find anyone in right now. The husband's at work, and the other three are off staying with a relative.'

'So no one's in?'

'Nobody's been in much for the last few days. Harry comes home late and is gone as soon as the sun is up. Poor thing. He must be so lost without the others.'

'All right, I've heard enough,' said Mum. She stood up and walked over. Tilly and I followed her lead.

'Afternoon, Mrs Lopez,' said Mum in her most charming voice. She didn't pull it out very often; it was a sign she meant business.

Mrs Lopez turned to look at us and beamed, clapping her hands together. She had on an ugly floral skirt and thick pink cardigan. 'Niamh! Edie! It's so lovely to see you both.'

'Thanks, you too,' said Mum. 'How've you been?'

'Can't complain. Have you spoken to Maggie? Do you know what's going on? I saw an ambulance here the other day. Are they OK? Is it true they're having marital problems? Are the two things related?'

After gossip, much?

'They're all fine. The ambulance was just a precaution. As for the martial problems, it's really not my story to tell, but…well, you can connect the dots,' said Mum. 'Not to the ambulance! Those dots aren't connected.' Phew. That would've been a hell of a rumour to accidentally start. Mum looked at Ben: 'is that for Maggie?'

Ben looked at the fake label we'd put on it. 'Yeah. Maggie Morgan.'

'I'll take it,' she said, grabbing the parcel from him. Mum turned back to Mrs Lopez conspiratorially: 'Maggie asked me to pick up some of her things while Harry was at work. Just on the off chance she ran into him, you know?'

Mrs Lopez nodded. 'I understand. I sent a friend to pack up my things when I left my first husband.' She shuddered. 'Terrible, terrible man. No idea what I saw in him. Anyway, I won't keep you. Have a good day.'

'You too,' said Mum.

Mrs Lopez disappeared back inside her house. Mum buried the gnome in the thick hedge which separated the two houses while I unlocked the front door. Looked like Mrs Lopez would get protection from evil too, if the gnome worked.

The three of us – sorry, four including Tilly – scurried inside, closed the door, and exhaled.

'That was close,' said Ben. 'Good thinking on your feet,' he said to Mum.

'Thanks,' said Mum, grinning. 'Although I have to admit, I planned it. The nosy sod is always after the latest gossip. Now, time to get started finding this vessel. Edie, you stay by the window. Ben, you're with me upstairs.'

'But can't I—'

'No, Edie. We need you on lookout.'

I sighed. 'Fine. Window duty it is.'

19
Niamh

Ben and I went upstairs, Tilly in tow. We sat on the landing. Everywhere around me were pieces of Maggie and Josh. Family photos on the walls of the landing; Maggie's favourite colour, a deep red, accenting their bedroom in throw pillows. Josh's rock band posters on the walls of his room. It pained me to be there when they weren't, and not knowing when they'd step foot in it again. If they ever did.

'So, what now?' I said to Ben.

'We need something with Maggie or Josh's scent on it.'

'But doesn't the whole house smell of them?'

'Probably, but that won't be focused enough for her to tell the difference and single out what we're looking for,' he said.

'All right,' I said. What could we use?

I got up and went into Maggie and Harry's room. The bedding had been changed since I'd last been in there, and the furniture had been rearranged. Had Harry rearranged everything to distract himself from what was going on? He wouldn't be the first person to need to keep his mind and body busy when he was anxious.

Not that he'd ever acknowledge having anxiety. Anxiety, to him, was like ghosts: illogical and therefore non-existent. Ugh.

I started with Maggie's bedside drawer. We had no secrets, so the vibrator I found in there didn't surprise me. She had to entertain herself somehow when her husband worked all the time.

I didn't just find that, though. The protection amulet I'd given her when Abigail was possessed was in the drawer, too. 'Fiddlesticks.' I picked it up and put it around my own neck.

'What is it?' said Ben. He hovered in the doorway, obviously uncomfortable in someone else's bedroom.

I held up the amulet that was hanging around my neck. 'Why wasn't she wearing it?'

'Maybe she thought the wards would be enough?' he suggested.

I scoffed. 'Yeah. Fat lot of good they did.'

'Don't blame yourself.'

'How can I not? Are you seriously telling me the attacks on them are random?'

Ben stared at his shoes. Yeah, I thought so.

I went into Maggie's T-shirt drawer. Her top collection stared back at me, filling me with guilt. Was this all my fault? Had they cursed my best friend and her son because of me?

It didn't matter. I'd fix it, then I'd hunt down the bastard responsible. I grabbed her favourite Madonna top, then went back into the corridor.

'Will this work?' I asked Ben.

'Worth a shot,' he said. He held it out in front of Tilly. She sniffed it, then sat on the plush grey carpet. We waited, watching her as she sniffed the T-shirt. She rolled over for a belly rub.

I stifled a laugh. 'Tilly, not now. What else can you smell like this top?'

She stared at me, willing me to give her a belly rub.

'Dammit, dog!'

'Is she trained to search for things?'

'She's barely trained to sit. You know westies only obey commands, like, 50% of the time, right?'

Ben ran his hand over his face. 'Tell me you're joking.'

'Um, no. She's stubborn, devoid of common sense, people smart, and cute to look at. She's Edie and me in dog form.'

Ben glared at me. 'Right now, none of those things are helpful.'

'Mum! He's home!'

'Fiddlesticks.' I shoved Tilly at Ben, threw Maggie's top back into the drawer, and met Edie and Ben at the kitchen door. 'We can get out this way. Quick!'

I unlocked the back door, then shoved the keys at Ben too, so that he could unlock the gate as he was the fastest. Tilly wriggled in his arms, but a quick 'shush' from him shut her up. Thankfully. The last thing we needed was for her to start barking or whining or growling when we were somewhere we shouldn't be.

Would Edie be OK to make a run for it with her back? Would it hurt her? We were about to find out.

'Go!' I said to Edie and Ben.

Edie hobbled away behind Ben, who seemed to make it across their garden in three giant leaps.

We didn't have time to lock the back door behind us. Hopefully Harry would just think he'd forgotten to lock the door and gate out of stress.

My heart beat so rapidly in my chest I was going dizzy, but I had to get everyone out of there. We weren't doing anything wrong, but I knew Harry wouldn't see it that way. How far was he willing to take his vendetta against us? It wasn't a risk I was going to take.

I closed the back door as Harry opened the front door. I dove across their – thankfully small but well-maintained – garden, reaching Edie and Ben as they unlocked the back gate. We ran through it, leaving it unlocked and running down the alleyway that ran behind their row of houses. We didn't stop running until we got home.

'Why do I feel like a fugitive right now?' Ben said, once we were back inside my place.

'Cause we technically just broke into someone's house?' said Edie.

Ben put Tilly down as Edie flicked on the kettle. A confused Tilly drank from her bowl, then went to her bed and curled up on it, all while still wearing her lead. Apparently I wasn't the only one tired from our escapade.

'Is your back OK from running?' I asked Edie.

'I'll be fine. I just won't do any running for the next couple of days. Not that I ever plan to go running,' she said with a small laugh. The grimace on her face said she was putting on a brave face. Was she doing that for me? I hoped not. I hoped I'd raised her to be honest with me, even if it was painful. But then, secrets seemed to be a part of my life, and I had them from her. It wouldn't be a massive stretch for her to have them from me, too. I was a terrible parent.

'Do you think he saw us? Or he'll notice someone has been there?' said Edie.

'Fiddlesticks! Where's the package?' I said, realising none of us were holding it, and I couldn't see it anywhere.

'In the living room. I put it near the piano. He doesn't really go near there, so if he sees it, he'll just think Maggie left it there,' said Edie.

'Good shout,' I said. Thank god Edie had thought of something. I'd planned to bring it back, but we'd left in such a hurry I hadn't thought about it.

The kettle finished boiling, and Edie automatically made us all drinks. We were so out of breath from running what felt like miles back to the safety of mine, we needed it. It wasn't much more than a five-minute walk, but clearly we all needed to go to the gym more often.

'Did you find anything?' Edie asked as she got the milk from the fridge.

'No. Apparently westies are terrible sniffer dogs,' said Ben.

I looked down at Tilly, who was asleep on her cushion. She was cute, and she was pretty good with ghosts, but she was a terrible search dog. Sigh.

Spectre jumped down from the bookshelf and over to Edie. Edie put her arms out and caught him, cradling him like she would a living cat.

Ben and I stared at her, wide-eyed.

It took her a couple of seconds to realise we were staring at her. 'What?'

'You're holding a ghost,' I said.

'Yeah?'

'Have you always been able to do that?' said Ben.

Guilt played across her face. Oh my god. She had, and she'd never told me.

'Why?'

'Most people can't do that,' I said.

'What do you mean by "most people"?'

I reached out to Spectre and tried to stroke him. My hand went straight through him, as if he wasn't there. Spectre didn't notice, since ghosts couldn't feel touch. 'I've never met anyone who can do what you're doing right now. Ever.'

20
Edie

Frazzle. What did it mean if I had powers my mum didn't? Had I inherited them from my dad? Was I secretly adopted? A changeling?

I'd always known I could touch ghosts and Mum couldn't, but I'd kept it from her because I knew it would cause her to freak out. Like she was right now. If I hadn't been so tired and distracted from the pain of running, I wouldn't have caught Spectre and she wouldn't have panicked.

I put Spectre down, then sat in one of the kitchen chairs, watching Mum and Ben. If they thought any harder, steam was going to come out of their ears. Clearly what I could do was totally new to them, but I'd never known any different.

'So, what does it mean?' I asked.

Mum sipped her tea. Delaying replying, probably. Which meant she didn't have an answer.

I looked at Ben. His expression was distant; he was in a far-off place inside his mind, wherever that was. I'd stumped the experts. What did that mean? If I could do this and nobody else could, did that mean I had other powers that nobody knew about?

Ben and Mum exchanged worried glances.

'What aren't you telling me?' I said.

Getting increasingly anxious from what they weren't telling me, I bent down to pick Tilly up and rested her on my lap. After licking my face a couple of times, she sat with her back against my stomach, facing Ben.

'How much do you know about your dad's powers?' Ben asked me.

'Um, he could see ghosts?' I replied.

Ben looked to Mum. Mum shook her head, refusing to look in my direction. 'That's all we know. His adoptive parents couldn't even sense ghosts, so we never spoke to them about it. That just left my mum, who's more powerful than me. But who wasn't exactly forthcoming with advice. Or tolerance.'

'Is anybody going to tell me what this all means?' I said.

'There's a possibility that it could mean you're more than just a ghost hunter,' said Ben.

'What's that supposed to mean? Like, I can do even more than exorcise ghosts?'

Mum nodded. Her lips were drawn into a tight line, and if she frowned any more she was going to make her forehead wrinkles worse. Her expression was one she only got when the topic of her mother came up. 'You should go back to college.'

'Mum! I deserve to know what's going on! I deserve answers too!'

'And you'll get them. Just as soon as I get the right ones.'

*

I was raging at Mum on the walk back to college, but she practically shoved me out of the door. While I wanted to argue with her, I knew I wouldn't get what I wanted from her if I did. I had to play the long game to get the answers I needed.

So, begrudgingly, I went back to college for my last class of the day.

Unfortunately, the last person I wanted to see found my on my walk to Chemistry class. Tessa. My arch nemesis.

'Hey Edie,' she said in a saccharine voice. Ew, what did she want?

Her cronies, Melanie and Laura, were a few steps behind us. Melanie met my eye and gave me an apologetic look. I shrugged. 'Where's Josh? I haven't seen him for a couple of days.'

Ugh. Her crush on Josh was painfully obvious. Even though Josh and I had been going out for almost a month, she still threw herself at him on a regular basis. The only reason she was talking to me was because she knew nobody else would know what was going on with Josh better than me.

'He's sick,' I said, trying to walk faster to get away from her. It didn't work. She upped her pace, too.

'Oh. Maybe I should stop by and drop off some chicken soup for him.'

Frazzle. I hadn't expected her to say that.

'Um, that's not a great idea,' I said, trying my best to think on my feet. 'He's contagious.'

Tessa flinched, taking a step back from me. 'Are *you*?'

'I don't know, want to try?' I leaned forwards, ready to sneeze in her face.

She flinched and ran away.

I stopped walking, laughing so hard I could barely breathe.

'What's so funny?' said Dominic, appearing out of nowhere and standing next to me. It felt like he was the first friendly face I'd seen all day after the way things had gone so far with everyone else.

We didn't run into each other much around college, since it was huge, so it was always nice to see him when I did. I still didn't know why I hadn't seen him the year before, but I guessed he'd transferred. I didn't want to scare him off by asking; I figured he'd tell me if and when he was ready.

'Just tormenting people,' I said, trying to compose myself. Easier said than done when I'd just terrified Tessa, someone who'd made my life hell since I'd arrived, purely because I was different.

Ever since facing off with a demon in Josh's kitchen, I hadn't been so afraid of Tessa anymore. Her bitching and backstabbing just annoyed me. She reminded me of a mosquito, constantly buzzing around, trying to get the blood she so desperately craved. But that blood – that attention – wasn't going to come from Josh or me anymore.

'Oh?' said Dominic.

I carried on walking towards Chemistry and he followed me.

'My boyfriend's sick. Tessa – the one who pushed me over and hurt my back – asked if I was contagious because he is. All I did was lean forwards as if I was going to sneeze in her face. I wouldn't have actually done it. Not that she knows that. She's been trying to make my life hell ever since I moved back here, so revenge tastes sweet.'

Dominic grinned, clapping me on the shoulder. 'I'm proud of you, standing up to her.'

I beamed. My stomach filled with butterflies at his compliment. Apparently I subconsciously needed his approval. What was *wrong* with me? I was with Josh! Or I would be when he was awake.

'Thanks. I just can't be bothered with her anymore.'

'Yeah, her attitude sucks.' He shook his head. His dark hair fell into his eyes, but he didn't seem to care. 'I hate people like that.'

'Me too.'

'Was everything OK, by the way? After you ran off the other day? I thought something might be wrong,' he said.

'Sorry about that. I've just got a lot on my mind right now, you know?'

'Like with your boyfriend?'

'Um, yeah,' I said. Why did talking to him about it feel so awkward? Was it me? Or was it talking about it with *him*?

'I'm sure he'll get better soon,' said Dominic.

'Yeah. I hope you're right.'

21
Niamh

'Maybe we should take Tilly for a walk,' suggested Ben.

I growled. It didn't matter what we did. None of it would change that my mother knew something and was hiding it from me. Was I less powerful than my mother *and* my daughter? Was that why my mother had always called me a failure? Why she'd never trained me properly? I had to know.

She was the only person who *would* know. I'd always had the feeling she was keeping something from me. And surprise surprise, I was right.

I started moving furniture ready for the seance. Ben put his hand on my arm. 'Why don't we walk Tilly to mine first? Do the seance there?'

'You're really obsessed with the idea of walking Tilly, aren't you?'

'I just think some fresh air will help you calm down before you talk to her, that's all.'

'Calm down? Calm down? Why do I need to be calm talking to someone WHO LIED TO ME? Who told me my daughter wouldn't be that powerful because I wasn't? Who spent her whole life making me feel inadequate? And now, who's managed to do it when she's been dead for over a decade, too?'

Ben bit his lip, looking anywhere but at me.

I sank onto the threadbare carpet. 'I'm sorry. I shouldn't be taking this out on you.'

'No, you shouldn't. And you're also more likely to get the answers from your mum if you don't attack her.'

Ugh. I hated the thought of not shouting at her. She'd shouted enough at me. Revenge would be sweet. But he was right. This was about Edie, not me.

I stood up. 'Fine. Let's go.' I went downstairs and put Tilly's coat on her. She glared at me, unhappy at the prospect of a walk. She hated walks and would rather lie on the sofa watching TV all day. It was like having a second teenager in the house.

After I'd put my shoes and coat on, I clipped Tilly's lead on to her collar and grabbed my bag on the way out. Ben followed and we walked in silence towards the park that offered a cut-through to his house.

I couldn't get my mother's sneering face out of my head. She'd always told me I couldn't do what she wanted me to; that I wasn't powerful enough. Now I knew why.

'She made me feel this big,' I said, holding my fingers an inch apart. 'Like it was my fault I didn't have the powers she did.' I kicked a rock in my path. It skidded along the tarmac then rolled down the hill we were walking on. 'Is that a thing? Can powers skip a generation?'

'I mean, people can be more powerful than their parents. It makes sense that some people are less powerful, too.'

'But you've never seen it?'

'No.'

I scoffed. 'Well, now you have.'

We carried on in silence for a little while. Since it was the middle of the day, the park was pretty quiet.

'Swing?' Ben suggested, gesturing to the children's play area at the bottom of the hill. It was empty. And he was walking towards it.

'Are you mad?' I said, scurrying after him. Even though she was off her lead, Tilly followed, curious to see where we were going.

'Why not?'

We reached the play area and each sat on a swing. Keeping my feet on the ground, I rocked the chair back and forth a little. It was comforting.

'I don't speak to any of my family,' confessed Ben.

'What happened?'

He sighed, staring at his battered black Converse. 'My sister. She fell in with the wrong people. And it got her killed.'

'I'm so sorry,' I said, reaching over to touch his hand. He smiled at me, but it didn't meet his eyes.

'My parents tried to defend her, saying she'd grow out of it and all that rubbish. No matter what she did, they always took her side.' He shook his head, blinking back tears. 'Like they couldn't see what was happening, or they didn't want to.'

'Both, probably,' I suggested.

'Yeah, I guess you're right.'

Tilly barked. We looked up and saw a bunch of teenagers approaching. Ugh. I called her to us. There was a fifty/fifty chance she'd come over; she loved attention. There must've been something about them that she didn't like as she ran over and sat at my feet. I clipped her lead on, standing up and hugging her to me. I didn't want to mollycoddle her and reinforce her anxiety, but I also wanted to keep her close in case the teenagers tried to hurt her. And calm my own anxiety.

'How cute. Old people on swings,' said one of them. The ring leader, no doubt.

There were three of them, and they were all trying to act tougher than they looked. They were slim, with almost shaved heads and fake tattoos on their bare arms. Yeah, they were so hard with their fake tattoos and naked skin in winter.

'You'll be old and wrinkly one day, too,' I said.

Ben, who was now standing beside me, shot me a warning look.

The ring leader met my eyes. 'Not as wrinkly as you.'

'That's because you already look like a dehydrated ball sack.'

His cronies sniggered. I was pretty sure Ben was trying not to laugh, too, but couldn't help himself. I smirked at our new friends.

'You ought to watch that mouth. It might get you into trouble.'

'Oh please. So far this week my best friend and her son have been cursed, I've met a guy who looks like a mummy but isn't one, and found out that my mother and daughter are more powerful than I am, and I have no idea why. So please, by all means make my week worse.'

The ring leader stared at me. 'What have you been smoking?'

I scoffed. Of course he had no idea. He had far more trivial things to worry about. If only he knew.

'Come on, let's go,' said Ben. He put one hand on me and another on Tilly, guiding us towards the edge of the play area.

The ring leader lurched. Ben held up his hand that had been touching Tilly. Everything around us rippled. A white haze surrounded us. The ring leader flew back, landing on his ass. Ha.

'What the—' He stared at Ben, his eyes wide.

'Leave,' commanded Ben in the sternest voice I'd ever heard him use. It was sexy. More please. Just of the voice. Not the threatening teenagers part. Although they'd totally deserved it.

The ring leader didn't need to be told again. He ran away, his cronies right behind him.

Once they were safely out of sight, I turned to Ben. 'What was that?'

He shrugged, walking off.

'Oh no you don't!' I said, jogging after him, Tilly still in my arms. I was too paranoid to put her down yet. 'You have an active power!'

He shrugged again.

I got in front of him, blocking his path so that he couldn't keep running off.

'Most witches do. It's not a big deal.'

'Wait. You're a witch? Also, thank you for using it to protect us.'

He blushed, his eyes on my walking boots.

'Why didn't you tell me?'

'I don't use my powers. What use are they when they couldn't save my sister?'

'Did she have the same power as you?'

'Yeah. We inherited it from my dad's side.'

'So if you don't use it—'

'It was a knee jerk reaction to protect us. It was nothing. Let it go.'

'OK,' I said.

I glanced behind us. The teenagers were already at the other end of the park. I was fairly sure one of them had a wet patch around his arse on his blue jeans. Ha. Had he peed himself? He deserved it.

Comfortable they were at a safe distance, I put Tilly down but kept her on the lead.

'I didn't mean to snap like that. I'm sorry,' said Ben after a few minutes.

'We're doing an awful lot of apologising today,' I observed.

'Mmm,' said Ben. 'It's been that kind of day.'

'You can say that again.'

*

I told Edie to meet us at Ben's after college. As much as I hated dragging Edie into anything, Ben had convinced me that she needed to be a part of the seance too, since it affected her past, present, and future.

'I love a good family drama!' said Fadil as we explained the situation to him. He watched as we reorganised everything up in Ben's lounge for a seance. It wasn't a massive lounge, as his house was only a two-bedroom terrace, but it was cosy and welcoming, and the space was plenty big enough for what we needed to do.

'Thanks. I'm glad you find my life so entertaining,' I said.

Ben laughed at me as he pushed the sofa back against the wall.

'Ready for another seance?' I asked him.

'You know, my life was far less interesting before I was cursed. And while I was in the sarcophagus.'

'Are you saying Ancient Egyptians didn't do seances regularly?' I asked.

Fadil glared at me. 'Less of the "ancient" please. I know I'm wrinkly, but still.'

'How would you prefer me to separate your generation from ours?'

Ben watched our exchange from a few feet away, an amused expression on his face.

'You just did. "Mine" and "yours".'

Ben laughed. Fadil was bettering me at my own sense of humour. Git.

'So, tell me more about this mother of yours,' said Fadil. He reminded me of a gossiping teenager. 'It seemed like there was a history there when we last met her.'

Oh, there was a history there all right. But it was *not* one I was going to talk about.

'No.' I walked off and went to put the kettle on. If I was going to face the dragon, I needed something to calm my nerves.

I poked my head through the living room door. 'Ben, have you got any camomile tea?'

'Top cupboard,' he said.

I opened the cupboard and took some out.

'Do you want any?' I asked him and Fadil.

'No thanks,' said Ben. 'I'm surprised you didn't go for the vodka.'

'I was tempted. But she'd probably notice and berate me for setting a bad example for Edie.'

'Sounds like a charmer,' said Fadil.

I flicked on the kettle. 'Yeah, the woman who told me I was worthless pretty much on a daily basis is a real ray of sunshine.' I opened the drawer for the tea strainer, slamming it a little too aggressively. 'Sorry,' I said to Ben as he joined us in the kitchen.

He shrugged. 'I'm sure the drawer doesn't mind.'

I laughed, meeting his eye. His gaze was filled with worry and compassion.

So I was angry. I was allowed to be, wasn't I? Who knew how much of our current – and past – drama could've been saved if the woman had been upfront with me decades ago?

But then, upfront had never been her style. She always did whatever she could to annoy as many people as possible.

22
Edie

When I was little, my parents never let me take part in a seance. But when they couldn't find a babysitter, I got to go with them. Even when the guests suggested it, though, I *still* couldn't join in.

Instead, my parents sat me in a far corner of the room with a book, where they could see me but the ghost couldn't get to me.

I never read the books they gave me. I was too hypnotised by what was happening in front of me. How could I not be? I knew that what they were doing was part of my family legacy. It had never occurred to me how much of one it was.

Mum wasn't in much of a better mood when I got to Ben's after college. Not that I blamed her. She'd never gotten along with Gran. To get the answers we needed, though, she'd have to be on her best behaviour. The concept alone was probably enough to give her nightmares, let alone actually kissing up to the woman.

Since Gran had died when I was really young, I didn't know her all that well. She'd always been kind of indifferent towards me, and since she hadn't been that close to Mum, I hadn't spent that much time with her. The main things I remembered were the smells of cigarette smoke and perming solution, and a blunt way of speaking that bordered on offensive. I'm sure some people interpreted it that way – Mum especially – but I was too young to notice.

'Edie! How are you?' said Fadil as I walked in. He opened his arms to hug me, and I leaned into him. It was weird, hugging someone who was alive before things I took for granted like clocks, antihistamines, and the internet existed, but it also felt kind of natural. Like I'd known him forever and not just a few days. He was a calming but fun presence in my life, and I needed that more than ever.

'Have you heard that latest?' I said as we pulled away from one another.

He nodded. 'Your mum was, uh, annoyed when she got here.'

'You sure? My mum doesn't do annoyed. She goes from zero to ten thousand in about three seconds.'

Fadil laughed. 'Must've been the walk and Ben's company that calmed her down.'

Hmm. Mum and Ben. Yeah, I could see it. I wasn't sure if they could, yet. It would happen if it was meant to.

If not, I was happy Mum had a friend she could talk to about all of this. She hadn't had that since my dad had died, and I knew she missed it.

Keeping all our secrets from Dumb Dan had destroyed her in more ways than one. But a relationship with secrets was never going to last. Especially a secret as big as being able to communicate with the dead.

But some people just won't listen when you tell them that. Especially when you're ten. Sometimes they still won't listen, even when you're almost old enough to vote.

*

Fadil stood on my left, while Mum was on my right, and Ben in front of me. We had no idea how she'd respond to being summoned, so we were on alert. Mum was convinced she'd get antagonistic. Or maybe it was Mum who'd get antagonistic…

'We call upon the spirits, to commune with us tonight, grant us your presence, come join us in the light.'

When Gran did, she looked like she could spit fire. Was that a thing? I was starting to think anything was possible. 'Do you mind? I was playing Bingo.'

Mum ground her teeth together. It was killing her not to lash out. That wouldn't be the way to get the answers we needed, though. 'You didn't have to answer.'

Gran looked down, first noticing me, then Mum, then Ben, then Fadil. She narrowed her eyes, turning back to Mum. 'You know, you could give a woman some time to investigate instead of rushing her. Time moves differently here.'

'That's not why we summoned you.' Mum said with clenched fists. Gran really did bring out the worst in her. 'Why can Edie touch ghosts?'

Gran recoiled. Horror, amazement, and fear played on her face all at once.

'So you *do* know something,' said Mum.

Gran stared at the wooden floor underneath her. 'I'd like to go now please.'

She turned away, her silhouette fading. Mum looked at me, jerking her head in Gran's direction. I reached out and grabbed her arm, pulling her back so that she couldn't disappear. Hopefully. Her arm was cold but soft to my touch. It didn't feel that different to touching any other old person with bad circulation.

Gran gasped. 'Edie, you shouldn't—'

'Shouldn't what?' I said, tired of Gran's games.

'We need to know why Edie can do what she can do,' said Ben. 'It could help answer a lot of questions.'

'Who are you to talk to me like that?' she said.

'I told you last time: he's a friend,' said Mum.

Gran narrowed her eyes at Mum. It wasn't like Ben had been rude or anything, but clearly he'd raised a topic she didn't want to talk about.

Gran looked down at my arm. 'You can let go. I'm not going anywhere.'

'With all due respect, I don't trust you to not try to leave again,' I said.

Mum sniggered beside me.

Gran huffed. 'Fine. Edie is a necromancer.'

All four of us gasped.

'I'm a what?'

'You know. Dead people magic.' She said it in such a nonchalant way, as if it was no big deal to find out I could do more than just see ghosts and cast a couple of basic spells.

'And you never thought to mention this before?' said Mum.

Gran shifted awkwardly, avoiding eye contact.

'What?' said Mum.

'You're not one! So I didn't think your daughter would be, either. Apparently she got it from her father.'

'Of course I'm not one. I can barely cast a basic spell,' said Mum.

Gran sighed. 'Yes. I was…perturbed when I found out our family legacy had mostly missed you. I thought that would be the end of our line and it would fizzle out from there. But it would appear that other factors played a role.'

'What factors?'

'Well, Javier's unknown lineage, of course.'

'You didn't think to mention that that could be a factor?' said Mum through gritted teeth.

'What was the point? You couldn't do most of it. We don't even know if Edie can. All we know is that she can manhandle ghosts,' said Gran, glaring at my hand on her arm.

I raised an eyebrow and smirked at her. I hated how she was talking to Mum, and I wasn't going to let her get away with her disrespect. Respect worked both ways and she'd never had any for Mum.

'How will we know if she can do any more?' asked Ben.

'I'm sorry, who is this gentleman?'

'Oh for the love of ghosts, Mum. He's a friend of mine. A witch.'

What? Ben was a witch? How much had I missed in one lesson?

Ben raised his head in greeting, even though he'd spoken to her several times already. It was amazing how my grandmother conveniently 'forgot' people she didn't think were important.

She floated closer to him, studying him like he were a museum exhibit. Sure, *now* he had her attention. 'A witch, huh? That could be useful.'

Mum glared at her. I doubted she liked her friend being referred to as 'useful'.

'How's your friend Maggie? And that reprehensible husband of hers?'

Well, at least we all agreed on how unlikeable Harry was.

'That's another reason we need you. Maggie and her son Josh are in a coma. They've been put into blood curses. But we're stuck as to how to find what's holding their items.'

Gran spun so fast to look at Ben I thought my arm was going to snap off. I let go, rubbing my wrist.

'Witch.'

Ben recoiled. For a moment, I thought he was going to leave, but he didn't.

'Ben?' Mum said.

Gran turned back to Mum and me. 'He can cast a finding spell.'

'He can?' said Mum.

'I told you: I don't do magic anymore,' said Ben.

'Even when someone's life is on the line?' said Mum, her face turning red. Oh no. As if she wasn't cranky enough already.

'Save the domestic for after your seance, please. I have bingo to return to and would like to finish this sooner rather than later,' said Gran.

'If time works differently on the Other Side, doesn't that mean you can return to your bingo game right where you left off?' said Mum.

I glanced at Fadil. We exchanged smirks.

Gran pursed her lips. She didn't answer.

Mum turned her malice back to Ben: 'What about earlier? You used your powers then.'

Wait. What powers? What could Ben do that I was missing? What was with people keeping so many secrets? At this rate I was going to discover Josh was a bloody werewolf.

Ben stared at the floor, avoiding Mum's death stare. If looks could kill, I was pretty sure Ben's heart would've stopped right then.

To try to get the conversation back on track and diffuse the growing atmosphere in the room, I addressed Gran: 'Is there anything else we should know? That I should know about my powers?'

I was both terrified and eager to learn more. It was weird, knowing I was capable of more than I knew or had ever dreamt of. It sounded cool on the surface, but what if those powers put me in danger? Or hurt someone? I didn't like the idea of that.

Gran floated closer to me, her remarkably lifelike face inches from mine. She looked me up and down, a judgmental expression on her face. I felt like I was under a microscope. 'Does your mother still have a locked box of mine?'

I nodded. 'We never found the key.'

'There isn't one. Not a physical one, anyway. You need an incantation to unlock it.' She leaned forwards, whispering the incantation into my ear. Then, with a puff of smoke, she vanished.

23
Niamh

'All this time, you could've done something to help, and you didn't once suggest it?' I growled.

Ben could've even given me a finding spell to try if he didn't want to do it himself. I wasn't *totally* inept when it came to magic. But no. He didn't say anything. He just got annoyed at the dog for being useless.

Ben's cheeks turned red. He looked anywhere but at me.

Edie, Tilly, and Fadil crept out of the room, leaving us alone.

I strode over to Ben, jabbing his chest as I spoke. 'You knew how upset I was about Maggie and Josh!'

'And I've been trying to help, haven't I?'

'And you've had a key way to help all this time and never once suggested it. You never even asked one of your witchy friends to cast a finding spell!'

'First of all, it's been less than a week. There are plenty of avenues we haven't explored yet. Second of all, I don't have any "witchy friends". I cut ties with most of them when I stopped practising.'

I huffed, completely unable to understand his logic. It was one thing to abandon his powers, but something else to detach himself from people who could help. Once you knew that things went bump in the night, it was important to have a network of people who could help when things went wrong. Coming from a family of witches, he'd know that, wouldn't he?

'So why even bother telling me you're a witch?'

'I didn't want to. But I wanted to protect you more.' Ben lowered his head, guilt washing over his features.

'Why? Why do you care about protecting me so much?'

'Isn't it obvious?' he asked my black ankle boots.

No. No it was not obvious, and that was why I was confused. And annoyed. And angry. And just... exhausted.

'I like you, Niamh. I like you a lot.'

I stepped back, the realisation hitting me. Oh my god. Ben had a thing for me. And I'd been too stupid to see it.

'But you're with Jaya,' I said.

'You've made it pretty clear you're not interested in anything right now. I didn't know if you ever would be. I figured there was no harm in hanging out with Jaya in the mean time.'

I clenched and unclenched my fists. 'What, so you're using her?'

'No! I genuinely like her.' He mumbled the next part, still staring at his tatty green Converse: 'Just not as much as I like you.'

'Is that why you've been sticking around? Why you've been helping me?'

He took a step closer to me, but I put my hand out and stepped away. Heartbreak was written on his face, but I was too angry to care.

'No, Niamh. I love spending time with you. And Edie. I want to help you. But you're so closed off.'

'I can't—I don't—'

What the hell could I say? What did he want me to say?

'Let me know if you want my help with the finding spell.' He walked out of the room without saying anything else.

So, what? He was going to use magic to help us anyway? After making such a big deal about *not* using magic? He wasn't making any sense and I was too tired and confused to keep arguing with him.

I stomped into the hall, grabbing my coat. 'Edie, Tilly, we're leaving!'

I heard her say bye to Fadil, then she arrived beside me and pulled on her coat. 'Are you all right, Mum?'

I grumbled in response. Truth was, I wasn't sure if I could say anything without crying.

*

We walked back to ours in silence. Edie tried to talk a couple of times, but I wasn't in the mood. After a while, she put her earphones in and bobbed her head along to some music. I didn't blame her. Walking in silence when she was used to constant stimulation was likely annoying for her.

Tilly ran over to us, barking. I turned around to see the guys from earlier approaching us. Frazzle.

I grabbed Edie's arm and began power walking. Tilly ran ahead a little, but always kept us in sight.

'Mum, why do they look like they're on the warpath?'

'Ben and I may have ran into them earlier.'

'What did you do?'

'Nothing!'

'Why does that high-pitched voice make me not believe you?'

We weren't fast enough. The three of them caught up to us, malice in their eyes. They got in front of us and blocked our path. They were probably younger than Edie, but they were considerably larger.

I bent down, picking up Tilly to keep her close.

'No boyfriend this time,' said the ring leader.

'So?'

'So, no whatever-it-was that he did last time to protect you,' he said.

I didn't have time for him trying to prove how big his dick was to his friends because we'd embarrassed him earlier.

'Look. I get it. You've had a crappy childhood. So did I. My daughter's wasn't great either. You don't need to take your self-hatred out on other people,' I said.

Edie elbowed me, staring at me with her eyes wide. Why did people keep giving me that look? What had I done this time?

'What. Are. You. Talking. About?' said the ring leader.

I opened my mouth to say something else, but Edie jumped in. 'Nothing. She's talking nonsense, like all parents do.'

For the first time, the ring leader's eyes fell on Edie. 'Well aren't you a regular Wednesday Addams?' He sidled up to her, making my blood boil. Picking up a strand of her hair, he sniffed it. She recoiled, shoving him away. He stumbled. When he went to push her back, she shoved him farther. Then, he started to gasp for air. It was as if he was being strangled, but no one was touching him.

I looked to Edie. Her lips were pursed and her eyes were narrowed in concentration.

'Edie!' I said, nudging her.

She shook her head, snapping out of whatever she'd been doing.

The ring leader gulped in air. It was like the noose around his neck had been unfastened and he could finally breathe again.

'You people are freaks!' he said, his hand on his throat as he ran off. His friends followed, confused looks on their gormless faces.

Edie turned to me, her eyes wide in horror. 'Mum, what was that?'

I grabbed her arm and we carried on walking. I wanted to get out of that park as soon as possible. Would that be the last time I ever took that shortcut to Ben's? Would I ever go to his place again?

Not after that argument. My heart fell into my stomach. How would I feel if that argument was the last time I saw him? Would I care?

Yes, yes I would.

'Mum?' said Edie, her voice still shaking. 'What did I just do?'

'I think…I think you almost killed him.'

'What?'

I stopped walking and turned her to face me. 'Not on purpose. But if you really are a necromancer, that means you can control death. And since we don't know how your powers work, we have some research to do.'

'Mum, I'm scared.'

Fighting back tears, since I was scared, too, I pulled her into a hug. She rested her head against my shoulder, her body shaking as she cried. Tilly, still in my arms, snuggled between us.

As the three of us stood there in the cold park, I realised there was one thing I knew for certain: everything was about to change. Forever.

24
Edie

Since almost killing someone the night before, I could feel the magic coursing through me. It was like electricity pulsing in my nerves. Had the incident the night before brought it to life? That was the first time I'd felt it, and it hadn't left me since.

If I could do that with little provocation and no spell, what else could I do? A part of me was eager and excited to find out. Another, bigger, part of me was terrified. I didn't want to be able to control death. It was too much responsibility. And what was the point, in the modern world? Wasn't that what medicine was for?

What would it mean for my future? Would people seek me out because they wanted me to bring back their loved ones? Would they try to get me to commit murder? How would I know I could trust someone and that they weren't just using me?

I kicked a few leaves on the path I was walking on, perching on a stone wall outside someone's house for a minute. My head was racing so much it was giving me a headache.

I was early for college anyway, because I'd been desperate to get out of the house. Mum had been seething ever since her argument with Ben. The floorboards had creaked with her pacing all hours of the night. Nobody in our house had gotten much sleep.

'Deep in thought, I see,' said Dominic. Where'd he come from?

I gave him a wan smile. 'It happens sometimes. Wouldn't recommend it.'

He massaged his wrist. It was wrapped in a thin bandage. Badly.

'What happened?' I gestured to his injury.

'Oh. Landed funny doing free weights.'

'Just proves my point: exercise is bad for you.'

Dominic chuckled. 'Yeah, maybe you're right.' He inhaled through his teeth.

I gestured to his wrist again. 'May I?'

He held his arm out. He really had done a terrible job of fastening the bandage, but then, it was on his right wrist, and he was probably right-handed. It was difficult to wrap your own wrist, and I had no idea if he had anyone around to do it for him.

I unfastened the safety pin, placed it in his free hand, then began to untangle the mess he'd created. The additional pressure from it being fastened tighter would hopefully help more with the pain.

When I was done, I smiled. 'Have to say, think that's one of my best bandage jobs so far.'

He spun his wrist, examining my handiwork. 'It does look a lot better than what I did.'

'It was good if you did it yourself,' I said, hoping I hadn't just insulted someone he cared about.

'Yeah, I did,' he said with a sheepish chuckle. 'Not easy.'

'Nope.'

He smiled, revealing cute dimples either side of his lips. 'Thanks.'

I tapped the back of my boot against the stone wall. Dominic sat beside me, starting at nothing in particular.

'So what had you deep in thought, anyway?' he asked.

'Doesn't matter. You think too much you'll end up with a headache like mine.'

'What does that mean?'

'Family stuff,' I said.

'Sounds like you've got a lot going on,' he said.

Frazzle. I forgot I'd told him about that. Had I gone into too much detail already? Was I putting him at risk just by insinuating stuff?

I nodded. 'I'd usually talk to Josh about it, but—'

I couldn't finish my sentence. Just thinking about Josh made me want to cry. So I did.

It'd been three days since I'd seen Josh in the hospital. I had no idea how he was, but I took solace in the fact that Fadil seemed fine and he'd been cursed millenia ago. Could I do a seance and ask the nurse from the hospital how they were?

Dominic stood awkwardly, looking around as if someone who could help was there. But the street was deserted. No human or ghost in sight.

'Josh is your boyfriend, right? The one who's sick?' he asked after my sobbing had subsided.

'Yeah,' I said, my voice cracking. 'We've been keeping it quiet, but the longer it goes on, the harder it is to do. And I think I can fix it, but I just can't connect the dots.'

'What do you mean? Shouldn't it be up to the doctors to fix him?'

'I have to find something and I don't know where to even start looking.'

'How will that help?'

'I can't explain.' I kicked the wall with the back of my boot in frustration. The less Dominic knew, the better. I'd already said too much. 'We should get going or we'll be late.' I stood up and carried on walking towards college.

'Smooth change of subject,' he said.

'Sorry. Even if I could tell you, I wouldn't know how. I'm still figuring everything out myself.'

He stuffed his hands into his pockets. 'Well, if you ever figure out a way and you can tell me, I'll always be a willing ear.'

25
Niamh

I paced my living room, my dead husband hovering over the sofa. Tilly and Spectre sat beside him. Tilly watched him, a doggy smile on her face. Spectre's face was indifferent. He was a dead cat, after all. A ghost was less interesting to him for many reasons.

'If your pacing could make me nauseous, it would have a long time ago,' said Javi.

Sighing, I stopped and sat opposite him on the coffee table. 'Why aren't you restless?'

'I'm dead. I don't have a heartbeat.'

'Your life is so much easier.'

Javi laughed.

I tried to kick him, but of course, my foot went through his leg.

'Nice try,' he said.

'Our daughter is a necromancer,' I said.

'Our daughter is a necromancer,' he repeated.

'How did this happen?'

'We were uneducated as children about who we really are and what our family histories are.'

'And as adults, it seems,' I added.

He nodded, giving me a sad smile. 'I wish there was more I could do.'

'Can you track down your birth parents? Find out what their powers were? What yours are?'

'In theory,' he said, his foot twitching. 'But I'm going in blind. My adoptive parents would be terrified if I turned up as a ghost, and I'm not sure they'd be willing to discuss what happened with you. No offence.'

'None taken.'

His parents weren't bad people, but they'd never been very open about discussing Javi's adoption. They'd adopted him in Spain – where his dad was from – then moved to the UK, where his mum was from, when he was a few years old. They didn't talk about Spain. Ever. Had something happened there, or were they just like my family and didn't like discussing the past? Who knew?

'They might open up to Edie, but I'm not sure she's ready for that,' said Javi.

'Me neither. She needs to digest her new powers first,' I said.

'I think the incident in the park confirms that she's got at least some necromancy powers,' said Javi.

'Well isn't that just great? Our daughter can kill people.'

'We don't know that for definite yet,' said Javi.

'But that's what necromancers do, isn't it? They control people's life essences.'

Javi nodded. 'I think so. Your mum knows way more than I do. My research sources are pretty much limited to her. Being a ghost is so frustrating.'

'At least you're here for me to talk to. I appreciate that more than you know.'

'Perhaps you could've avoided your second marriage had you spoken to me beforehand,' he said, his tone saying he was only half-teasing me.

'Shut up,' I said.

'I'm only teasing. I just want you to be happy. Speaking of which—'

'Let's not talk about Ben,' I said, cutting him off. 'That door is closed.'

'But Neevie—'

I crossed my arms, daring him to continue the conversation. 'He's with Jaya.'

Javi blew a raspberry. I didn't even know ghosts could do that. '*Please*, he's not even that into her.'

How did he even know that? He was a *ghost*. And not even friends with Ben.

'Doesn't matter. That door is *closed*.'

Javi glared at me, but didn't say anything else.

I stood up, brushing myself off. 'I need to get to work.'

*

Could today just end already? I hoped beyond hope that the finding spell worked and we could get Maggie and Josh out of their comas. And my exorcism went according to plan. So much to do, so many deadlines.

Eamon warned everyone away from the house – even though nobody living ever bothered me except him anyway. His way of warning them was to say I had horrific PMS and they needed to leave me alone so I didn't take it out on them. I pointed out how sexist that was, and he asked me to suggest an alternative. I didn't have one.

'Is there anything I can do to help?' said Eamon as we walked towards the house.

'Stay away,' I said. 'It gets dangerous and I don't want anyone getting hurt.'

'Is there someone I should call if it does go wrong?'

Reluctantly, I passed him Ben's number as an emergency contact. I didn't want to use him as backup, especially after our argument, but I also knew that he'd help if he needed to.

And it wasn't like I could tell Eamon to summon Javi if I got into trouble. Knowing Javi, he'd probably be watching anyway.

Eamon left me at the front door. Before I went inside, I took the candle from my bag and lit it. It was in a silver holder, with just the top poking out so my hand wouldn't get covered in wax. In theory, anyway.

I put my bag by the front door, read through the spell on my phone, then pocketed it. I figured taking a photo of the spell would be more covert than carrying a book the size of my rucksack around. Plus, I didn't want to risk it getting damaged. It was too valuable. And the less stuff Peter had to throw at me, the better.

'He's mad,' said Gwendoline, appearing in front of me as I walked in.

'You don't say,' I grumbled.

Getting rid of a poltergeist was different to exorcising a person. It was more complicated. There were more anomalies to take into account. Meaning there were also more things that could go wrong.

I hadn't exorcised a house since Javi had been alive. It had been a house exorcism that had killed him. The only reason I'd agreed to do this one was because I didn't want anyone else to get killed like Javi.

'You're shaking. Are you OK?' Gwendoline asked me as I began walking through the house, waving the candle. Its purifying properties helped to cleanse the site and make it toxic to the malevolent spirit.

'Got to get on with things,' I said.

'Just can't stay away, huh?' said Peter, appearing in front of me.

'Guess not,' I said, not looking at him.

Like it or not, I needed to do the exorcism. And I was on my own for this one. Should I have asked Edie for help?

No. I didn't want to risk her. And it wasn't like I could just bring her on to a building site unauthorised. It wasn't that simple. I was on my own.

As I reached the edge of the dining room, Peter wailed. It was one of those long, haunting moans that some people assume is the weather, but is really an angry ghost.

'What are you doing?' he said, getting in my face. I waved the candle in front of him. He jumped back, snarling.

Holding the candle in the air, I recited the spell. 'Cleanse this house, cleanse this place, from any spirits who make it unsafe.' I repeated it over and over as I walked through the space. It didn't seem to be affecting Gwendoline, which I took as confirmation she was a friendly ghost. Peter's wails grew louder. It was pretty windy outside, so I hoped if he made the noise at a level your average human could hear, they'd blame that. I hadn't thought to cast a soundproofing spell beforehand.

Then again, I wasn't sure I'd have enough magic to be able to do that.

I walked through the dining room into the kitchen, where a window was open. Fiddlesticks. All windows needed to be shut for the spell to work, or the effectiveness of the fire would be diluted. And it may not work. Particularly if the ghost was super-nasty, and I had a feeling Peter was.

Peter, who'd been following me around the house, saw the open window at the same time as me. I ran to close the window above the sink, but he was faster. He got there seconds before I did. Then he slammed my head into the sink.

I fell on to the floor, seeing stars. Everything around me blurred. How strong was this guy if he could do that? I was in big trouble.

Gwendoline wailed. Her usual friendly, warm expression had been replaced by anger. 'Leave. Her. Alone.'

Peter scoffed. 'What are you going to do?' he asked as he pulled me up by my ponytail. Knew I should've tied my hair into a bun.

'Who are you to tell me what to do? You're nothing but a useless, immature, weak, woman.'

Oh no he didn't.

I started to wave the candle around again, but either the impact or the draft had blown it out. It was no longer alight, which meant it couldn't cleanse the house. The window was still open, too. Without closing the window and somehow getting to the lighter in my pocket, I was screwed. Especially when I could barely stand up without everything spinning.

Not to mention I had no idea how to do either of those things without him noticing what I was doing.

His parlour tricks had meant I'd underestimated his power, but he'd been testing me. I was rusty, and he'd shown just how rusty I was.

Peter laughed, knocking the candle out of my hand. It fell to the tiles, wax melting on to the floor. 'You're pathetic, you know that? All of you. You're weak. Helpless.'

Gwendoline scowled. She looked like a rhino about to charge. But what could she do? He was bigger than her. He was stronger than her.

'You caused me pain for centuries,' she growled. 'You will not hurt my friend.'

His eyes on Gwendoline, I took the chance to take the lighter from my pocket, grab the candle, and relight it. It would be watered down with the breeze coming straight in through the window, but hopefully it would be enough to weaken him.

I leaned over the sink to close the window, forcing back the dizziness.

Gwendoline charged at him, screaming as she did so.

I wobbled, wanting to check behind me to see what was happening, but I couldn't. She'd given me an opening and I needed to take it.

I slammed the window shut.

'NO!' screamed Peter. He pushed me out of the way. I slammed to the floor. But, no matter how hard he tried, he couldn't reopen the window. He'd drained too much of his energy. And since ghosts were pure energy, he didn't have the strength to make himself corporeal again. Which also meant he couldn't hurt me.

Instead of resorting to the spell I'd been using, I took the lighter from my pocket, relit the candle, then switched to an incantation that I hadn't used in a decade. It was an intense, risky spell that I'd only used on one other occasion. It obliterated anything in its path.

I jerked my head at Gwendoline, hoping she could get out safely. She shook her head, grabbing on to Peter instead. 'Do what you need to do,' she said, tightening her grip on him. Having saved her energy – and being filled with rage – she had more power than he did. Which meant, for a limited time at least, she could hold him.

'Save this house from the ghost inside, remove this spirit from where they preside, give them no right to the Other Side.'

Nothing happened. Why had nothing happened? I'd used it on the poltergeist that had killed Javi and it had saved everyone inside.

Peter laughed. It was an evil cackle, one that belonged to a supervillain. But he only liked to think that he was one.

'Gwendoline, can you help me?' I asked her.

'Help you do what?'

'Say the spell. Repeat after me.' She'd alluded to being part-witch. Now it was time to see if she had her powers in the afterlife, too. 'Save this house from the evil inside, remove this spirit from where they preside, give them no right to the Other Side.'

Peter tried to wriggle, but that just made her tighten her grip on him. She recited the spell, then we repeated it over and over together, our voices falling into a creepy harmony. 'Save this house from the evil inside, remove this spirit from where they preside, give them no right to the Other Side.'

Energy filled the room, spirits I didn't know circling around us and homing in on Peter. They flew inside him and he screamed. Gwendoline let go, running over to me. I tried to force her to stand behind me, but she wouldn't.

Peter screamed, pulling at his ghostly clothes and figure as the spirits writhed inside of him. He was growing weaker; fainter. He screamed. Then imploded. Bits of black energy scattered around the kitchen, then disappeared.

The ghosts that had filled him dissipated, returning to wherever it was they'd come from.

I sank down against the kitchen counter, gasping for air.

'Are you OK?' asked Gwendoline.

I laughed. 'Are you kidding me? After all that, you're checking on me?'

She laughed too, hover-sitting beside me.

'That was some badass power you showed,' I told her.

She smiled. 'I was always weak. I never stood up to him. But when I saw him hurting you, after you'd been so nice to me…'

'Glad I could help. What I don't get is why I couldn't do the bloody spell.'

Gwendoline frowned. 'Maybe it's stress-related?'

'As if stress doesn't cause enough problems already.'

But was she on to something? Was that why I couldn't sense ghosts *or* exorcise them? Or do anything bloody useful? Wouldn't that just be marvellous?

26
Niamh

'So, uh, how'd it go?' asked Eamon, hovering outside the front door with his hands stuffed into his pockets. He glanced around, I assume to make sure nobody else was listening.

He narrowed his eyes at me. 'You have a black eye.'

I gritted my teeth and lifted my T-shirt to just below my bra. My ribs were purple. 'Think I've bruised my ribs, too.'

'Can I get you anythin' for it?'

'Thanks for the offer, but I'll be fine. I've done worse.' I lowered my top and brushed the dust from my clothes. My ribs protested as I caught them with my hand. I gasped. Avoiding that spot for a few days or weeks would take some getting used to, but I didn't have time to speak to Doc, so I'd have to make do.

'Did it work? Is it safe to go in there now?'

'Yeah, it's safe.'

His eyes darted from one side to another, as if he expected a ghost to appear in front of him. People always did that, when they found out about ghosts. It always amused me. Just because they found out about ghosts, that didn't mean they could suddenly see them. 'Are you sure?'

'I'm sure.'

He didn't need to know that it hadn't gone according to plan. The how wasn't important. It would only freak him out or confuse him. Or both. It was safest to stick to the basics when talking to people who didn't really understand – or need to understand – ghosts.

His body relaxed. 'That's grea', thanks.' He stuffed his hands into his pockets, his eyes glancing around nervously. Why did I get the feeling he wanted to ask me something else?

'What is it?'

'The rest of the site. Do you think…I mean, the accidents the lads keep gettin' into. Are they really accidents?'

I sighed. 'Probably not.'

'Do you think you could…fix tha'?'

'Your building site is at the centre of it. You know that, right?'

He nodded, looking somewhere between ashamed and embarrassed.

'But I'll see what I can do.'

His expression turned into a smile. 'Thanks.'

'Do you mind if I take a slightly longer lunchbreak? There are some other ghostly matters I need to sort for a friend.'

Not completely true, but it was close. And again, safer to leave out the scary and unnecessary details.

'Not at all! Take as long as you need.'

'Thanks.'

*

I could do a basic finding spell. It only took one ingredient and an incantation. It was easy. Wasn't it?

I refused to ask Ben for help after our argument the night before. I'd managed without a man before, and I'd managed again. *That* would show Mrs Brightman.

Well, subconsciously to myself it would. She'd never actually know I'd done something important on my own, but still. The sentiment was there. In my head.

I didn't do much magic. Ghosts didn't usually require much more than a seance and an exorcism. A finding spell was totally new to me. But I had to try. For Maggie and Josh.

Since I spent so much time in Maggie's house, and we'd known each other forever, I convinced myself I wasn't breaking and entering. Maggie paid half the mortgage, and she loved me. And it was her I was there for. Harry could get stuffed.

Just so long as he didn't come home for lunch. He never had before, so I really hoped his wife and son falling sick wouldn't change that.

Oh god. What was I doing?

Nope. It was too late to back out. Maggie and Josh needed me.

Suppressing my anxiety, I positioned myself in their hallway. There were no windows there for nosy neighbours to see what I was doing. The spell was saved on my phone, so I flicked to the photo and read through the spell. *Light the incense while reciting the following spell. Replace the second instance of the word object with what you're trying to find.* All the page had said was that and the spell. Which meant it had to be simple. Right?

My hands shaking, I lit the incense then recited the spell. 'Objects are lost and the answers are bleak, find me the cursed object I seek.'

Nothing happened.

Since I didn't know what I was trying to find, the closest I could come up with was 'cursed object'. Clearly it hadn't been specific enough.

I let the incense burn for a little longer. The smoke permeated the hallway, seeping into each of the open bedroom doors. I waved it about, hoping that it might somehow guide me to the room where the object was hidden. But it didn't.

I repeated the spell. But it didn't make a difference. Had I messed up somehow? Was I missing something?

Turned out it wasn't a basic finding spell after all.

That was two spells in a couple of hours that had failed me. I was pretty sure the second exorcism would've failed me if Gwendoline hadn't chimed in, too. What was wrong with me? I'd been able to do magic before, hadn't I?

Fiddlesticks. It was probably too far for Gwendoline to travel, and as a ghost, she was probably too drained to help with the spell even if she *could* travel. Especially after earlier.

I only knew one other witch. And we weren't exactly on good terms. But he was a good person. He wouldn't want to see people suffering unnecessarily. He'd help. Wouldn't he?

*

Guilty. That's how I felt when I begged Ben to come over to help with the spell. But he was on his lunchbreak, so he agreed to help. I met him at the front door and ushered him inside.

'Hi,' he said, not looking at my face.

Was this how it was going to be, now? I hated the thought of things being awkward between us. He was the first person I'd been able to be open with since Javi, and it wasn't something I wanted to lose.

Sure, I'd had Maggie, but it wasn't the same. She couldn't experience what I was going through, only understand it from what I was saying. I couldn't go to her when I was stuck, or needed supernatural help.

'Hi,' I said back.

'Oh my god. What happened to your eye?' he asked, genuine concern in his chocolate brown eyes.

'I'm fine. Just side effects of an exorcism.'

'Oh. Well, at least you're OK.'

Awkward. So. Awkward.

'Is there anything you need me to do?' I asked, wanting the awkwardness to stop but knowing I'd at least partially created it.

'No. I'll go upstairs and cast the spell. I'll let you know if I find anything.'

'Oh. OK.'

So he didn't even want me present when he cast it. That burned. But then, hadn't I burned him first? For not understanding why he hadn't used his magic in so long?

I started to say something to him, but I didn't know what I could say. I didn't get how he could turn his back on everything he'd grown up with. But then, had he? He clearly still had an interest in the paranormal, he just didn't want to use his powers anymore. Could I resent him for that?

No, I couldn't understand it because I'd never been lucky enough to have active powers, and I'd been punished for it growing up.

Ben had already gone upstairs, so I sank onto the sofa and stared into my lap. No wonder I'd lashed out at him. I was jealous he'd stopped using his active powers when I'd never had any. How bad of a person did that make me?

I didn't even want to begin to think that over.

But it was too late.

My brain said no. It was going to berate me for punishing Ben for doing something totally understandable.

I sighed, listening to him chant from upstairs. I couldn't work out what he was saying, but I could tell the intent. Magic filled the house, swirling around me and the objects in the room. I watched as each object emitted a golden glow. After a few seconds, the glow moved on to the next object. Then the next. Then the next. And so on.

After about half an hour, the objects downstairs stopped glowing. Assuming that was a sign he was done, and bored of sitting downstairs on my own, I went upstairs.

Ben was already packing up. Based on his expression, he hadn't found anything.

'Sorry,' he said without even looking at me. 'The spell just kept gravitating to Abigail's room, probably because it was looking for evil and there's still some leftover from when she was possessed. It's hard when we don't really know what we're looking for.'

My shoulders fell. Another dead end.

I'd made Ben use his powers, and for what?

'Listen, Ben, about yesterday—'

'It's fine.' His tone was so dismissive it caught me off guard. 'I have to get back to work.'

I was so startled by his tone I didn't say anything else. I just watched him leave. Would that really be the last time we ever saw each other?

27
Edie

There was only one way to find out what was going on with Josh and Maggie. Why hadn't Mum thought of it? I guess she had other things to worry about. If I wanted answers, I'd have to take the lead on this one.

Mum finished work a couple of hours after I finished college, so I had some time on my own. I used that time to research how to do a seance in the Book of Shadows.

I had a vague idea of what I needed to do, but I wanted to check to be on the safe side. I didn't have anything of Anna's to summon her with, so I hoped the fact we'd met would help.

I would've invited Fadil, or even gone to Ben's, but I didn't want to make things awkward after Mum's argument with Ben. I didn't know where that left me. Or where that left Fadil. I knew Ben wouldn't abandon him, but he wasn't technically Ben's problem either. Everything was a mess.

My powers were doing strange things, so obviously I was nervous, but I was also desperate. And the desperate side of me overrode any anxiety I was feeling about conducting a seance. I could touch ghosts. That meant I had more power over them than most people, right?

Or did it mean I was in more danger?

Whatever. I didn't care. It'd been too long since we'd had an update on Josh and Maggie's conditions and I needed one. Now.

The spell said that if I was doing a seance alone, I needed to draw a salt circle. A group of people doing a seance automatically created a boundary, but that was impossible on your own. You could include them for group seances, but Mum seldom did. Clients hated them and so did she because of the clean up.

My circle was wobbly and not even remotely circle-shaped, but I wasn't an artist. Josh was, and he was the one I needed to help. As long as it set a solid boundary, that was all that mattered.

I settled Tilly in the kitchen with some peanut butter so that she wouldn't interrupt or get hurt. Not that I thought either of us would get hurt, but you could never be too careful with ghosts.

Dog in kitchen. Furniture relocated. Book of Shadows in front of me. Salt circle drawn. It was time.

'I call upon the spirits, to commune with me tonight, grant me your presence, come join me in the light.' The words spewed from my mouth, merging into one long word as I panic-read them. Would that affect if the spell worked or not?

Nothing seemed to be happening. Maybe I really did need something of Anna's to summon her. Maybe our short meeting at the hospital wasn't enough after all.

A figure appeared in front of me. For a split second, I thought it was Anna. But no. It was male. And very, very familiar.

'Dad?' I said.

'You shouldn't be casting spells without your mum's supervision,' he said.

'Since when did you become the boring one?'

'Since we don't know the scope of your powers yet. Using them could make you a target and put you in more danger.'

'Who says I'm in danger?'

Dad folded his arms. 'Who are you trying to summon?'

'The nurse from the hospital. Her name is Anna. She helped me get in to see Maggie and Josh. I was hoping she'd have an update on them.'

He paused, clearly weighing up what I'd just told him. 'Wait here.'

He faded out. Where was he going? What was he doing?

I sat on the floor and waited.

Not a moment later, Dad reappeared. With Anna beside him.

I jumped up. 'Dad! Thank you thank you thank you!' I hugged him, squeezing him tight to show my gratitude. He ruffled my hair.

'Your dad here says you'd like an update on your friends?'

I nodded, still holding on to my dad.

Anna shook her head. 'They're the same. No better, no worse. Harry looked terrible the last time I saw him. I don't think he's sleeping.'

'Good,' I said.

'Edie!'

'What? He's banned us from visiting. He should feel terrible,' I said.

'He prays for them whenever he's there,' said Anna.

I scoffed. 'He can believe in God but not in ghosts or curses? Unbelievable.'

'Everyone believes what they need to,' said Dad. I'd never known him so philosophical.

'There's something you should know,' said Anna, wringing her hands.

'What? What is it?'

The look on her face was making me more anxious. Which didn't help anything.

'They're being moved next week to a different hospital.'

'What? Why!'

'So that they can do more tests, see if there's something they're missing.'

'But their tests won't pick anything up!' I said.

'They don't know that,' said Dad. 'Do you know where they're being moved to?'

'No, I'm sorry. I think they're exploring a few specialist places. It depends where they can get beds. They may end up getting split up and going to different facilities.'

'NO!'

Dad rubbed my back. 'We'll find a solution before then. It won't come to that.'

I really hoped he was right.

*

'How did the finding spell go?' I asked Mum as she walked through the front door that evening. She'd ignored my texts asking her for an update, which I took as a bad sign, but I had to know. I looked up. 'Oh my god, Mum. What happened to your eye?'

Tilly jumped up at her to greet her. Mum dumped her bag onto the floor and sank onto the stairs. Tilly sat on the step next to her, waiting for some fuss. Mum rubbed her side and Tilly leaned into it. With her other hand, she pulled her jumper up to reveal purple ribs. And inhaled, a pained expression on her face.

'What the hell happened?' I said. 'Does it hurt?'

'Only if I move,' she said, lowering her jumper. 'Exorcism. Now you see why I didn't want you to get involved?'

I didn't remember Mum or Dad coming home with any ghost-related injuries when I was younger, but then, would I have noticed? Would it have been easier for them to hide it from me? An exorcism was definitely easier with two people, that much I'd learned.

'Do you want me to get some ice or something?' I offered.

'Maybe in a bit. The finding spell was a dead end, by the way.'

I perched on the stair below them and stroked Tilly too. 'So…now what?'

'I don't know. That was our last hope. We can't keep turning up at Maggie's. It's going to look suspicious and one of the neighbours is going to say something to Harry soon.'

'So, what? That's it? We stop looking?'

'No! Of course not. But we need a better plan. Or a stronger spell. Or…something. I don't even know anymore.' She sighed, looking up at the ceiling and resting her head on one of the steps. 'I'm going to go shower the smell of smoke and incense off me.' She stood up.

'I thought I'd make pasta for dinner.' It was a simple but effective comfort food. After everything that had happened, it felt like a good choice.

'Thanks,' she said, kissing the top of my head. Tilly joined in, licking my cheek. I giggled.

Mum rubbed Tilly behind the ears. 'You're a cute one, little dog.' She licked Mum's hand.

*

Another dead end. But that couldn't be it. Someone had freed Fadil, which meant there was a way to free Josh and Maggie, too. I refused to give up.

While dinner cooked, I read through every page of the Book of Shadows to see if one of us had missed something. Then, when that failed, I switched to the internet. It wasn't always the most reliable source, but with the library shut and Mum and Ben not speaking, it was the only source of information we had left.

I stayed up until I passed out, but I didn't find a thing.

28
Niamh

'Niamh? You're back?' said Gwendoline the next day, when I re-entered my own personal house of horrors. Hopefully to finish painting it this time.

'Just today. I hope,' I said.

The house definitely felt better than it had yesterday. The smell of smoke still hung in the air, so I went around and opened all the windows. It would get hot painting anyway, so might as well make it freezing before I started. 'You know,' I said to Gwendoline when I'd opened the window in the box room, 'you can't haunt this house, right?'

Gwendoline lowered her head. 'Where am I supposed to go? I don't have anywhere else.'

'You could cross over,' I said.

She shook her head, her blonde hair falling into her face. 'No. I don't want to do that.'

'But—'

'No. I'm not ready yet. I didn't get to enjoy my time on this earth properly. I want to do that now.'

I leaned against the wall, just beyond the window, and crossed my arms. 'But you're limited to where you can go. How is that living?'

'I'm not looking for a life, per se. Just freedom. A sense of purpose, I guess.'

I smacked my lips together. 'I think I have an idea.'

*

Turned out, painting was painful with a bruised rib. But I needed to keep going.

At lunchtime, I took Gwendoline to the park near the house I'd been painting. It wasn't massive, but it wasn't small, either. It was a good vantage point, and just the right size for what I had in mind.

The site was busier now, with families starting to move in to the finished houses over the last few days, so I took my phone from my pocket and pretended to talk on it while I sat on a bench. Gwendoline joined me.

'I think we should establish a place for ghosts like you to hang out and feel less alone,' I said.

'You mean ghosts from First Pit?'

I nodded. 'And any others who might be lurking. You could help them. Like you helped me.'

Conflicting emotions played across her pretty face. She settled on a smile. 'Yes. I think I could do that. What do you need me to do?'

'We need to find the rest of the ghosts haunting the building site. Do you think you could find them and bring them here?' My hope was that it would give her the sense of purpose her first life had lacked, and that she was searching for in the afterlife.

She nodded. 'Yes. I can definitely do that.'

'Then we can cross them off the list, safe in the knowledge they're not hurting anyone,' I added. Javi and my mother had helped us cross off a few more, but tracking down people on the Other Side took time. It wasn't easy to find people. Still, it was progress.

Noticing me in the park, Eamon walked over. He gave me a wide berth, as if I had a contagious disease. 'All righ', Niamh?'

I rested my phone on my lap. 'Why do you look like you're afraid of me?'

Gwendoline chuckled.

'Well, I mean, are there any—y'know?'

'Ghosts?' I said, laughing.

He nodded.

'None that you need to worry about,' I reassured him.

*

By the end of the day, there were ten ghosts hanging out in the park. Most were dressed in similar outfits to Gwendoline, but some looked far more modern. As I drove past on my way home, I nodded my head at Gwendoline. She waved, as did the other ghosts. I didn't recognise the others, but I knew they'd be in safe hands with her to look after them. I'd get their names from her to cross off the list on Monday. She'd had a calming effect on me, even when Peter had been trying to kill me.

Should I have let him? Would I have finally been able to join Javi?

But what about Edie? Edie needed me. Especially when we still had so many questions about her powers.

Maggie and Josh needed me too. I couldn't leave, even though sometimes I felt like it would've been easier. Javi was so much calmer now that he was dead.

It would be so easy to drive to the motorway bridge and go off the side…

'Don't you dare!'

I flinched, slamming the breaks on. Thank god nobody was in front of, or behind, me.

'Javier, what the bloody hell are you doing here? You have *got* to stop showing up unannounced! It's not normal!'

'I saw that look on your face.'

'You saw a look on my face, but you didn't come and help me during a bloody exorcism? What happened to Super Ghost?'

'Spirits who've crossed over are supposed to be neutral. We're not meant to intervene in the problems of anyone still on earth. But I can get inside your head. So to speak.'

As if he hadn't interfered already. It felt more like he was picking and choosing when he showed up. It was all right for some.

'Well isn't that just marvellous?' I said, pulling away again. My heart continued to thunder in my chest. Clearly I was still jumpy from yesterday's encounter.

'Edie needs you. Maggie and Josh need you. This whole town needs you,' said Javi. 'You've got so much to —'

'Don't you dare finish that sentence,' I said. 'Don't you think I know I have responsibilities? That doesn't mean I have to like it. That doesn't mean I have to always want it. Do you have any idea what it's like to be the boring, responsible one all the time? No, you bloody well don't, because you were always the fun one. And you died too young to ever have any real sense of responsibility. So don't you go giving me a lecture about giving up when you never had the chance to.'

'It's not my fault I was killed, Niamh.'

'Isn't it? It's someone's fault. One of us failed that day, and it resulted in your death. And I'm just supposed to keep going? Pretend everything's fine? Act like I want to deal with all this ghost stuff on my own? When I don't even know what our daughter is capable of, and apparently my mother kept our lineage from us all this time because she was embarrassed at how pathetically powerless her only daughter is?'

'It's more complicated than that,' he said.

'Is it?'

I indicated left, away from home, as I was heading to see Mrs Brightman. Even though she kept insisting on setting me up, most of the time, she still made me smile.

And I'd promised her I'd take a look at her creaky floorboards at the top of her stairs, which she said were annoying her.

'There's a lot neither of us understands. Your mum still hasn't explained it all to me.'

'And I wouldn't trust half of what she says. That woman could win an Oscar for her lies,' I said.

'She's our best bet to getting the answers we need. Especially when it comes to Edie.'

'Well isn't that just great? The easiest way for us to get answers is to trust a liar. We're screwed. The lot of us.'

'Don't think like that.'

'Like what? What am I *supposed* to think? I've hit another dead end with Maggie and Josh. Ben and I aren't speaking. My mother holds all the answers, but won't tell us anything straight. So tell me, Javier, how am I *supposed* to bloody well think?'

He sank farther into the passenger seat, his black hair falling over his face. Who did he think he was, lecturing me from the Other Side because I'd had a moment of self-doubt?

'You know what? I'm not going to do anything. I had a confidence crisis, that's all. But I'll be fine. I always am.'

Javi faded from view without another word.

*

'Hello, dear,' said Mrs Brightman as I walked into her house. It was Friday evening, and I'd organised to have a catch up with her. It'd been so busy the last few days I'd barely seen her and I felt guilty. It was harder when I spent all day on a building site and all night trying to get my friends out of comas.

I was still desperate to find ways to save them, haunted by my argument with Ben, and annoyed at my dead husband, but that was no excuse to neglect one of the few people left in my life who wasn't comatose or angry at me. She was one of the few connections I had to a normal life, and I didn't want to take that for granted, or have her think I'd forgotten about her.

'Oh my! Your eye! What did you do?'

'Work,' I said. 'Is it that bad?'

She cringed. 'Well, dear. It's nothing a little concealer won't disguise. I'd offer to lend you some but, well, I can't see to apply make-up these days. I stopped buying it years ago.'

And I didn't wear it because I was too lazy to apply it. But she was trying to be nice, which I appreciated. 'Thanks. How was your day?' I asked, changing the subject.

Her husband lingered nearby, as usual. He'd once told me he tried to give his wife space when she had guests over, but since he'd discovered Edie and I could see him, he'd stopped bothering. I wondered if it was because he liked being able to talk to us in a roundabout way, even if the main way we communicated to him was facial expressions that his wife couldn't see because of her declining eyesight.

'Wonderful and enlightening,' she replied, guiding me into the front room. Enlightening? Had she been to church?

I entered the beige living room and froze. Martin was sitting on the sofa, tea in hand. Oh no she didn't.

'I ran into Martin after church, and he told me you'd been awfully rude at the restaurant the other day. I said that wasn't like you and I'm sure you have a legitimate reason for leaving him so abruptly.'

Oh fiddlesticks. The little old lady had conned me. Could I use Edie as an excuse to get out of there? 'I thought I was here to fix your flooring.'

'Oh yes. That does need fixing. It makes the most awful noise. But some things are more important. Sit, sit.' She practically shoved me onto the sofa beside Martin.

I looked up at her husband and glared.

'Sorry,' he said. 'She really did run into him after church. But she…strong-armed him into coming over, shall we say?'

His response just deepened my glare. He lowered his head. What was the point in being able to see the man who haunted her if he couldn't warn me before I walked into an ambush?

'I'll go pop the kettle on.' She disappeared into the kitchen, her husband close behind her, no doubt trying to avoid my wrath. Good.

I'd been blindsided and I had no idea what to do. The last thing I was interested in right now was a bloody date. Let alone with someone who could help me fall asleep without so much as a potion.

'I know you don't like me,' he said, once the kettle was boiling and our matchmaker was out of earshot.

Guilt filled me. It wasn't that I didn't like him…

OK fine. It *was* that I didn't like him. I'm sure he was a nice person, but he was so far from the type of person I needed more of in my life. And I was done putting people at risk because of ghosts. Mrs Brightman was protected, in a way, because she had her husband. But Maggie and Josh had been hurt enough. I'd failed them. I needed to be finding a solution, not sitting on a sofa drinking PG Tips.

'It's not that,' I lied. 'I have a lot of things going on in my life right now.'

'Don't we all?' he said.

No, not like this.

'My best friend and her son are in comas and her husband won't let me see them. He also won't let my daughter see them, and she's dating their son. And did I mention I can see ghosts? Mrs Brightman's husband haunts her, waiting for the day she crosses over so that they can be together again.'

Martin's eyes went so wide I thought they were going to pop out of his sockets. Before he could reply, Mrs Brightman walked back in with our cups of tea. She pulled a little table out from a nest of them in the corner and placed it, along with the tea, in front of me.

'Now, isn't this lovely?' she said, sitting in her armchair opposite us. I felt like I was on trial for something. If I said no, she'd interrogate me until I explained why.

There was no sign of her husband around, so I assumed he was hiding from me. Or he couldn't bear to see the drama unfold. Neither could I. Could I go hide somewhere too?

'Mm-hm,' said Martin with a mouthful of tea. He gave me a sideways look, seeming terrified of me. If he moved any farther away, he'd be sitting on the arm of the sofa.

Had I scared him off? Oops.

It wasn't like he'd believe what I'd just said. Not the second part, anyway. But I was hoping it'd make him think I was crazy enough to avoid. Permanently.

There was nothing worse than people who did the whole, 'I know your pain,' crap. Most people who said it really had no idea. It was just fake empathy; them saying what they thought you wanted to hear. And projecting how they felt on to you, to make themselves feel better and pretend they actually cared. When really, most people only care about themselves and their emotions.

Martin just proved my point. He had no idea how it felt to have someone he knew in a coma – let alone two someones in a supernatural coma – or to be able to see ghosts. And have to exorcise them.

In good news, I supposed, at least he wasn't haunted. That would've overcomplicated things and might've even made him believe me. And we couldn't have that.

'Niamh, why don't you tell this fine young man what you do?'

Er, what?

Mrs Brightman stared at me, clearly waiting for me to fill in the gaps. How could I get out of the situation? Could I fake a call from Edie?

'I'm a handy woman.' And a ghost hunter. 'Could you excuse me for a minute, please? I need to use the bathroom.' Even though I'd asked for permission, I didn't wait for anyone to say yes. I dove out of my seat, went upstairs, and locked the bathroom door. Peace. Finally.

Without hesitation, I took my phone from my pocket and called Edie. She didn't answer. Fiddlesticks.

Who else could I ring?

Ben! Would he still be at work? Should I ring his mobile or landline? I rang his landline, unsure of whether I actually wanted him to answer or not. Which was worse? Interrupting him again, after everything that had happened, or being ignored?

It was Fadil who picked up, just as it was about to go to answerphone. 'Ben's residence. How may I help you?'

'You can use phones?'

'Yes, I have fingers and thumbs and a voice. I can use a phone. What do you want?'

'Can you ring me back in about two minutes please?'

Could he even tell the time? I guess I was about to find out.

'Why?'

'If I promise to come over and give you a story where you can laugh at me, will you do it?'

He hesitated. Those few seconds made me want to reach through the phone and strangle him, but that wasn't a possibility. 'Yes.'

'Do you know how to ring me?'

'Yes.'

'So, ring me in a couple of minutes. Yes?'

'Yes,' said Fadil.

I hung up, desperately hoping he'd actually do it. Did he hate me enough that he wouldn't? Surely not. I gave him a voice! Well, the ability to speak modern English, even if he didn't know what most stuff was.

I faked flushing the toilet and washing my hands, then went back downstairs. Mrs Brightman was talking animatedly about something they'd discussed in church. Martin tensed up again as soon as I walked into the room. At least I'd had some sort of impact on him.

There was nowhere else to sit, and I knew I'd look questionable if I kept standing, so I returned to my spot on the sofa, conscious of sitting too close to Martin.

Fidgeting with anticipation, I almost spilled my tea down me. Mrs Brightman was so busy talking about church she didn't seem to notice. At least we'd found something she was more interested in discussing than matchmaking.

I checked the clock above the TV. It'd only been a minute. How literally would Fadil take my 'couple of minutes'? Would he make me wait longer, just to torture me? Did he even know what a couple of minutes looked like? How did they tell the time in Ancient Egypt, anyway?

'Niamh, is that your phone vibrating?' said Mrs Brightman.

I jumped. I hadn't even noticed it!

It was on vibrate, so I pulled it from my pocket and answered it. 'I expect a full, in-detail explanation of what happened. And also a coffee please,' said Fadil.

'Will do,' I said, before hanging up and trying to hide my relief. He'd come through! I turned back to my awkward tea party. 'I'm really sorry, but Edie needs me. I have to go.' I stood up.

'I hope everything is OK?' said Mrs Brightman. She sounded genuinely concerned.

'She's stressed about her boyfriend, and now having some school issues. Teenagers. You know how it is.'

She nodded. 'Send her my love.'

'Will do.'

'I'm sorry your time together has been cut short twice now,' she added, a hint of judgment in her voice. Ugh. 'Perhaps you could do it again some time.'

Without looking at Martin, I was practically at the front door already, showing myself out. 'Perhaps.' Not.

*

I handed Fadil the disposable coffee cup and resisted the urge to hug him. He didn't seem like a big hugger. Not that I was, either.

'Thank you,' I said.

He took the coffee from me and inhaled it. 'Black coffee is one of my favourite smells.' He looked up. And clearly noticed my black eye, as he flinched. So it *did* look as bad as I thought. I'd been avoiding mirrors so that I couldn't see how bad it really looked, but Fadil's reaction told me everything. 'Do I want to know?'

'Poltergeist,' I sighed.

'Ah.'

How long was my eye going to be a talking point for? It didn't even hurt that much. My ribs did. But nobody could see them to comment on them. Thankfully. They probably would've told me to slow down, and I refused to do that with so much going on.

We went inside and sat in Ben's living room. His house felt empty without him in it, but I wasn't sure I could face him yet after what we'd said to each other. Had I overreacted? Probably. Did I have more important things to worry about? Definitely.

'How are you feeling?' I asked.

'More…human, I guess, every day. It's hard to explain. My senses flit between being overwhelmed by everything, and completely numb to everything. I'd ask if that was normal, but I guess you have nothing to compare it to.'

'No, I don't, I'm afraid. But I'm sure your body is adjusting after being in such a sterile place for so long.'

He nodded, sipping the hot liquid and smiling. 'Yes. So, tell me about what I was saving you from.'

I explained what had happened at Mrs Brightman's, going into as much detail as possible. I felt bad that he couldn't really go anywhere without being seen as a science experiment, so I wanted him to feel like he was living as vicariously through me as possible. I couldn't do much, but I hoped I could at least offer him an escape.

He laughed most of the way through, and was still laughing when I finished.

'I'm impressed you told him you can see ghosts,' said Fadil.

'I knew he wouldn't take me seriously.'

'But he'd think you were nuts.'

I nodded. 'Which means that I don't need to reject him. He'll tell Mrs Brightman for me that he isn't interested in the crazy woman, and I can continue enjoying single life.'

'And fawning over Ben.'

My back stiffened. What was he talking about?

'I'm four thousand years old, not an idiot. Despite what you seem to think,' said Fadil.

Could I strangle him yet?

'Ben has a girlfriend. I saw him with Jaya.'

'Doesn't mean you can't be interested in him,' the soon-to-be-actually-dead mummy pointed out.

'Ben and I are just friends. That's all,' I said.

Fadil sighed. 'If that's what you need to tell yourself.'

Keys jingled in the front door. I tensed. But, before I could move, the noise stopped.

'Jaya, come on,' said Ben.

'Come on what?' said Jaya. 'Do you really like me, or are you just bored?'

'That's not fair!' said Ben.

I felt like I was encroaching; eavesdropping. But I couldn't turn away. And it seemed neither could Fadil, as he was sat up like a meerkat on guard, trying to catch every word.

'Admit it: you're just using me to keep your bed warm until Niamh wakes up and realises you have a thing for her.'

My back tensed. Oh fiddlesticks.

Fadil turned to look at me, but I couldn't meet his gaze.

'You've cancelled lunch on me twice this week to spend time with her, or help her with something, or day dream about her, or whatever it is you do that involves her. It feels like the two of you are part of some secret club I'm not privy too.'

She was kind of on to something, there. It wasn't like we could tell her about ghosts. Even if Ben had told her about Maggie and Josh's comas. Without mentioning they were caused by curses, obviously.

'It's not that simple,' said Ben.

'Isn't it?' Her voice was rife with accusation.

'Jaya, I—' Ben's voice cracked, but it felt like he didn't know what else to say. It sounded a lot like she was right and he didn't want to admit it.

Not wanting to eavesdrop anymore, I snuck out the back door, waited until Ben was inside the house, then left through the back gate.

29
Edie

Mum kept insisting there was nothing to find at Josh's house, but the more she said it, the more I wondered if she'd missed something.

What if the spell hadn't failed? I mean, it had gravitated to Abigail's room. What if the reason it had done that was because there was so much dark energy in there, it permeated the whole room?

Mum kept her spare key to Josh and Maggie's on a hook in the kitchen. Stealing was wrong, but it was a life or death situation. What choice did I have? I had to try. It was annoying enough Mum hadn't let me sit in while she'd cast the spell, but Mum kept insisting she didn't want anything supernatural to interfere with my studies. As if it hadn't already.

Also, my grades were still fine, thank you very much.

Having borrowed Mum's key, I approached the front door.

Unfortunately, Mrs Lopez was sitting in a chair by her window and poked her head out when she saw me. 'Edie!' She ushered me over.

Begrudgingly, I walked around the hedge and to her window.

'Is there any update on the Morgans? I've only seen Harry around here lately, and I barely see him.'

Gossipy old woman. Couldn't she mind other people's business?

I needed her to not say anything to Harry, though, so I had to pretend I was on her side. 'I didn't tell you this, but Maggie asked me to check on a couple of things for her. She can't bring herself to come home right now.'

Mrs Lopez tapped the side of her nose, a conspiratorial expression on her face. Satisfied, she returned to her chair in front of the TV.

I exhaled, running around the hedge, which was still home to a snorkelling gargoyle, and heading into the house before I lost my nerve. So I was breaking and entering. It was for a good cause! If I could spot something the others couldn't, it was worth it, wasn't it?

And I mean, we *had* established I was more powerful than Mum. Maybe I was more powerful than Ben, too?

The lights were off inside, which was a good sign. But then, what if Harry was home, but asleep?

That wasn't his style, though. He didn't believe in naps. He thought they were for the weak. He was so narrow-minded and careless with his words sometimes that it made me want to gag. The guy didn't have an ounce of compassion in his body, and I'd never get what Maggie saw in him.

I kept the lights off, using the torch on my phone to navigate my way around. I didn't want to accidentally stand on anything, but I also didn't want to draw attention to the house by turning on a light, either.

It was almost five, so, assuming Harry went straight to the hospital from work, I had just over an hour. Hopefully I wouldn't need that long.

As soon as I reached the top of the stairs, I felt it. I hadn't noticed it before. I wasn't sure if that was because nobody else was there, or because of the finding spell. But it felt like something was sucking the air out of upstairs. I turned the corner. That's when I sensed the direction everything was being pulled in. It tried to drag me in, too, but I fought it, focusing my energy on finding whatever it was.

All the air and energy was being dragged in the direction of Abigail's room. Keeping my back against the wall in case I wasn't alone, I went in. It was just as My Little Pony as I remembered. Except for one thing. The bed. All the energy in the space was being pulled towards the bed. Negative energy radiated from it. Energy I hadn't noticed before. Was that why Harry had been such a grump?

Nah.

He'd always been that.

But there was nothing *on* the bed. Except a topsheet over the unmade bed, so that it didn't get dusty while Abigail was at her grandparents' house. That made it feel like Harry knew this was a long-term thing. You didn't put a topsheet on a bed when you were expecting someone back in a couple of days. I'd mostly only seen them when we'd gone to super old, haunted houses that nobody wanted to spend time in. I shuddered.

Is that what the Morgan house would become?

No, I wouldn't let it.

I'd save Josh and Maggie. They'd done too much for me. There was no way I was giving up on them.

I gravitated to the bed. The pull became stronger. It was dark, too. I'd never felt so much darkness from something before. But I still couldn't see anything that could be sucking the energy from the room.

Pulling the topsheet back revealed nothing but an unmade bed. I tapped my foot. It had to be around the bed somewhere.

Abigail's bedframe lifted the mattress about a foot off the floor. There were a couple of boxes underneath, so I moved them, then knelt down to look underneath it. Taped to the bottom of bedframe was a fluffy giraffe.

30
Niamh

'Edie! Edie where are you?' I called.

I stood in the doorway, shivering. I'd been so desperate to get there when Edie had rang and said she'd found something, I'd ran out of the house without grabbing a jacket. So I stood on Maggie's doorstep in nothing but a flimsy T-shirt. Idiot.

'Did you touch it?'

'No. I didn't want to risk it.'

'Good,' I said. I held out a pair of dirty gardening gloves. 'So we don't touch it. You can never be too careful with objects like this.' I mostly used the gloves for weeding, but sometimes curses were contagious, and I didn't want to chance that for either of us.

We ran up the stairs, two at a time. Edie pointed under the bed. My joints protesting, I knelt down to look underneath it. Sure enough, there was a toy duct taped to the underside of Abigail's bed. The vessel was a toy?

Well I'd be damned. Ben's spell had worked after all. Why hadn't mine?

After putting the gloves on, I reached out and tugged at the giraffe. My ribcage protested at the movement. No amount of pain I inflicted on myself made a difference.

That tape did not want to move. It was also stuck to some of the fur.

Fiddlesticks.

'Edie, can you lift the bed?'

'Um, no?'

It was a heavy wooden thing. Even without a bad back, I wasn't sure she'd be able to lift it. And I didn't want to put her in any more danger than she was already in.

'Put these on,' I said, removing the gloves and passing them to her. Using the bedside table as leverage, I pulled myself up. I was going to pay for this tomorrow, but we didn't have a choice. 'I'll lift the bed. Get the giraffe off without damaging the bed, if you can.'

'Are you sure?'

'What choice do we have?' I said.

Edie put the gloves on. I hated this plan. It put her in more danger than me, but what choice did we have?

Deep breath. I squared my muscles, reminding myself to put the weight onto my legs, and not on my arms or my back. My back would love for me to screw that up.

'Go!' I yanked the bed up, using all the strength I had. It didn't lift far, and I couldn't hold it for long. Hopefully it was enough. It wasn't like there was anyone else who could help us.

Edie tugged and pulled at the base of the bed as my arms quivered under the weight of it. The damn thing was heavier than I thought.

'Hurry. Up,' I said through gritted teeth. Sharp pain shot through my ribs. It took the little energy I had left not to scream.

'I'm trying! There's a lot of tape here!' said Edie.

Deep breaths. Focus on the breathing, not on the quivering limbs.

'Can't—'

'Got it!' said Edie as I dropped the bed to the floor with a thud. Thank god it was a detached house so the neighbours wouldn't feel it.

'Mum, are you all right?' said Edie, leaning over me as I rested my hands on my knees, panting. In her hand was the giraffe, still covered in duct tape.

'Fine,' I said through gritted teeth. Well, I would be. I just needed a minute. 'Is there an opening?' I gestured to the giraffe.

Still wearing the gloves, Edie turned it around. There was velcro on the back. Casting me a glance, she opened it. There was nothing there.

'What? But I was so sure,' she said. 'I can still feel it.'

'Feel what?'

'The dark energy from it. Can't you feel it?'

'No. It just looks like a giraffe toy to me. Are you sure this is Abigail's?'

'No,' she said. 'She's not into giraffes. I don't get it.'

'Maybe it's enchanted,' I said.

'Like Fadil's jars?'

I nodded. 'It makes sense, doesn't it? Whoever cursed Maggie and Josh would likely create Fadil's curse as close as possible, especially if said person wanted them to stay that way.'

'That would explain why I can feel the darkness but there's nothing there.'

But why did it mean I couldn't feel anything? Last time there'd been bad energy in Abigail's room, I'd been drawn to it. Which I hadn't told anyone and which still freaked me out, but that wasn't the point.

I couldn't feel *anything* this time, but Edie insisted the giraffe was the source of it all. Was I losing my powers? Or was something else going on?

'Could you cast a spell to undo it?' suggested Edie.

'Um…'

'What's that mean?' said Edie. She sat on the floor, placing the giraffe on the rug beside her.

'It means my powers have been wonky lately.'

'So then who did the finding spell?'

I avoided eye contact. Telling her I'd failed multiple times was hard enough. Admitting I'd asked Ben to help after a massive argument which was totally my fault? Mortifying.

'You asked Ben,' she said, practically reading my mind.

'I didn't know anyone else who could help. And I was desperate. Until you found that—' I gestured to the giraffe '—I didn't even think it'd worked.'

'Perhaps the finding spell removed part of the enchantment, but not all of it?'

'Well, it's a finding spell, right? It helps us find what we want. It doesn't necessarily reveal what it is.'

Edie picked up the giraffe from beside her and stood up. 'So. To Ben's?'

*

Every bone in my body and all my emotions protesting, we went to Ben's house.

He answered, poe-faced.

Until Edie held up a carrier bag. It was opaque, but you could see the outline of a giraffe inside.

'What's that?'

'Our vessel,' said Edie.

Ben's jaw fell. He stepped aside to let us in. I knew that, no matter what happened between us, his academic curiosity would always trump his emotions.

'Edie? Niamh? What are you doing here?' said Fadil when we walked into the living room. He was sitting on the sofa, his legs crossed, a sudoku on his lap.

'We found it,' I said.

'Oh my god,' said Fadil. 'Why does it have the outline of a toy?'

'Because it is one. Sort of,' I said.

Fadil stood up and walked over to us. 'May I?' He gestured to the bag.

'We haven't touched it, just in case. It was hidden under the bed.' I put the carrier bag on the table, and the vessel on top of it. 'So your spell worked, Ben.'

'Huh,' was all he said to that.

There was a tension in the air. An awkwardness that was undoubtedly my fault. But we had to stay focused.

'We don't know how to destroy it,' said Edie, keeping the conversation on track.

'And you were hoping I would?' said Ben.

'You or that library of yours. Or Fadil. Or someone you know. Or—' Edie started crying, tears running down her porcelain skin. I put my arms around her as the guys stared on awkwardly.

'We're almost there, Edie,' I reassured her.

'But what if we can't destroy it?'

'Hold on. I think I know a book that might help,' said Ben.

He went into his library and returned faster than usual. Had he already had the book out, to try to find the cause?

'Ever since you gave me that ash sample, I've been cross referencing what was in it with what's in my library,' he said. He'd still been looking? Even after our argument? Must not cry. Must not cry.

'Did you find out what was in it?' I said.

'Lavender, oregano, cinnamon. An odd mix, but they all have purifying properties.'

'Do you have them now?' said Edie.

Ben lowered his head. 'No. I'm not very green-fingered. And they're all out of season.'

I went into my pocket and began detaching my house key from my keyring. 'I grow lavender and oregano in my greenhouse for Maggie. There should be some cinnamon in the drinks cupboard for hot chocolates. It's dried, though.'

He took the key from my hand. 'That should do it. Thanks.'

'If Tilly bothers you, just give her a treat from under the sink. She'll leave you alone and love you forever,' I said.

Ben caught my eye and smiled. There was a twinkle in there, one I hadn't seen since our argument. I returned his smile as my heart fluttered.

'Are you sure this will work?' said Edie, her voice wobbling.

He put his hand on her shoulder. 'We're nearly there.'

She smiled, wiping at her watering eyes with the back of her hand. Fadil and I reached out and put our hands on her back. She nodded, looking up so that she didn't cry even more. If she cried any more, I was going to end up joining in. Then we'd be no good to anyone.

'So what do we need to do?' I said, trying to keep us on track.

'Break the enchantment on them first so that we can figure out what we're dealing with.' Ben picked up a book from the coffee table and opened it to a tabbed page. 'This one is just an incantation. Obviously only someone with magic in their blood can cast it, but beyond that, it's pretty basic.'

'Wait, what did you just say?' I asked.

'It's a basic incantation?'

'No, about magic in someone's blood.'

'Only someone with magic in their blood can cast the spell.'

I sank onto the sofa. Hadn't Gwendoline said something similar?

'What is it, Mum?' asked Edie, sitting next to me.

'You know I told you my spell failed?'

She nodded.

'I think what Ben said might be why.'

'You don't have magic in your blood?'

Was that really why my spells weren't working? Was that why I could only see ghosts, but beyond that I was pretty powerless?

'Think about it. We know my dad – your granddad – was human. What if that watered down my powers somehow? And you get most of your powers from your dad, who had no idea what he was capable of because he was adopted?'

Ben nodded, pacing the length of the coffee table with the book still in hand. 'It makes sense. Magic is genetic, and just like any other genes, it can be watered down. Maybe even skip a generation entirely.'

As if my mum hadn't screwed me up enough already.

'But I thought you used to be able to cast spells, like with Dad and stuff?' said Edie.

'What if that was because he was with me? I haven't really done anything since he was alive. Maybe he was the real power.' He'd *love* that. He already thought he was Super Ghost.

'Edie, why don't you try the spell?' suggested Ben.

Edie's eyes went wide. 'Why me?'

'Humour me,' he said, handing her the spell book.

We put the giraffe on the table, then Edie leaned over it and read out the incantation as Ben, Fadil, and I held our breaths and watched.

'Reveal what cannot be seen, show us a view that is clean.'

Pop.

The giraffe in front of us changed to a canister. If I hadn't seen it, I wouldn't have believed it.

Wearing the gardening gloves, Edie unscrewed the lid. Inside was one of Josh's paint brushes. Maggie's engagement ring. And some perfect, brown and blond hair. And two vials of blood.

'Someone went all out on this,' said Ben. 'Two lots of DNA shows they really want to be sure it works. It's additional insurance.'

'Why did you ask me to cast that spell?' said Edie.

'I think we need to talk to your dad about your powers. But for now, we need to focus on saving Maggie and Josh. Is that OK with you?'

She stood up. 'What do we need to do now?'

'Set it on fire,' said Ben.

'All of it? Even the ring and paint brush?' I said.

'*All* of it,' said Ben. 'Some of it may survive, I don't know. But I doubt she'd want that thing back anyway.'

'Why?' I said. It was her engagement ring. Of course she'd want it back.

'Because the dark magic won't leave it. It will always be a cursed object, attracting darkness to anyone who uses it.'

'What was your object, Fadil?' Edie asked.

'It's been so long I can't remember. It wasn't there with the smashed canopic jar, I guess because it got destroyed with the rest of it.'

'So, what? We set it on fire and they wake up right away?' I said.

'Thereabouts,' said Fadil.

'Someone needs to be there to explain to them what's happening,' I said.

'And they need to wake up at the same time, or they'll get freaked out seeing the other one still comatose,' added Edie.

'I'll do it,' said Ben. 'You two go to the hospital. We'll do the preparations here. Ring me when you're there.'

'But what about—'

Ben cut me off before I could finish my question. 'If I can help Maggie and Josh, I will. They don't deserve this any more than Fadil did.'

'Hear, hear!' said Fadil, punching his fist in the air. He'd probably learnt that from watching too many films.

'Do you have everything?' I asked.

'Yeah. I have an iron cauldron I can set everything on fire in.'

'So cool!' said Edie.

'I'll bless the room first so that none of the negative energy can escape. I'm not taking any chances with a spell this dark,' said Ben.

'Is there anything I can do to help?' asked Fadil.

Ben smiled at him. 'Don't worry. There'll be plenty for you to do.'

'All right then,' I said. 'Let's get this show on the road.'

31
Edie

'I'm not sure on this,' said Mum.

'It worked last time,' I said. We were standing around one of the back entrances, near the ward that housed Josh and Maggie. Hopefully it wouldn't for much longer.

'Anna!' I half-whispered, half-shouted.

Mum paced in front of me, a worried look on her face. Her cheeks were pink from the cold. Ben had offered to lend her a coat. She'd said no. I'd suggested picking one up on the way to the hospital. She'd said no. She was so desperate to fix Josh and Maggie she wasn't going to stop until it was done. Pneumonia be damned.

'Edie!' said Anna, appearing in front of me. She looked at Mum. 'Is everything all right?'

'Is Harry with the Morgans?'

'No. I haven't seen him for a couple of days.'

'Really?' said Mum, turning to look at Anna. 'That's odd.'

'Two people who can see me in one week. Who'd have thought?' She bobbed up and down, floating slightly off the ground. 'Do you need to see them?'

'Yes. Urgently,' said Mum. She stopped pacing and stood directly in front of Anna. 'We can wake them up, but we want to be there.'

'Of course,' said Anna. 'There's no one there now. I can show you in the back way so that nobody will notice you're there, and I'll keep an eye out in case anyone tries to come in.'

'Thank you,' said Mum.

Anna nodded, then floated towards the back door. We followed her through the hospital. She recited the codes we needed for each door, like our very own ghostly guide.

A few doors later, we got to the ward.

Mum stopped, taking a deep breath. 'You ready?'

I punched in the code and held the door for her. 'Let's do this.'

We meandered our way through to Josh and Maggie's room. It was still in darkness. Mum hadn't seen it before in person, so when she saw it, she gasped. While their vitals were normal and hadn't changed, they looked ill. Really ill. Their faces were gaunt and pale. Their eyes were sunken, surrounded by purple bags.

'Oh my god,' said Mum, walking over to Maggie. 'Maggie, I'm so sorry. We'll get you fixed, I promise.' She took her phone out and rang Ben. 'We're here.' After putting her phone on speaker, she placed it on Maggie's bedside table, then sat in the chair beside her. I sat next to Josh, my back to Mum and Maggie, her back to me.

Josh's touch was cold. It sent a shiver through me. Was it because of the curse, or the temperature in the room?

It was definitely getting colder in there. Was that normal?

'Mum, do you feel that?' I said.

'Yeah. Stay focused. We have to trust that Ben and Fadil know what they're doing.'

'Let's not forget Ben and Fadil haven't done this before,' said Fadil through the phone.

'You're supposed to be reassuring,' I grumbled.

'Sorry. Not my thing. Try a different person.'

I laughed. What else could I do?

I'd always known my life would be weird, but I'd never thought it could be this level of weird. What could I do, though? If I tried to run away from it, we wouldn't be about to wake Josh and Maggie up. They could be in comas forever. And that was *not* an option.

Josh's hand twitched in mine. I jumped up, leaning over him. 'Josh, are you there?'

His hand twitched again.

Ben screamed.

Mum jumped up. 'Ben! Fadil! What's going on?'

'The magic…it's so…the darkness….' stuttered Ben.

'He's trying to control it, but it's strong,' said Fadil. 'He's using his forcefield, but it's trying to break through. He needs to hold it off until the hair and blood has burned.'

'What about the items?' I said.

'They're less important. The other stuff is burning slower than usual, as if it's fighting it.'

'Is that normal?' said Mum.

'I don't know. Why don't I go ask the person who released me? Oh wait. I don't know who it was!'

'Now isn't the time for sarcasm!' said Mum.

Someone let in a sharp intake of breath. I turned around. Josh was awake.

I stood up, leaning over him. 'Josh?'

I reached out to him, but he jerked away from me. Something tugged at my heart, but I convinced myself it was just a subconscious reaction from waking up. 'What's going on? Mum? Niamh?'

'What do you remember?' I asked.

Before he could reply, Maggie woke up, too. She sat upright, a horrified look on her face. 'Oh my god. What happened?' She looked at Mum. And recoiled. It looked like she was going to throw up.

'What do you remember?' Mum asked her.

'We were in the kitchen, talking. Then I was…no. That's not right. It can't be real.'

'What can't?' I said.

I tried to reach for Josh's hand again, but he pulled it away. He couldn't even look at me. I swallowed back how hurt I was, knowing it was no doubt because of how confused and traumatised he was.

'I was tortured,' said Maggie.

'Me too,' whispered Josh.

'What?' chorused Mum and me.

'You couldn't hear anything happening here?' I said.

'No, nothing,' said Maggie. Her voice cracked as she spoke. 'They—they looked like you, and they…they set fire to me.' She sobbed. When Mum tried to comfort her, she turned away.

'It wasn't me, Mags.'

'But it was because of you, wasn't it?' said Josh. The look he gave me turned my blood to ice. My heart broke in two. He was blaming us for what had happened? After everything we'd done to help them? How hard we'd tried to find answers?

'We worked our arses off to free you!' I said.

'But if you weren't in our lives, none of this would've happened. Abigail wouldn't have been possessed, and

Josh and I wouldn't have been—' She couldn't finish her sentence. She was too busy sobbing.

'This isn't because of us, Maggie. You have to believe me,' begged Mum.

But, judging from the looks on Josh and Maggie's faces, they didn't.

32
Niamh

Edie and I drove home in silence. When we got in, I ignored Tilly and went up to my room. Edie came in a little while later, Tilly in tow. The three of us curled up on my bed, Edie and I crying. Tilly tried to lick our tears away, but we were crying too much. There wasn't anything the fluffball could do, but I loved her for trying.

After everything I'd done to protect Maggie since we were little, and she was blaming me? Surely she knew I'd never put her in harm's way?

No doubt that smug bastard Harry would be happy to see us gone. But would that really be it? No, it couldn't be. I'd talk to her in a couple of days, when she'd calmed down. I'd find her a supernatural counsellor. They had to be a thing, didn't they? Supernatural trauma was bound to be a thing. Maybe it could help Abigail too. And Josh. And Edie. Hell, even Ben and me.

Edie, Tilly, and I fell asleep, curled up together on my bed. I didn't know what time it was, but we got woken up by a knock on the front door.

My eyes blurry from crying, and my ribcage protesting, I went downstairs to see who it was. Ben and a hooded figure – whom I assumed was Fadil – stood on our driveway. Ben held up a carrier bag. 'Brought comfort food. And painkillers. Thought you might need it.'

'Bless you,' I said, fighting back tears. 'Edie! Food!' I called up the stairs.

The clock on the stairs said it was nine. Not as late as I'd thought.

'I didn't think you'd want to cook,' said Ben as he and Fadil followed me into the kitchen.

'I'm not sure I want to eat, either,' I said as I took some plates from the cupboard.

Tilly circled us, hoping to get herself a chip or two.

'You might find you feel better after you have,' said Ben. 'It's been a draining few days.'

'You can say that again,' agreed Edie, walking in. 'Thanks for the food, Ben.'

'Of course. What are friends for?' He smiled at me and it sent a fire through me. He didn't hate me after all! We were still friends!

'Before I forget, here's your key back.' He placed my house key on the table. I'd forgotten I'd given him my key in the panic of everything else going on. It'd felt so natural I hadn't even thought twice about it. A part of me didn't want him to give it back. Which was dumb, because then I wouldn't have a key to my own house. I kind of needed one…

'I'm going to go eat this upstairs,' said Edie. She chucked some chips on to each plate, then topped them off with minted mushy peas.

'Found any good YouTube documentaries lately?' said Fadil.

'There's one on the Victorians you're going to love. It's about how everyday household objects could kill them.

Come on.' Edie grabbed a plate of chips and bottle of pop from the side, completely oblivious to how twisted she sounded, then she and Fadil took their food upstairs. Leaving Ben and I alone in the kitchen. I couldn't help but feel like it was intentional.

We put our plates on the dining table, then sat down.

Tilly sat under the table, watching us. Ben picked a chip up from his plate and gave it to her. She munched on it merrily.

'I want to ask how you're feeling, but I know it's a stupid question,' said Ben. He and Fadil had heard the whole exchange between Maggie and Josh.

'Do you have any idea how it feels to go out of your way to protect someone, only to have them shoot you in the face with it?'

Ben lowered his head, his hands in his pockets. 'Yeah. My sister. It was like the more I tried to help her, the more evil she got.'

'I'm sorry. I'm sure it wasn't your fault,' I said.

'Are you sure?' he said.

'Are you sure Maggie and Josh aren't mine?'

'Touche.'

'I just don't get why someone would do something like that,' I said, dipping a chip into some minted mushy peas.

'Me neither, but that amount of black magic wasn't normal. Even for a curse.'

'What do you mean?'

'I felt it. I fought it. And it took all the strength I had. I passed out after you hung up. Fadil woke me up a couple of hours later.'

I reached over and touched his hand. He smiled up at me. 'I'm so sorry. I had no idea. You shouldn't have put yourself at risk like that.'

'It's not about that. I'm worried for you and Edie.'

'What do you mean?'

'Well, Josh's grandfather warned Edie about protecting his family. And Javi warned you about protecting Edie. Doesn't that seem coincidental to you?'

'Are you saying Edie and I could still be at risk? That someone really did do that curse to get to us?'

'They added another layer to it that we didn't see until we tried to undo it. It was difficult because I wasn't pulling them out of a coma. I was pulling them out of another dimension.'

I gasped. 'No. No. That can't be right.'

'Think about it: they said they were tortured. What other reason is there?'

My appetite gone, I stood up and paced the kitchen. 'But…no. Parallel dimensions aren't real. They can't be.'

Ben laughed. Actually laughed. 'Your mum really didn't tell you anything, did she?'

'No,' I half-growled.

'Well, it's real. And it's very possible to trap the souls of someone you don't like down there.'

'And that's what you think happened to Maggie and Josh?'

'I'm almost certain of it.'

I sank back onto the chair opposite him. 'But why Maggie and Josh? What have they done?'

Ben sighed. 'Proximity.'

My shoulders slumped. 'So it really is my fault.'

Ben reached out and put his hand on my arm. 'Not like you're thinking. If I were to guess, I think someone wants to isolate you and Edie.'

'From what?'

'The people you're close to. You're more vulnerable if you're alone, and the Morgans are your oldest friends.'

I fought back tears. The last thing I wanted was to start sobbing in front of Ben. Again. 'In that case, you and Fadil need to stay far, far away.' I stood up and started to walk to the door.

Ben got up too, blocking my path. He looked me dead in the eyes as he said, 'I can't do that, Niamh.'

'But—'

Before I could finish my sentence, he leaned in and kissed me.

33
Edie

I wanted to text Josh and see how he was, but I knew it'd be pointless. Was his phone even charged? Probably not. Harry wouldn't see the point if Josh was comatose.

But he hadn't actually been comatose. He'd been tortured.

'What are you thinking?' Fadil asked, studying me.

I crossed my legs, staring at the plate of chips sitting in front of me, on my bed. 'Josh and Maggie were tortured. Not just cursed. *Tortured.*'

'Yeah, it's messed up,' said Fadil.

'But what if that means Josh and Maggie can't look at us ever again? What if that's it?'

'You've known each other a long time. By your standards. Right?'

I nodded, picking up a chip and biting into it.

'They wouldn't be that stupid.'

'Depends what happened. We don't know what they went through. And their torturers *looked* like us. That's screwed up on so many levels.'

'That sounds like someone was intentionally trying to ruin your relationship with the Morgans.'

'What?' I'd never considered that.

'They'd have to know about you to imitate you and not have Josh get suspicious, right? They can't do that without intimate knowledge of you and Josh.'

Oh my god. 'Do you think someone's been watching us? Taking notes?'

Fadil shrugged. 'It's a possibility, don't you think?'

'I really hope you're wrong. But it makes sense.'

'I'm sorry. I hope I am, too.'

'I know,' I said. 'It's not your fault. I just hope that Josh and Maggie don't give whoever's behind it what they want. It would destroy Mum to lose her oldest friend. And after everything we went through to get Josh and Maggie back, to lose them anyway—'

I started sobbing. Fadil took a box of tissues from my desk and handed them to me.

'Thanks.' I took one and wiped at my eyes.

'We've lost them, haven't we?'

'You don't know that until you've spoken to them.'

*

Fadil was right. So, early the next morning, I went to the hospital. It was so early everyone had barely had breakfast.

Anna had confirmed that Josh and Maggie were still there. They'd been kept in overnight for more tests and observations. The doctors couldn't work out how they'd recovered so rapidly. And they never would.

I snuck past everyone and into their room, Anna keeping lookout again.

Maggie was curled up facing the window, fast asleep. Josh was awake, flicking through his phone. He looked up when he saw me, but his face turned white. He couldn't have looked less happy to see me if he'd tried.

'How are you feeling?' I said, pushing down the doubt I was feeling. I carried on into the room, standing beside his bed.

He swallowed, the terror still evident on his face. 'Fine.'

Was he really that afraid of me? That he couldn't even *look* at me? When we'd known each other practically our whole lives?

'Josh, you know it's really me, right? None of what you went through was real.'

'Wasn't it? It felt real.'

'We got you out of there as soon as we could, I swear.'

'How do we know it wasn't you who cursed us?' said Josh.

I frowned, trying to hold back tears. Did he really think I'd do something like that to him? 'You don't mean that.'

'Don't I?'

I took a deep breath, stuffing my hands into my coat pocket and curling them into fists. If I dug my nails into my palms, maybe I wouldn't cry.

'Things like this will always happen with you around,' said Josh.

'What's that supposed to mean?'

'You and what you can do. You attract it.'

'Because I can see ghosts? Why does that make me a target?' I crossed my arms, resting my weight on my left leg. And trying really, really hard not to show Josh how much he was breaking my heart.

'No. You're a necromancer, aren't you?'

'Um, how do you know that?'

His eyes darted around the room as he tried to look everywhere but at me. Whenever his gaze landed on me, he cringed, then immediately looked away again. Did he know he was braking my heart every time he did it? 'They told me.'

I waved my arms in the air, totally confused at what he was talking about. 'Who?'

'The demons!'

Seriously? Did everyone know I was a necromancer but Mum and me? How would demons know, but not us?

'Is that who tortured you?' I said. I really, really hoped it wasn't.

'Why are you asking so many stupid questions? You know all the answers.' He crossed his arms and turned away from me. My heart began to shatter.

'I really don't. Talk to me.'

'Whatever.'

'Josh—'

He shook his head. 'No, Edie. What we went through was because of you, whether you want to admit it or not. I think you and your mum should stay away from us from now on.'

'You don't mean that,' I said.

'Yes, we do,' said Maggie. She'd rolled over and turned to look at me while I spoke to Josh.

I looked at her through tear-filled eyes. 'Why? Why are you punishing us for something we didn't do?'

'*We're* punishing *you*?' said Josh. He scoffed. 'That's rich.'

'If we didn't have you in our lives, this never would've happened.'

'You don't know that!' I said.

'The demons said so,' said Josh.

'They're demons! They lie! You saw that with Abigail!'

'Did we, or was that just you?' said Maggie.

'What on earth are you talking about?' I said.

'You and your mum have lied to us about so many things. How do we know we can trust you?' said Maggie.

'Lied to you about what? Putting some wards on your wall? My powers? We didn't know about my powers. Everything we do is to keep you safe!'

Josh scoffed. 'Some good it did.'

'I think you and your mum have done enough damage, Edie. It's time for you to leave.'

'But Maggie—'

'Goodbye, Edie.'

My head spinning, I left their hospital room. I'd waited for Josh for so long. We'd been together for a month. And my heart had been ripped away from me because of something that wasn't even my fault. How was I going to tell Mum they never wanted to see us again? My heart was shattering into a million pieces. And it would never be the same again.

Just for you...

Discover how Niamh's powers were outed to her classmates in an exclusive short story, just for mailing list subscribers. Visit https://www.kristinaadamsauthor.com/the-mothers-lesson/ to download your copy today.

The Necromancer's Secret

Niamh and Edie may have freed their friends from demonic torture, but that doesn't mean their friends don't blame the mother/daughter duo for it happening.

Searching for comfort, Edie starts hanging out with her handsome, mysterious classmate Dominic. Is he really who he seems to be, or is there more to him than she first thought?

Niamh and Ben, meanwhile, are trying to make their new romance work. But it's not going to be easy. Especially with Niamh's dead husband trying to give her romance advice, and a live ex back in her life and begging her for help. Will their fledgling romance be able to survive so much interference?

Find out what happens next for Niamh, Edie, and the rest of the gang in The Necromancer's Secret, the third book in the mother/daughter paranormal mystery series Afterlife Calls.

Visit https://www.kristinaadamsauthor.com/the-necromancers-secret/ to preorder your copy today.

Acknowledgements

Thanks to everyone who read *The Ghost's Call* and was so lovely about it. I was nervous about my first foray into fantasy, but I needn't have been: it seems you all love Niamh, Edie, and Tilly as much as I do. I won't lie, I got a little emotional reading some of your reviews.

This series feels like it was a long time coming. It's a combination of my love of writing about all kinds of relationships in a way that's realistic, but weirdly unique to fiction; my desire for escapism and fantasy; my love of a good romance, and my teenage years, which were spent rewatching *Charmed* an unhealthy number of times.

Thanks to Alexa, Ellie, Chelle, and Mary Beth, for your comments and suggestions on different aspects of the book. It really helped to bring the world and characters to life. I couldn't have done it without you!

As always, thanks to Carl for all your support. And to Millie, for continuing to provide inspiration for Tilly.

About the Author

Kristina Adams is an author, poet, blogger, and podcaster from Nottingham in the UK. When she isn't writing, she's baking or spending time with her west highland terrier, Millie.

Also by K.C. Adams

Afterlife Calls

The Ghost's Call

The Necromancer's Secret (coming soon)

The Witch's Sacrifice (coming soon)

Writing as Kristina Adams

What Happens in...

The Real World (free prequel about Liam)

What Happens in New York

What Happens in London

Return to New York

What Happens in Texas (free blog series about Astin)

What Happens in Barcelona

What Happens in Paphos

Spotlight (*What Happens in...* spin-off about Cameron and Luke)
Behind the Spotlight (runs alongside *What Happens in London* and *Return to New York*)

Hollywood Gossip (*What Happens in...* prequel spin-off about Tate and Jack)
Hollywood Gossip
Hollywood Parents
Hollywood Destiny
Hollywood Heartbreak
Hollywood Romance (coming soon)
Hollywood Nightmare

Nonfiction for Writers
Writing Myths
Productivity for Writers
How to Write Believable Characters

Printed in Great Britain
by Amazon

48123204R00179